THE RANCHERO'S LOVE

LAND OF PROMISE

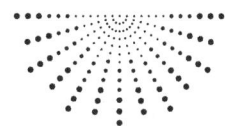

NANCY J. FARRIER

Copyright © 2018 by Nancy J. Farrier

All rights reserved.

Cover art by Ardra Farrier.

River Ink logo by Ardra Farrier.

No part of this book may be reproduced in any form or by any electronic or mechanical means, including information storage and retrieval systems, without written permission from the author, except for the use of brief quotations in a book review.

Published by River Ink Press, Apple Valley, CA 92307

Scripture quotations from the King James Version of the Bible.

Publisher's Note: This is a work of fiction. Names, characters, places, and incidents are a product of the author's imagination. Locales and public names are sometimes used for atmospheric purposes. Any resemblance to actual people, living or dead, or to businesses, companies, events, institutions, or locales is completely coincidental.

Library of Congress Control Number: 2018947003

ISBN- 10: 0-9990547-3-2 (Print)

ISBN- 13: 978-09990547-3-4 (Print)

ISBN- 10: 0-9990547-2-4 (E-book)

ISBN- 13: 978-0-9990547-2-7 (E-book)

❧ Created with Vellum

*To my son, Adrian, his wife, Heather,
and their wonderful children:
Bree and Dom,
Hunter,
Billy,
and Tiffany.
I am so blessed to call you family.*

CHAPTER ONE

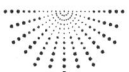

"THIS COULD BE TROUBLE." Ramón motioned with his chin toward the waiting wagons. The quirk of his head *vaquero's* mouth twisted Lucio's stomach into a knot. What now? He swiveled around.

Icy dread sluiced down his spine. This couldn't be right. In all his preparation for this trip, no one mentioned Rosalinda and her children going along. No one.

His teeth grated as he strode toward the wagon where the young mother swung the last of her three children aboard. The toddler, Luis, grinned at Lucio as he approached. The child's innocence and delight squeezed his heart. He'd tried hard to avoid this trio for the past three months since they'd arrived at the *rancho*. And their mother.

Especially their mother.

Despite all they had been through in the *bandolero* camp they'd been rescued from, these children retained their delight in living. Luis, shy at first, had come out of his shell in the past few months and often raced through the barnyard chasing after his sisters, who were more willing to include their baby brother than Lucio and his brothers had included their younger sister.

1

Lucio intended to focus on his job, but he often found himself following their antics and smiling.

Lucio reached the back of the wagon and swung Maria, the oldest sibling, to the ground. "Rosalinda, we are getting ready to leave. I can't have your *niños* playing here." Maria's squeal of delight at the sudden drop had him biting back a grin. It wouldn't do to let their mother see that he cared about her brood.

Isabel, the middle child, jumped toward him, arms outstretched. As soon as her feet touched the ground, Luis yelled, "Me!" and raced across the wagon bed, arms outstretched. The little boy flung himself at Lucio, who caught the child in mid-leap. It took all his will to not to hug the boy to his chest. Luis's dark eyes shone. He clapped both palms to Lucio's cheeks and grinned. Lucio set him on the ground and frowned. Where had Maria gone?

He straightened to see the little imp back in the wagon. Rosalinda flipped her dark hair over her shoulder as she reached for Isabel and lifted her back up with her sister. Lucio froze, unable to take his eyes from that mesmerizing cloud of shimmering brown.

Rosalinda smirked at him as she reached for Luis. Lucio forced his thoughts away from her and onto the problem at hand. He grabbed Maria and swung her back down. The child's laugh bubbled in the air, nearly shattering his frown.

"What are you doing?" The question came out harsher than he intended as Rosalinda glared at him. She lifted Maria back up with her siblings.

"We are pulling out soon. I can't have your children playing in the wagon and getting in the way." Lucio swung Isabel down. Rosalinda lifted her back up.

"We are going with you." Rosalinda shifted in a way that made him want to forget everything but looking at her. This happened way too often as she sashayed around the hacienda or the ranch grounds. He found his gaze tracking after her and his thoughts going adrift from the work at hand.

"You are *not* going with us." Lucio tried not to shout at her since her children were taking in every word. "You can't go."

Even if he had been told, he would have argued against her coming along. When his father proposed this trip to take some livestock to the Santiagos, and to transport some goods to Lucio's sister, Yoana, Lucio had been delighted to get away from the temptation Rosalinda presented. She was not the type of woman he wanted to be attracted to. Not at all.

And truth be known...

He. Was. Not. Attracted to her.

He pictured his mother. Her innocence. Her love for his father. Her love of God. That was the kind of woman he wanted. One who would treasure him as much as his mother had treasured his father. Not a woman who flirted with every man who crossed her path.

Of course, Lucio hadn't witnessed Rosalinda flirting lately, but what did that mean? Enticing men must be part of her nature. Hadn't she had been taught this behavior at an early age?

Not that it was her fault. He understood. He truly did. Still, she had been that way for so many years, how could she change now? How could she ever belong to one man alone?

"We're up here." Maria jumped up and down, clapping her hands. Lucio started from his reverie as all three children laughed and clapped. Luis leaped for him, and Lucio barely had time to lift his arms and grab the boy. He almost lost his hold and pulled the toddler against his chest to steady him. The scent of child and soap and boy made him want to hold Luis longer. Instead, he set him on the ground—only to have Rosalinda sweep him back into the wagon.

"Me." Isabel launched toward him. She slammed into his chest, her thin arms wrapping around his neck. She smacked a kiss against his jaw, and his heart clenched. He'd wanted a family of his own for so long but hadn't found the right woman. Why did he have to be so attracted to Rosalinda? Did he just like her for her children? One glance into the woman's hazel eyes gave him a clear answer.

No.

She shook her hair back over her shoulder again. Her full lips pursed in a feigned pout. On any other woman the expression would look childish and ridiculous, but on her, those lips only made his heart race and his thoughts drift into dangerous territory.

"I am going with you. Maria wants to see her friend, Teo." She leaned forward the slightest bit. Lucio almost swayed on his feet. He snapped his thoughts back.

"This is not a pleasure trip. The going will be rough and we could encounter dangers. Your children would be at risk." He would not give in, no matter what wiles she used.

"I would see my friend, Yoana. I can help on the journey." Her chin tilted up just a bit. Her eyes darkened. Lucio almost snorted at the thought of Yoana being Rosalinda's friend. He'd heard about the rivalry between them when Yoana was held captive in the bandolero camp.

"I can take a letter to Yoana from you. I'm sure she will love hearing from you." He flinched inside. He couldn't imagine Yoana being glad to hear from her nemesis.

"I am going with you." Rosalinda took a step closer. "My niños are going too." She took another step. He could see the gold flecks among the green and brown in her eyes. Her full lips reddened.

His heart pounded harder than a blacksmith's hammer.

Around them the noise of horses stamping, men shouting, and cattle lowing faded. The sight of this fiery woman filled his world. He couldn't breathe. He wanted to shake some sense into her. To give her an order she would obey. To kiss her until she understood they shouldn't be in close proximity to each other.

He stepped back. What was he *thinking?* She'd never shown

any interest in him, not any more than she'd shown in every man on the ranch, no matter the age. She even flirted with the few visitors they received. The woman was shameless.

Rosalinda glared at him as if she wanted to turn him to stone. The *niños* jumped up and down in the back of the wagon clamoring for more rides to the ground.

He took a step back and saw triumph flash in her eyes. She thought he had given up. Perish the thought. He would win this battle.

Taking another step back, he watched as Rosalinda put her hands on her hips. Her bright lips tipped in the start of a smile. She lifted her chin just the slightest as if to tell him he didn't measure up.

Without losing eye contact he reached over and plucked Maria from the wagon and set her on the ground. She squealed. Isabel already had her arms out when he swung her down too. Rosalinda's smile turned to a frown.

He didn't have to reach for Luis. The toddler leaped to him. Before he could set the boy beside his sisters, his mother grabbed onto him, halting Lucio's downward swing.

They stood, once again almost nose-to-nose, Luis dangling between them. He could feel the heat of her hands just below his. Their fingers almost touched. He only had to move his little finger down an inch to make contact with hers.

"We are going."

"You're not going."

They spoke in unison, glaring at one another. He wanted to close his eyes and avoid getting drawn into the mesmerizing depths of hers, but he could picture the exultation on her face if he did. She would see it as him backing down. He would not back down. They were not going.

He tugged on Luis. She pulled back. Luis giggled. Lucio lifted the boy higher. She pulled him back down. Luis didn't seem to understand the gravity of the situation. He flung his head back and laughed with childish delight. Despite his annoyance, the sound of the child's laughter lightened Lucio's mood. Rosalinda's glare softened.

"There you are. I see you are ready to go."

ROSALINDA WANTED to weep with relief when she heard Leya speak. Lucio's *tía* had invited her to come along, saying she needed another woman on the trip with her. Plus, she'd said Teo would love to see his best friend, Maria. The children had been inseparable in the bandolero camp.

Without letting go of Luis, she looked over her shoulder and smiled at Leya. "We are just getting the children in the wagon." She tried to guide Luis closer to the wagon. Lucio resisted.

"Lucio, thank you for helping Rosalinda with the children. I meant to be here earlier but was delayed. Can you help me with my bag after you put Luis down?" Rosalinda saw the hint of a smirk through Leya's *mantilla*.

"Luis must have put on a lot of weight if it takes the two of you to put him in the wagon." Leya chuckled.

Rosalinda wanted to laugh at the absurdity of both of them having to lift her son. He weighed almost nothing. But she refused to let go because Lucio would not give up telling her they couldn't go. She wasn't even sure why going to visit Yoana and Teo had become so important to her. Whatever the reason, it certainly wasn't because she wanted to spend time with this one man who refused to acknowledge her wiles and went out of his way to avoid her.

No, she would *not* be intrigued by him. She knew men. If anyone knew them, she did. They wanted only one thing from a woman. Well, maybe two. They also liked to be waited on by a subservient woman. Which she was not. Lucio might appear different, but he would be the same as all the others. Perhaps this trip would prove her right.

Lucio didn't let go but shifted to look at his *tía*. His dark brows drew together, and a frown creased his forehead. Rosalinda could only imagine his distress over seeing Leya with her bag packed. She hadn't told him she intended to visit the Santiagos.

"Tía, what are you doing?"

Rosalinda glanced over her shoulder to see Leya trying to lift her heavy leather satchel into the wagon. Lucio released Luis and jumped forward to help his tía. Rosalinda set her son back beside his sisters, who had climbed up on their own. She shooed the trio toward the far end of the conveyance so Lucio couldn't reach them.

"I am traveling to see my niece." Leya's light tone conveyed her excitement over the trip. She must be ignoring the thundercloud of emotion hovering over her nephew's head. Rosalinda half expected lightning bolts to shoot out from him and drop them all in their tracks.

"This is not a pleasure trip." Lucio's jaw clenched tight. "The journey will be long and arduous. You can't go. Neither can Rosalinda and her children. Children! What are you thinking taking them?" His eyes flashed as he turned to see the objects of his wrath too far in the front of the wagon for him to reach. Rosalinda smirked at him. He focused on his tía.

"Don Armenta has given his permission." Leya stepped closer to Rosalinda and held out her arm. Rosalinda slipped her hand through her cohort's. She sent Lucio a saucy smile and let her hips sway more than usual as she rounded the buckboard to climb to the seat.

"No." Lucio hurried around to face them before they could climb aboard. At the front, one of the vaqueros lined up the horses that would pull the wagon and then hitched them to the traces. The wagon jolted, and the children squealed.

"I will not put my family in danger by taking you on this trip." He held his palms out to them.

"You consider me family?" Rosalinda widened her smile to the one that usually had men stuttering and forgetting what they intended to say or do.

Lucio stared at her, mouth agape. He blinked. The vaquero behind him paused in his duties to ogle her. In fact, most of the vaqueros had stopped to watch the drama unfold.

"You're right. She is *familia*." Leya patted Lucio's stubbled cheek. He blinked and focused on her. "Now, help me up." She reached for the wagon seat and climbed aboard. As if in a daze, Lucio lifted her up. He reached for Rosalinda when his tía had settled but shook his head.

"No." He expelled a breath. "Tía Leya, get back down here. You are not going with us. Neither is Rosalinda or her niños. That is final."

"Lucio, there are dangers here at the ranch. We can't be safe all the time." Leya's words sobered them all. From his expression, Lucio had to be remembering a few months ago when his sister and tía were abducted by bandoleros and held captive for months. He had become overprotective since their return, knowing his tía suffered at the hands of outlaws as a young woman. That capture resulted in her ruination for marriage and in the ropy scar that went down her cheek and neck, the reason she always wore a mantilla.

"If you stay close to home, there is a better chance to protect you." The anger faded in Lucio's eyes to be replaced by anguish. He took his duties to care for his family members very seriously. From all Rosalinda had heard, he'd sacrificed much to keep hunting for his tía and sister when they were taken. They would have been sold to a horrible fate if he hadn't persisted despite the objections from his father, the don.

"*Mijo.*" Leya leaned down to cup his cheek in a gesture so tender Rosalinda's chest tightened, and she struggled to breathe. Had anyone ever touched her with such tenderness and love? Never.

"Mijo, we must remember God is in charge of what happens.

As much as I love and appreciate you, God is my protector." She pulled her hand away and sat upright. "Now, lift Rosalinda up so we can get started before the day is past."

"Wait."

Rosalinda turned to see one of the servant girls hurrying toward them, a pile of blankets in her arms stacked so high she could barely see over them.

Lucio groaned. "Not another one." His mouth pinched as he turned to Rosalinda. "Are you planning to bring every female on the ranch?"

"Maybe." She gave him a sly smile. His face darkened, and he ducked his head.

She always had such power over men. Most of them would give her whatever she wanted as long as she pleased them. That hadn't been as true of the bandolero, Cisto, who bought her and took her to the camp where she met Leya and Yoana. She could manipulate him some, but he had a violent temper and hurt her more often than not. He took pleasure in hurting women. She didn't regret his death in the desert.

Besides Cisto, only Lucio resisted her charms. She never would have convinced him to take her on this trip if Leya hadn't decided to go. He loved his tía and would do most anything to please her.

"I brought blankets for your children to sit on and to keep them warm at night." The girl's breath huffed in and out when she stopped beside them. Rosalinda grabbed the blankets and dropped them into the wagon bed. Maria and Isabel spread them in the open area.

"I wish you a safe trip and ask you to give my greeting to Yoana." With a small smile the girl backed away. Lucio's shoulders lost some of their stiffness as she left. He must have realized the young woman wouldn't be traveling with them.

"We're ready to go, boss." Ramón strode up to them. He gave Rosalinda a wink, his droopy mustache lifting as he smiled at her.

She winked back at him just to see Lucio's reaction. His face flushed again, this time maybe not in embarrassment. Could it be…? Did he avoid her because he found her attractive? A thought to consider.

While she had no romantic feelings for Ramón, perhaps she could use him to manipulate Lucio. After all, that's what a woman should do with a man. If they wanted to use her, she figured she was justified in doing the same to them. She had to provide for her children somehow.

"Have the lead wagons head out. We're almost ready here." Lucio shifted, and his spurs jangled.

"If you want, I can ride with the women and see that they are safe. Someone needs to drive the wagon." Ramón gestured to where Leya waited.

Lucio glanced up as if he hadn't considered who would drive them. His dark eyes were unreadable. Did he trust his head vaquero enough to let him be around the women all day?

"You go get the herd and lead wagons started. I'll see to my tía." Lucio watched as Ramón left, then turned to Rosalinda.

His visage revealed he was as angry as she'd ever seen him.

CHAPTER TWO

THE AFTERNOON SUN had burned away any lingering morning chill. Sweat trickled down Rosalinda's back. She wanted to scratch, but Luis drowsed in her arms. If she moved, the toddler would be climbing all over just as he'd done since they'd gotten on the road.

From the corner of her eye, she could see Lucio's stoic expression. Did he really not care to look at her, or was he making himself ignore her? Leya insisted they switch places when Luis kept crawling all over Lucio trying to "help" guide the horses. Rosalinda knew the switch had been a ploy on Leya's part, but she didn't mind. She intended to figure out this man while they traveled, and sitting next to him would provide opportunities. Maybe this time flirting would catch his attention as it did every other man.

She overheard him talking to Leya about which vaquero he would trust to drive the wagon with the women and children. Not that he didn't trust his vaqueros. She knew he did. Leya had whispered to her that Lucio didn't want any other man to sit next to her because he was sweet on her.

Ha! Sweet on her. When had a man ever had such innocent thoughts about her? Not in her memory. She doubted Lucio had them now.

He glanced her way and caught her looking at him. She smiled. He blushed. For a man who ran a large operation with many men answering to him, he didn't have much experience with women. Still, his men all respected him. She'd never heard anyone say anything negative about him. From the servants who cooked and cleaned to the men who rode with him every day to check the herds, they all loved him. A testament of his character...but she would see. Many powerful men were one way in public but much different when they were alone with her.

Luis relaxed even more. His deep breathing told her he slept. Finally. Since leaving the bandolero camp, Rosalinda had struggled to learn how to mother these children. In the mountains they had run wild, but that wouldn't do at the Armenta hacienda. Leya had been a huge help in teaching her how to corral her niños and keep them entertained. She'd also helped Rosalinda teach Maria her letters and numbers. Since Rosalinda herself had had no schooling before, she appreciated Leya's pretense that she was only teaching the children. In the past few months she'd learned to read and write a little and could add simple figures.

Maria stuck her head between Rosalinda and Lucio. "Mama, how soon will I see Teo? Are we almost there?" Her hazel eyes shone, and Rosalinda's heart clenched. Maria would become such a beautiful young woman. Men would want her just like they wanted Rosalinda. She would do all in her power to protect her daughter from the fate she'd endured.

"It will be many days, mija. We have far to travel."

Lucio smiled down at her daughter, but his smile didn't contain even a glimmer of the predatory gleam Rosalinda saw in the men who visited her. She relaxed a little.

"Days? I want to be there now. It's been long." Maria's lower lip stuck out.

Rosalinda tensed. Would Lucio strike out at the child as Cisto always did? His face softened, and a slight smile crinkled the corners of his eyes.

"Teo." Isabel pulled up to the back of the seat, stretching on her tiptoes to be as tall as her sister. Almost four-years-old, the younger girl wanted to do everything Maria did and often mimicked everything her sibling said, much to Maria's annoyance.

"You both need to sit down." Rosalinda gave her daughters a stern look as the wagon jounced and they stumbled to one side. Only their grasp on the seat kept them from tumbling to the wagon bed.

"Sit down before you wake your brother." She kept her voice pitched low as the toddler stirred in her arms.

"Do as your mother says." Lucio started to turn but had to guide the horses around a rut in the road as he spoke. Maria's eyes widened, and Rosalinda knew her daughter remembered Cisto and his volatile temper.

"Hurry. Sit down." Fear laced Maria's command as she tugged at her sister.

Rosalinda's heart hurt. Oh, if only she could have changed things for the better for her niños! They hadn't deserved the life they'd lived. Had she? What could she have done that was so horrible she deserved the cruelty and degradation that had been visited upon her for years?

"Ramón." Lucio waved a hand at the man who cantered toward them. Maria and Isabel lifted back up on their knees to see the vaquero. They were always in awe of the cowboys and the horses.

"Sí, boss." Ramón pulled his horse to a walk beside them. He nodded at Rosalinda and Leya.

"I have a job for you." Lucio glanced as Rosalinda as if he wanted to ask her something and then turned back to Ramón. "I have a couple of passengers who are tired of riding in the wagon and could use a change of scenery. Do you have a couple of vaqueros who could help with this?"

"Hmmm." Ramón twisted the tip of his mustache. "Would these be small passengers?" His eyes gleamed, and Rosalinda could see his teeth through the droop of his mustache as he grinned.

Did Lucio mean her girls? What did he want the vaqueros to do with her girls? Maria wasn't even seven-years-old! What did he mean to do with them?

"Don't worry." Leya's hand on her arm stopped Rosalinda. She looked at the older woman, unable to put her fear into words.

Leya leaned close. "I think Lucio means for the girls to ride around the wagons with the vaqueros. These men would take very good care of the niñas. They would not hurt them."

"I believe I have room on my *caballo* for the two you have in mind. A small one in front of me and a bigger one behind me." Ramón tipped his sombrero farther back on his head and leaned over to look at the girls in the wagon. He winked at them. Maria giggled. Isabel mimicked, putting her hand over her mouth just like her *hermana* did.

"¿Está bien, señora?" Ramón addressed Rosalinda, and the kindness in his eyes eased her tense muscles. She trusted Ramón. She knew him well enough to hope he was not at all like the men she'd known before she came to the ranch.

"Sí. If you will be careful with the passengers." Rosalinda watched her daughters. They still didn't understand what was being said. She watched to see their excitement when they realized they would get to ride on a horse.

"Maria." Lucio tugged the reins, bringing the team of horses to a stop. He turned to smile at the little girl. "Do you think you are big enough to climb on behind Ramón and hold on tight to him?"

Maria's mouth made an O. "I could ride his horse?" Her eyes shone.

"Me. Ride a horse." Isabel clapped her hands.

"Come here, Maria. I'll help you on." Lucio reached over the seat back and lifted Maria as if she weighed nothing. He turned her around. Ramón edged his horse closer. Lucio held Maria so she could get her leg over the back of the saddle. Ramón reached behind him to steady her.

"*Yo también.*" Isabel's eyes welled with tears as she reached one slender arm over the seat back toward her sister. "Yo también."

Lucio swung around, his hand swinging toward Isabel. Rosalinda's throat tightened in a stranglehold. "No!"

She clasped Lucio's arm before he could touch her daughter. Behind her, she heard Leya say something, but the buzzing in her ears cut off all other sound. She could only see Cisto's hand bearing down on her and the threats he made toward her niños.

No man would ever hurt her daughters again!

Lucio's gaze focused on her. His mouth moved. She couldn't hear his words. She dug her fingers deeper into his arm.

He smiled at her. Not the sadistic *I-will-hurt-you-later* smile Cisto had used, but a genuine *I-care-about-you* expression. She fought to breathe. Realized he was doing exaggerated breathing with her. In. Out. In. Out.

Sound rushed back in. Isabel crying. Leya praying. Lucio murmuring, "Está bien. I won't hurt her."

Tears burned her eyes. A wave of exhaustion washed over her. He hadn't meant to hurt Isabel. Of course, he hadn't. She knew that. All the times she'd been around him, he'd never reacted in anger. But would he be the same in private?

She turned to Isabel. "Mija, you have to stop crying. You can't ride the horse if you are making so much noise."

In an instant, Isabel was all smiles. Lucio grinned at the child as he lifted her over the divider and onto the saddle in front of Ramón. Oh, if only she could turn her emotions off and on as easily as her little one.

Would she ever be free of this fear and distrust?

15

Lucio watched Ramón ride off with his precious cargo, making sure his friend was taking care with the two little girls. The joy on their faces didn't bleed over onto their mother. Rosalinda looked as if she wanted to snatch them back.

Rosalinda always seemed so sure of herself, so confident and in charge. But there for a moment, she'd seemed frozen with fear. From what his sister, Yoana, and her husband, Gabrio, had shared with him about the bandolero camp, Lucio was sure it was because of Cisto. The bandit was so evil he would do anything and not be bothered by his conscience, and he had beat Rosalinda and threatened everyone one in camp.

Cold chills snaked through him. Did she really think he could be a monster like Cisto? He started to demand how she could think that but held himself in check, taking a moment to pray.

"Rosalinda." He kept his voice low and controlled, but he knew Leya heard him too. Rosalinda had curled around Luis as if drawing comfort from the child in her arms. "Rosalinda, I want you to know there is nothing one of your children could do that would make me strike them in anger. Do you understand?"

He watched her nod, but she kept her head bowed, so very different from the sassy woman he'd seen around the ranch. What horrors had she experienced to make her behave this way?

Leya lifted aside her veil, and he could see the concern in her eyes. His tía must understand more than he ever could.

Perhaps Rosalinda struggled because she had never been in a situation where she had to guide her children instead of simply keeping them alive. The tales Gabrio told about that camp nauseated him. Perhaps her bravado at the ranch was an act, something she learned at the camp…a way to stay alive. Could it be…?

Did she have no idea how to react to kindness?

He wanted to touch her. To comfort her. To pull her close—

He shook his head. Give him the saucy, talk-back-to-him woman any day, because with her he wanted to keep his distance.

This vulnerable señora...was dangerous to his heart. He tightened his hands on the reins.

"Mama." Luis batted sleepy eyes and reached up to pat his mother's face. He popped up, wide awake and ready to go. Lucio could almost see the niño's mind working at a lope as he tried to decide what to do next.

A long-forgotten memory surfaced as the young boy squirmed on Rosalinda's lap. Lucio shifted the reins to his left hand.

"*Ven acá.*" He held out his right hand to the toddler. Rosalinda's eyes were moist with unshed tears as she looked from Luis to Lucio. "Luis, come help me drive the horses."

The young boy's mouth fell open. He stared at Lucio briefly before scrambling to get to him.

Lucio smiled at Rosalinda. "Está bien. He will not be so jealous when his sisters return." He situated the young boy on his lap and then took the reins back in both hands.

"Here, Luis. Put your hands on mine and hold the reins like I do." He showed the boy how to gently tug the lines to guide the team around any rocks or other obstacles. Luis listened with studied intent for one so young. Lucio peered at the boy's face. The toddler's wide smile warmed his heart. His mother had insisted on fun times for her family. He hadn't realized until he'd grown up that those times were actually showing him important jobs or lessons in life.

"*Gracias.*" Rosalinda ran her hand down Luis's hair, brushing her fingers across Lucio's arm. His breath caught even at the light touch. Her smile, different from her usual come-hither one, set his pulse racing.

"Maria! Isa!" Luis bounced on Lucio's lap, excitement vibrating through him. "*Mira!* Look!"

Ramón guided his mount next to the wagon as Lucio, with Luis's help, pulled back on the reins to halt the team. The two girls were grinning, their cheeks flushed from their ride. Ramón chuckled as he helped Isabel into the wagon first. "Looks like we have a new driver."

"*I* want to drive." Maria leaped for the wagon, and Ramón almost lost his hold on her. Rosalinda gasped but didn't say anything as her daughter landed in the wagon bed.

"Yo también." Isabel clapped her hands and tried to climb over the seat back. Rosalinda shushed her, telling the girls to stay put.

Ramón smiled at his patron. "We are almost at the camping spot for the night. Carlos will bring your horse as you asked. He'll tie him to the back of the wagon. Want me to take the wee one for a short ride?" He nodded his head toward Luis.

Lucio turned to Rosalinda. He could see the trepidation in her eyes, but she nodded.

"Luis, let go of the reins, and you can ride with Ramón like your sisters did." Lucio grinned at Rosalinda when the boy almost jumped into Ramón's arms. Her *niños* had been so shy and withdrawn when they'd first come to the rancho, but every day he could see progress as they relaxed among people who cared about them. Even Isabel talked more like a child than a baby.

"There you go." Ramón settled Luis in front of him and let the boy take the reins--or at least he let him hold the ends of the reins. Luis bounced up and down, eager to get the horse moving.

Rosalinda laughed at her son's antics. *Laughed.* Such a free, delightful sound. Lucio nearly tumbled from his perch at the edge of the seat. Everything she did or said on the ranch had been designed to get attention of one sort or another. Usually male attention. Perhaps he was right, that her behavior was a ploy because she only knew that type of behavior. Maybe she just needed to learn new conduct.

"I want to go too." Maria poked her head beside Lucio's arm. "He has room for two. I could sit behind again."

"No, you've had your turn." Rosalinda gave her daughter a stern look that had Maria sinking down onto the blankets beside Isabel, an adorable pout on her sweet face.

When her mother turned back toward the front, and Ramón rode off with Luis squealing in front of him, Maria stood and cupped her hand to Lucio's ear. *"Me gusan caballos."*

He chuckled and turned to put his mouth next to her ear. "I know you like horses. I'll see that you get to ride every day when we return to the hacienda. Pretty soon you'll be experienced enough to ride your own horse." Her smile warmed him clear through. Nothing like a delighted child to make a man's day.

"Boss." Carlos cantered up leading Lucio's dun. Lucio halted the team and motioned to the back. He waited until Carlos tied his mount and took off. He chucked the reins and the wagon jerked into motion.

The girls settled down onto the blankets, their voices a soft murmur. They must be tired after the long day. They would be glad for the stop tonight when they could get down and run off a little energy, which he knew from experience they would have stored for later. He remembered trips from his own youth when they had visited the Santiago familia. Like Maria, he thought they would never arrive.

"I am glad we'll be stopping soon." Leya lifted her mantilla and made a face at him. "I am getting tired of this hard seat. Perhaps tomorrow I can walk for a while, if that won't slow us down too much."

"Me too." Rosalinda shifted on the bench. "We can let the children walk with us. They will become hard to manage cooped up in a wagon. Sometimes I think they could run for miles and not get tired."

"That is the way of children." Leya chuckled. "My sister's niños were that way for sure."

"Hey." Lucio tried to pretend offense, but he knew she spoke truth. He, Yoana, and his brothers had been hard to corral. Leya often told stories of their antics. She hadn't been much older than his eldest brother, but after his mother died, Leya had taken on the señora's duties. She hadn't been visible to company because of her scar and shame, but she had been there for them.

"There comes Luis." Leya pointed at Ramón's horse across the camp. "I think the girls have fallen asleep. They are so quiet." She turned...

...and gasped.

CHAPTER THREE

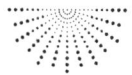

"¿Qué es?" Lucio swung around at the same time Rosalinda did. He froze, staring in disbelief. "How?"

"No." Rosalinda looked like she wanted to scream, but the sound came out in a whisper.

He realized he hadn't heard the girls talking for several minutes. Maybe longer. Somehow, they had pulled his dun up beside the wagon. They were both in the saddle, Isabel in front and Maria behind her. The rein tethering his horse to the wagon hung loose, the loop almost undone.

"Stay calm." Lucio kept his tone even as he reached across Rosalinda to give the wagon reins to Leya. He knew she could handle the horses. "Ease them to a stop." She nodded at his instruction.

"Rosalinda, get Ramón's attention, but don't make any sudden movements. I'll go over the back of the seat and try to get the horse's reins before they come free." He squeezed her arm, hating the panic that tightened her features. Her wide eyes begged him to save her niñas.

The dun snorted. Lucio saw Maria kicking her little heels into the horse's flanks. "Maria, don't kick. He won't like that." She grinned at him and kicked again. Isabel tried to imitate her sister, but her little legs were too short. The scene would have been comical if the situation weren't so dire.

The horse snorted again. As Lucio approached, the dun backed away and jerked his head. The rein dropped free. For a frozen moment, Lucio held his breath. *Sit still, little ones. Sit still. Please, God, don't let the horse take it in his head to race off to join the other horses.* Where was Ramón? Would he be able to help since he had Luis with him?

"I'm behind you, boss. Handing off Luis." Ramón sounded as calm as if this happened every day. As if little girls who didn't know a thing about riding could climb on a feisty mount and just take off. Sometimes even Lucio had trouble keeping his dun in check. How could he expect these little niñas to come out unscathed?

"I'll go around the front." Ramon's horse's hooves clopped in the dirt. Lucio waited until he could see the vaquero's chestnut mare rounding the wagon. Then he eased forward again.

"*Vámanos, caballo!*" At Maria's yell, the dun laid his ears back.

"Vamso, ballo." Isabel's imitation didn't come out quite right, but she waved her arms. The dun snorted and shied farther away from the wagon.

"Easy." Ramón sidled his mare alongside Lucio's stallion. The dun calmed. Ramón leaned down to gather up the reins. Lucio breathed out his relief. Behind him, Rosalinda shuddered out a breath that echoed his.

"You girls heading for an adventure?" Ramón plucked Isabel from the saddle and handed her to Lucio, who hugged her and kissed her on the cheek before setting her down. He kissed Maria and held her a moment longer, his eyes closed. *Thank you, God. Thank you.*

He turned, expecting to see a weeping Rosalinda, a mother ready to hug her children. Instead, she stared at him with a fiery gaze that threatened to burn him to cinders. He almost backed up a step.

Almost.

"You put my niñas in danger." Rosalinda stood and leaned over to set Luis on the blankets beside his sisters. "My niñas. I trusted you with them, and you almost killed them. Her voice rose to a near shriek. Leya put her hand on Rosalinda's sleeve, but the younger woman shook her off.

"Why didn't you tell me they could reach your caballo? Why?" If her ire hadn't been directed at him, Lucio would have been standing back admiring this woman. Here was the one who captured his attention around the ranch. *This* woman could conquer countries. He liked the quiet version, the one who inspired his protection, but the woman he faced now was a danger to him. To his heart.

"I had no idea--"

"You had no idea?" She swung her leg over the seatback, giving him an enticing view of a shapely calf. He jerked his eyes up only to meet flashing hazel eyes.

"You had no idea." She stalked to him across the wagon bed. Her finger poked him in the chest. From the corner of his eye, he could see Ramón swipe at his mouth as if trying to keep from laughing.

"You put my niñas in danger because you didn't *think*. They are children. You knew they wanted to ride the horse again, and you left yours where they could reach him. A dangerous horse." She poked him again. He couldn't tear his gaze from hers.

"I've seen you when that beast is giving you trouble and you're fighting to get him under control. How did you expect my girls to ride him?"

Before he could say anything, she poked him a third time, continuing her rant about how he endangered her children. For a moment he almost responded with a firm reprimand, but then he looked beyond her words and saw her mother's heart in her eyes.

She was afraid.

Afraid her daughters could have died or been injured. It wasn't anger that had her shaking. It was fear.

Ignoring everything and everyone, he pulled her close. Her fists battered his chest. Her accusations became more choked and incoherent. Wrenching sobs shook her. He held her until the storm passed, until she'd spent all her fear and collapsed against him. Even then, he didn't want to ever let her go.

"Está bien." He murmured to her, as though soothing a horse, although he would never tell her about the comparison. "Está bien. I didn't know, but they are all right."

He rubbed his hand up and down her back in a motion he remembered his tía using when he was a child and distraught over something. When Rosalinda pushed away, brushing her hair back from her face, he wanted to pull her back to him.

"I will start tomorrow teaching Maria some of the basics of riding." He held up a hand when he saw her objection coming. "If she is this forward with horses, she needs to know what she is doing. I don't have any children's mounts along, but she can ride with Ramón or with me. I can teach Isabel too."

"But they could get hurt."

"They could fall out of the wagon and get hurt." He couldn't resist wiping a tear from her cheek.

"Mama, *por favor*." Maria tugged on her mother's skirt. "I will be a good rider. I can show Teo when we see him. He knows how to ride too. He asked Leya to tell me that. Please."

Rosalinda glanced back at Leya. His tía nodded.

"I will think about this and give you my answer tomorrow." Rosalinda smoothed Maria's hair, and her tone was firm but gentle. "You scared me, mija. You scared us all. Lucio's horse is not a horse for children."

"I'm not a child." Maria stomped her foot. "I am *not*."

"You are not an adult either." Rosalinda's frown silenced the niña. "Now, we will walk the rest of the way to the camp. ¿Está bien?" She directed the question to Lucio.

"Yes. We aren't far." He could barely get the words out. How could a woman be so beautiful when her nose had reddened and there were tear tracks on her cheeks? He had to find someone else to drive this wagon. His resolve to find a woman like his mother was slipping fast. He had to get his heart back on track.

In the distance he could see the lead wagons stopping and the men scurrying around setting up camp. If Rosalinda and her children were walking, he would take this wagon on to the camp. Otherwise, he would take his dun and let Leya bring the wagon in. She could do it.

"Ramón, take my horse. I'll catch up to you." He nodded at the vaquero as he took off with the dun in tow.

He jumped from the wagon to help Rosalinda down. He swung the children to the ground, not finding their squeals of delight as intriguing as they had been earlier. When they were taken care of, he rounded to look up at Leya. "Do you want to walk or ride with me?"

"I believe I will accompany Rosalinda and the niños." She took his hand and stepped down, always the lady.

He climbed back up to the seat, picked up the reins and paused. Rosalinda came alongside and stopped to look up at him.

He cleared his throat. "Tomorrow, I will have Ramón drive the wagon." Lucio fought to find a good reason that didn't sound like he was trying to avoid the most enticing woman he'd ever met. "I need to oversee the livestock and make sure everything is running smoothly. Ramón will do a good job."

He flicked the reins before she could object.

THE NEXT MORNING, the smell of the campfire made Rosalinda's stomach churn. How many months had she lived in the mountains with the bandoleros after Cisto bought her? So many mornings she had struggled to even walk down to the fire to help with the cooking as expected. The memory of his cruelty shuddered through her. Would she ever be free of him? Of what he'd done to her? She closed her eyes. Leya spoke of a God of love. If He existed, He could make sure her children would have no lasting memories of that time. She would pray for that, if Leya's God would listen.

She slitted her eyes open. The children and Leya were still asleep, as was most of the camp. The pearly gray of dawn lightened the night sky. Within moments everyone would be stirring, and another day of travel would begin. She almost regretted coming on this trip. Had she stayed at the ranch, these memories wouldn't have plagued her. She wouldn't have shown Lucio and Leya her weakness and fear.

Her face warmed at the thought and made her shift in her blankets. The wagon bed creaked. She froze as Leya stirred. She needed a few more moments alone to sift through the events of yesterday. How had she become such a mewling weakling?

Her earliest memories were of standing her ground against bullies who attacked her younger sister. She'd been about Maria's age then, maybe a year older. It wasn't long before that horrible day. Even the beatings and degradation she'd suffered in the past years had only served to strengthen her resolve. So what was different yesterday?

Lucio.

Lucio had been different. Instead of raising his hand to her or to her children, he'd reacted with kindness. Not one man in all she'd known had ever shown her any compassion. Ever. She did what they demanded of her or she suffered. Or, worse, her children suffered.

When Lucio kissed her girls instead of beating them, she couldn't cope with it. How was she even to react to such a response from a man? Her anger had surprised even her, but she hadn't been able to stop it. Should she apologize to him? What would she say? No matter what words she went over in her mind, they made her sound weak. Lucio would then take advantage of her. Wouldn't he?

Her boldness, even her belligerence, had served her well up to now. How could she possibly change? She squeezed her eyelids tight as the need to shed tears burned at them. Why her? Why couldn't her life have been one of family and a home? Maybe going to church and believing in a loving God like Leya and Yoana. Why did her life have to be so horrible? A solitary tear leaked out to trickle down the side of her face. She held her breath against the sobs that wanted to come.

Voices drifted to her. The vaqueros starting to round up the stock and hitch the wagons. The smell of coffee made her sigh. Leya touched her arm, squeezing it. Rosalinda stilled. Had the woman seen her tears? Heard the suppressed sobs? Noted the shudders that wracked Rosalinda? She hoped not. The last thing she wanted was to try to explain this sudden bout of emotion.

"I forgot how hard a wagon bed could be." Leya groaned as she sat up and stretched. She reached behind to rub at her back before picking up her mantilla and putting it on. Rosalinda understood Leya's need for the privacy the covering provided. So many people recoiled at the sight of the scar that marred her face. In the bandolero camp, Leya had been forced to go without her mantilla and had become used to doing so. But the outlaws were used to seeing people who were not perfect.

"Mama, good morning." Maria shoved aside her blanket and scrambled to her feet. Rosalinda's moments of reflection were over. Another busy day had begun. She pushed all her doubts and hesitations to the back of her mind as she helped her children down and herded them into the trees. She herded them back to help Leya with morning chores.

"Are you riding or walking?" Ramón tipped his hat as he tied his horse to the back of the wagon. He frowned at Maria, Isabel, and Luis. "You are not to try riding my horse without permission.

Is that understood?" Three solemn niños nodded. "So, ladies, riding or walking?"

"I am so stiff this morning." Leya lifted her shoulders and let them drop. "I think I will walk first to limber up. Rosalinda?"

"The niños and I will walk with Leya. That way no one will be tempted to take your caballo." She smiled at Ramón, and he blushed like a young boy.

"If you want me to stop the wagon for you, just wave or call out. I won't be far ahead." Ramón climbed up onto the bench seat and slapped the reins.

The wagon gave a loud creak. Rosalinda smiled. Maybe it had muscles as sore as hers.

"Let's have a treasure hunt." Maria pointed at the road in front of them. "We'll see who can find the best treasure to bring to Mama and Tía Leya." She clapped her hands and led the way, with Isabel and Luis close on her heels. Leya smiled and hooked her arm through Rosalinda's.

"Your niños are a delight. I enjoy having them around the hacienda." Leya chuckled as Luis bent to pick something up and almost toppled over.

"I am..." Could she find the words to express what she wanted to say? "I am learning to enjoy them." She glanced at Leya. Why had she said that? What must the older woman think? "I mean, I have always loved my children but haven't always been able to enjoy them."

Leya tipped her head to look up at Rosalinda. She lifted the veil, and her deep brown eyes glistened. "I understand. You have always done what you could to protect them. I am glad you are having this time now when you don't have to fight to exist."

Rosalinda's throat tightened. She swallowed hard. Fighting to exist. Yes. That explained her life since that dreadful day in her seventh year. All these years, she'd been existing, not living.

They walked in silence for a while, watching the niños scamper from one possible treasure to the next. The sun climbed in the sky, chasing the shadows the trees cast along the trail. Through the undergrowth of brush, Rosalinda caught a glimpse of a coyote trotting past them. She glanced to where Luis toddled on chubby legs, trying to keep up with his older sisters. He shouldn't be by himself.

"I would like to speak on behalf of my nephew." Leya smoothed her skirts before glancing at Rosalinda. She lifted the mantilla to the side again, and her eyes were sad.

"Lucio would never do anything to endanger your niños, or you. He is an honorable man."

"I know." And she did. So why had she reacted the wrong way every time yesterday? When she should have been strong and spoken up, she'd been weak. When she should have been grateful and thanked Lucio, she'd harped at him like the worst of harridans. She didn't understand her own reactions, how could she explain them to Leya?

"Lucio is interested in you, Rosa. I can see it in his eyes. The way he looks at you."

She snorted. "Men are always interested in me. All of them. It is the curse of having this face and this body. I don't know why Lucio would be any different."

Leya gasped, her hand covering her mouth. Shame hit Rosalinda, hot and punishing. She shouldn't have shared that truth so crudely. She hadn't meant to hurt Leya when she'd become a friend. The first true friend Rosalinda had ever had.

Maria and Isabel bent over something in the road. Luis had a fist full of flowers and trotted toward his sisters, his face alight with excitement. Her heart thumped at the joy on his face.

The wagons had drawn away from Rosalinda and the others. That was good. They didn't have as much dust to breathe. She also liked the quiet away from the men and animals.

"Lucio would be trustworthy and never view you in the way you mean." Leya's fingers gripped Rosalinda's arm, digging in as she pulled her to a stop. The intensity on her face spoke volumes.

She covered the older woman's hand with her own. "You must understand. I will never be anything to Lucio. I can never be anything good to him. My past...dishonors him. If he were with me, he would be shunned by all of his friends and peers. I am not for him, no matter what he might feel."

Leya's mouth pursed. The purple scar puckered the side of her face. Her eyes glittered. She didn't say a word, but Rosalinda knew she understood the truth of her words. Lucio was an upright man.

Precisely why there could never be anything between him and Rosalinda.

On impulse, Rosalinda bent down and hugged the older woman. Leya squeezed her tight. The embrace warmed Rosalinda in a way she'd never felt before. Had her own mother ever hugged her when she was a young girl? Not that she could recall.

"We'd better get going or we'll be left behind." Leya released her and they turned to walk on. Maria and Isabel still knelt together in the road. But, Luis—

Luis had disappeared.

CHAPTER FOUR

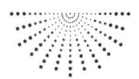

THE HERD of horses did not want to keep up the pace. They wanted to mosey. To stop and graze on the thick grass along the trail. To skitter away from the vaqueros trying to keep them on track. Lucio shook his head. Maybe it would have been better to put them on a line and lead them.

Of course, he hadn't been able to keep his mind on the job at hand. His brilliant decision of last night didn't seem so smart this morning, but he couldn't back out. Not without a valid reason for changing his mind, and not wanting Ramón to sit beside Rosalinda on that narrow wagon seat wasn't a good excuse.

All morning he'd had that picture in his head: Ramón sitting close enough that his arm brushed against hers. Rosalinda looking at him with lowered eyelids and that smile that turned intelligent men into imbeciles. Leya choosing to walk with the niños so the two could have time together.

His teeth gritted, sending a shock of pain through his tightened jaw. He had to get his thoughts in check. He knew the women had started out walking. Maybe they still were on foot. Besides, he had no reason to suspect his good friend would make a move on Rosalinda when he knew Lucio was attracted to her. He did know. Didn't he? Even though he *wasn't* attracted to her...

Stop! Enough of this battle between his mind and heart.

Lucio waved at the vaquero in charge of the herd and reined his dun around to check on the wagons. In the distance, he could see Ramón hanging back with the last wagon. He'd told him not to get too far from the women as they walked. The trail through here was safe enough, but he didn't want to take chances. He hadn't heard of any new gangs of bandoleros or trouble with bears or cougars, but that didn't mean there wasn't danger.

Ramón stood up on the wagon and turned around. A frisson of unease shivered through Lucio. Why was Ramón standing? Lucio nudged his horse to a trot. Ramón waved his arms over his head in Lucio's direction and leaped from the wagon, running to mount his chestnut. Lucio leaned forward in the saddle and slapped the reins against the dun's neck. Something was wrong.

His heart pounded in time with the horse's hooves. Rosalinda. Leya. The niños. What could have happened? Why had he let them get so far behind?

He rounded a curve in the road. Cries filled the air. He couldn't make out the words, but he heard his tía and Rosalinda. At the frantic timbre of their cries, he pushed his mount to go faster.

Ramón wheeled his horse to race toward Lucio. Maria and Isabel clung to their mother's skirt, but he didn't see Luis anywhere. Was he behind her? His heart thrummed against his ribs.

"The boy's missing." Ramón shouted as soon as Lucio was close enough. Lucio and Ramón skidded their horses to a stop.

"What happened?" Lucio looked through the undergrowth. At least they weren't near water where the niño could have fallen in.

"Luis was running to Rosalinda with some flowers. She and Leya looked away, and then he was gone. She said they looked away only for a moment." Ramón pulled his horse back around. "I don't know if I can pick up tracks here after all the wagons and horses have gone through."

"Luis is so light he wouldn't make much of an impression in the dirt." Lucio could feel the urgency building. They had to find the boy.

"I'll get the women and niñas to the wagon. They'll be safe there. Go get as many of the men as you can spare to help us search." Lucio shared a look with his friend. They both understood the desperation of the situation.

"I'll see if I can figure out which direction he went." Lucio reined the dun toward where Leya and Rosalinda stood calling Luis. They clung together, and the sight tore at Lucio.

When he swung out of the saddle, Rosalinda hurried to him. Her eyes were wide, her face pale. He'd never seen her like this.

"My baby. He's gone." She grasped his arm, digging her fingers in until it felt like she might touch bone. She shook him. "You have to find him."

"Stop." Lucio pried her fingers from his arm and wrapped her chilled hands in his. "Stop." He commanded again, his voice firm but calm. She blinked. Focused on him. Her eyes appeared glazed with what he assumed was worry.

"You can't panic." He gentled his tone. "Stay focused and help me find Luis. ¿Está bien?"

She jerked her head in a quick nod. Drew in a deep breath. Nodded again. He felt her relax. Released his grip on her fingers.

"Bien. Tell me what you saw. Everything."

Behind Rosalinda, he noted Leya biting her lip. She must not remember she had brushed her mantilla aside. Or maybe she didn't care since he was family and had seen her many times without the covering.

"We were walking, and the children ran ahead to have a treasure hunt." Rosalinda's breath caught in a half sob. She closed her eyes for a moment and then went on, telling about their walk and watching the children. When she came to the part where she and

Leya weren't watching, she glanced at his tía and stopped as if she couldn't say more.

"Did you see anything odd or different? Hear any sounds? Where was Luis the last time you saw him?" Lucio had to stop before he overwhelmed her with questions.

She gasped. "The coyote." She covered her mouth with her hand, her eyes widening. "There was a coyote trotting along through the brush going the same way as we were." She looked behind her.

He tilted his head toward a patch of brush. "Is that where you last saw Luis?" He took her hands in his again to help her focus.

She nodded, tears glimmering in her eyes. "Leya, please watch my niñas. I have to go find Luis."

Before he could react, she yanked her hands from his grasp and raced into the trees.

"Go, Lucio. I'll get the girls to safety." Leya herded the niñas toward the wagon. They had begun to cry, a reaction to their mother's angst.

Lucio swung onto the dun and urged him through the brush and trees in the direction Rosalinda had disappeared. A coyote. Mostly they were harmless, but he knew of instances when they had dragged off, or tried to drag away, small children.

Like Luis.

He caught up to Rosalinda. Her skirt had caught on a prickly brush. She was tugging frantically when he rode up. He swung down. "Stop." Once again, he covered her hands with his and waited for her to look at him. "Let me."

He loosened the twigs that had tangled the material into a knot and freed her. She gave a strangled sob. He gathered her against him. Felt her tears dampen his shirt. Reveled in the feel of her in his arms, all the while feeling guilty for wasting time.

"I'll take you back to the wagon." He stroked his hand down her loosened hair. "I need you to stay there with Leya. I can't search for Luis if I'm worried about you. My men will be here soon to help with the search."

"I'm sorry." Her breath shuddered. "I should have listened and stayed home."

He wanted to agree, but he couldn't deny he also wanted her here. "Come on."

By the time he got her back to the wagon where Leya and the girls waited, he could see Ramón and several of the vaqueros were reining to a stop beside his tía. He rode to meet them, explained the circumstances, and divided them up to search.

For the next hour he rode in a quadrant close to Ramón, peering under bushes and behind rocks, searching for one small boy. Cries of, "¿Luis, donde está?" rang through the trees. He saw no sign of a coyote or of Luis.

"I'm going to check on the other men." Ramón nodded and veered off through the trees, the grim set to his face saying what he wouldn't put to words.

No. Lucio refused to accept that they wouldn't find the boy.

He turned the dun back toward the starting point. If that was where Luis entered the trees, it had to be the best place to look.

About a hundred yards from the road, a spot of color caught his eye. He swung down from the dun to peer under a bush.

In a clump of grass rested a crumpled bouquet of flowers.

ROSALINDA'S EYES ached from staring into the trees searching for a glimpse of her little boy. She could see his sweet smile. Hear his laugh. Feel his arms wrapped around her neck. Would she ever have him with her again?

She clutched Isabel to her. Maria sat on the blankets beside Leya listening to a story about a coyote. The memory of Yoana telling the children Bible stories in the bandolero camp washed over her. She hadn't wanted to listen to the tales. Thought they weren't true. But Yoana showed a bravery in the face of danger that Rosalinda admired. She never gave up. Never backed down. Never lost hope.

Isabel's breathing softened as she slept. Rosalinda caught Leya's eye. "I need to go look. I'm putting Isabel down. Will you watch her?"

Leya looked like she wanted to argue but nodded.

"Can I go?" Maria rose up on her knees.

"No. You stay here and listen to Leya's story. I'll be back as soon as I find Luis." Rosalinda wanted to be as brave as Yoana. In truth, her bravado was a front. Deep inside lived a coward she did her best to cover up.

The wagon rocked as she jumped down. An uneven rut threatened to turn her ankle, but she caught herself in time. She hurried to the point where Luis disappeared.

She closed her eyes. Thought about Yoana talking about God and how He guided their footsteps. She'd read that in a song. In the Bible? Did the Bible have songs? She thought it was only words. Words she still struggled to read because she'd never had the chance for schooling.

"God, if You guide my footsteps to my bebé, I will consider You being real. I know You helped Yoana, and Leya loves You too. Please, help Luis." She opened her eyes. Nothing was different. Would God even listen to someone like her? Did he care about a woman who had done so much wrong? Who had lived a lifestyle––though not of her own choosing––that went against everything Christians thought was right?

She took a step toward the trees, uncertain what to do. If God guided her footsteps, wouldn't there be some direction? Nothing told her which way to go. She closed her eyes again and listened to the sounds around her. The chirp of birds. Bees buzzing. The flutter of leaves in the breeze. No niño's voice. No human voice at all.

"*Dios*, por favor." She put her whole heart into the plea. Kept her eyes closed. She didn't want to look and see no answer again. To be rejected by the One who supposedly loved everyone.

She slitted her eyes, afraid to open them fully. Movement. Her eyes snapped open. Lucio rode toward her through the trees. His dun picked his way around a large bush, and the ranchero smiled at her.

She squinted. He had something in front of him. Her heart leaped. Her hands flew up to cover her mouth. Luis. Her *bebé*. Lucio had found him!

She picked up her skirts and raced toward them. Her chest ached. Tears blurred her vision. "Luis."

Lucio pulled to a stop and turned his mount so she could approach from the side. She reached up, and he lowered Luis into her arms. She'd never felt anything so sweet as the small, warm body against hers. She buried her face in his neck and breathed deep. The scent of sweat and boy centered her. He was safe. Alive. *Thank You, God. Thank You.*

Lucio swung down. She could feel his movement and the warmth of him beside her. When he put an arm around the two of them, she leaned into him. She wanted to thank him too but couldn't find the words. Couldn't find her voice.

"I found him asleep under a bush." Lucio's chest vibrated against her shoulder. "He went looking for the `dog,' and found more flowers for his mama. He couldn't find the road again."

She opened her eyes. Met Lucio's gaze. Touched her son's soft cheek. The coyote. Luis went after the coyote, thinking the wild beast was a dog.

Luis grinned and held up a bouquet of bedraggled flowers for her inspection.

"These are lovely, mijo. Thank you." She took the bouquet and pressed a kiss to his brow. "Shall we go show your hermanas?"

He nodded.

She looked up at Lucio. He was so close. So strong and handsome. And so wrong for her. She stepped away. "Thank you. I'll take him to the wagon. I'm sure you need to tell your men he is found."

A fleeting expression crossed his face. She had hurt him. She hated doing it, especially now. Still, she owed this man the truth, even if it hurt. His kindness deserved as much. She wasn't the right woman for him.

Without looking back, she hurried to the road and the waiting wagon. Leya sat up straight before Rosalinda was halfway there. The woman said something to Maria, and the girl leaped to her feet. She jumped from the wagon and raced to her mother.

"Luis. Luis! You found him." Maria barreled into her, hugging her legs and nearly toppling them to the ground. Luis giggled, a sound Rosalinda knew she would never again tire of hearing.

A flurry of activity surrounded them as the vaqueros all came by to see Luis. They offered to help with giving the niños rides, which delighted Maria and Isabel, who woke at all the commotion.

Ramón tied his chestnut mare to the wagon and climbed on the driver's seat. Rosalinda and Leya sat on the blankets in the bed with the children curled up next to them.

"I want Yoana to be here." Maria frowned up at Leya. "I miss her Bible stories. Can you tell one?"

"Yoana does have a gift." Leya nodded, her expression turning thoughtful. "I might be able to come up with one though. Is there a story you would like to hear?"

"I don't know. Maybe a boy one. Luis would like that." Maria snuggled close to Leya.

Rosalinda smiled at the sight. Her niños had never had anyone they could trust like this, an older woman who cared about them but didn't want to use them in a horrible way for profit.

"Yoana told you about David, who fought the giant, Goliath, right?" Leya asked.

Maria nodded.

"Did she tell you about Joseph, whose brothers didn't like him?"

"His brothers didn't like him? What about his sisters?" Maria frowned as if she couldn't understand such a thought.

"I don't know about his sisters. They aren't mentioned in this story, only his brothers." Leya smoothed Maria's wild curls.

"Why didn't his brothers like him?"

Rosalinda used to love when Yoana told Bible stories because Teo always asked the questions she wanted to know, just as Maria did now. That way Rosalinda could learn without seeming ignorant or stupid.

"Joseph was a special young man. He had eleven brothers." Leya chuckled as Maria's mouth dropped open.

"I can count to eleven." Maria held up her fingers and proceeded to show them how much she had learned about counting. Twelve brothers is a lot."

"You are very good at counting." Leya kissed Maria's brow. "And that *is* a lot of brothers."

"My mama would have to remember all their names." Maria giggled. Rosalinda rolled her eyes at Leya and laughed. Maria was right. Sometimes —a lot of times— she mixed her children's names up.

"So, Joseph was special to his father, Jacob, and his brothers didn't like that. They were jealous. Do you know what that means?" Leya tilted her head as she watched Maria.

Maria shook her head, and Leya explained the concept to her.

"Jacob asked Joseph to go to his older brothers, who were out tending their sheep very far from their house."

"Did Joseph have to walk a long way? Did he have a horse like Ramón?" Maria pointed to the chestnut pacing behind the wagon.

"I don't think he had a horse. He probably walked to find his brothers." Leya pulled Isabel over to sit on her lap as the niña headed for the horse. "Joseph had a special coat given to him by his father. It was a valuable coat with many colors in it. One that set him apart as a favorite. His brothers were jealous of that coat too."

"What happened when he found his brothers?" Maria asked. "Did they take his coat?"

"They saw him coming from a long way off, and they talked about how they didn't like him. Some of them wanted to kill him and steal his coat."

Maria's eyes were huge. She gasped. "They *killed* him?"

"Maria, let Leya tell the story." Rosalinda's patience snapped. She grabbed Maria's arm and her daughter cringed away.

CHAPTER FIVE

MARIA HUNCHED her shoulders and put her face against her knees. Rosalinda's heart sank. When would she learn not to be so harsh with her children? She hadn't meant to sound that way or to dig her fingers into Maria's tender flesh, but she wanted to hear what happened. "Sorry, mija." Rosalinda shifted Luis to the side and rubbed her daughter's back. "Go ahead, Leya, and tell us what happened."

"The good news is they didn't kill him. When he arrived at the camp, his brothers threw him into a dry well. He couldn't get out by himself."

Maria gaped at Leya, her upset at her mother apparently forgotten. Rosalinda shuddered at the thought of being trapped in a well.

"But, one of the brothers, the oldest, didn't want them to kill Joseph. While he was away from their camp, the other brothers decided to sell Joseph to some passing traders who would take him to Egypt and sell him into slavery."

"A slave." Rosalinda's head swam. She could hear the bartering. The brothers asking for more money. The buyers examining him like a piece of livestock, unwilling to pay so much. All the while

Joseph awaited a terrible fate. She closed her eyes as dark memories made her lightheaded with the horror of it all. Why would God allow this to happen to Joseph?

To her?

"He must have hated his brothers." Maria sounded so sad. What would her daughter say about her mother's past and what had been done to her?

"But you remember how Yoana told you that God has a purpose for those who trust in Him?"

Rosalinda opened her eyes to see Maria nod. She couldn't imagine how God could ever have a purpose that involved being sold into slavery. The degradation. The stripping away of a person's rights and choices. How could that be turned for good?

"I remember." Maria sat up straight, eyes shining.

"Joseph was sold in Egypt and many things happened to him, but he trusted God. God made a way for Joseph to become a very powerful man, second only to the ruler in Egypt. Joseph was in charge of preparing the country for a famine. Do you know what a famine is?" Leya smiled when Maria shook her head. Isabel still rested against Leya, twirling one of her curls around her finger.

Leya explained the famine and continued the story. "When the seven years of plenty passed, the people were glad Joseph had stored all the food. In the next few years, even the countries around Egypt suffered because they didn't have enough food. Guess who else needed food."

Rosalinda shifted until her back was against the side of the wagon. Luis might not weigh much, but even he got heavy after a while.

"Who?" Maria asked.

"Joseph's father and brothers! They didn't have enough to eat. God told Joseph's father to go to Egypt for food, so he sent all of the brothers except Joseph's youngest brother." Leya smiled as Maria covered her mouth with her hands.

"When his brothers arrived, Joseph knew them, but they didn't know him. He ended up giving them the food they needed and having them bring his father and all their families to Egypt where he could provide for them." Leya paused as if knowing Maria would have a question.

"Did Joseph beat up his brothers? Was he mad at them?" Maria asked the very questions rattling around in Rosalinda's head. If she ever saw those responsible for what she had endured, she didn't know what she would do.

"God taught Joseph much in those years he was a slave. He taught him the importance of forgiveness." Leya brushed her hand down Maria's cheek to cup her face. "Joseph's brothers were afraid of what he would do to them, but he told them, 'What you meant for harm, God meant for good.'"

Maria's brow furrowed. Rosalinda realized she had the same expression on her face. How could being sold into slavery be something good? How could selling your child into a nightmare situation be right?

"God used what they had done to Joseph to provide for Joseph's family when they had a need. God can bring beauty out of a horrible situation when we trust in him." Leya leaned back, hugging Isabel to her.

Rosalinda studied the older woman. She'd been so calm in the bandolero camp. Had she lived out the same hope Joseph had when she and Yoana had been kidnapped? They had almost been sold to men who would have done detestable things to them, but in the end, they had been rescued. And then, when it looked like Yoana's fiancé, Gabrio, would be hanged with the other bandoleros, he had been saved at the last minute. Had that been God intervening?

No. It was all just stories. Such things didn't really happen.

Maria leaned up against Leya, her eyelids drifting down. Isabel had already fallen asleep. Leya smiled and shook her head when Rosalinda offered to situate the niñas on the blankets so Leya could relax.

Rosalinda watched the countryside pass. Overhead the blue sky stretched without a cloud, a blue so pure and beautiful she wished she could capture the color.

By the time they stopped for lunch, Rosalinda was ready to walk again. Every bone in her body ached from jouncing over the rough trail in the wagon. As she dropped to the ground and turned to help Leya and the niños, she could see her friend needed to walk too.

They ate a meal of dried meat and tortillas left from breakfast while the horses rested. Several of the vaqueros came by to see Luis, or that is what they said. Rosalinda suspected they wanted more than to show their concern for the boy who got lost. She was so tired of men looking at her that way. Maybe if she wore a mantilla like Leya, they would treat her with more respect.

She watched for Lucio but didn't see him. Ramón stuck close as the others drifted in and out of their area of camp. Did he have orders to watch over them? Or maybe he also had an ulterior motive. He did send glances her way more than he needed to.

The afternoon dragged by. Rosalinda and Leya walked until the niños were tired and then climbed back in the wagon. She didn't know what was worse, the ache in her muscles from miles of walking or the ache in her bones from the jarring ride. And this was only the second day.

The quick cadence of hooves jolted her from a light sleep. Rosalinda blinked at the young *vaquero* who brought his pinto alongside the wagon. He grinned at her, his broad nose wrinkling at the sides.

"Carlos, what are you doing here?" Ramón's gruff question had the stocky vaquero kneeing his mount to move up beside Ramón.

"I came to relieve you. I can drive the wagon, and you can take your caballo and help Lucio."

Ramón's heavy brows drew together. "What does Lucio need?"

"He could use your help." Carlos grinned at Ramón, but his

glance flicked to Rosalinda and back. She suspected Lucio hadn't sent him at all.

"Why does he want me?"

Ramón must not believe the swarthy vaquero either.

Carlos shrugged. "I was riding beside him, and he mentioned you might like a break from the wagon. I came to give you that break. He also mentioned you giving the niña a riding lesson."

Ramón seemed to mull over the suggestion. Rosalinda wanted to object to the young man driving them. Carlos was pleasant enough. He had a boyishness about him that the older vaqueros didn't have. Still, his gaze followed her all the time and made her uncomfortable. She'd learned to listen to her instincts, not the man's appearance. Not that she would ever let on that she didn't trust Carlos. If a woman appeared vulnerable, men took advantage every time.

She braced as Ramón pulled back on the reins and the jouncing stopped. Surely Ramón wouldn't fall for this vaquero's story? But he did. She pasted on her usual saucy smile as Ramón climbed down and rounded the wagon to his horse.

"Can I ride with you?" Maria jumped up and trotted across to the back. Isabel and Luis were both asleep.

"I can help guide your caballo." Maria put her hands, palms together, under her chin. Even from a side view, Rosalinda could see her daughter's widened eyes begging for permission.

"Come on." Ramón lifted the child in front of him and let her take the reins. He glared at Carlos as the younger man tied his horse to the wagon back and jumped up to the bench seat. "I will only be gone a short time."

Maria and Ramón cantered off. The chestnut looked eager to do more than plod at a walk. Maria's laughter floated back to them.

Carlos turned from the seat. "Why don't you señoras come up here to sit for a while. The niños are asleep."

"I think that is a good idea." Leya stood and dusted her skirt. "Come, Rosalinda. A change will do us some good."

ONE OF THE mares from the remuda broke away, trotting toward a lush bit of greenery that must have looked like *pan del cielo*, bread of heaven, to her. Lucio urged his dun into a slow canter to herd her back before she roamed too far.

So far, they'd made good progress with the trip. The trail had been in better shape than he expected. Lack of rain kept the road from getting churned up, plus very few people passed this way. If the travel conditions held, and the wagons didn't require repair, they should be at the Santiago hacienda by the end of next week. At least this trip didn't have them going over any mountain passes or dangerous terrain. That was good.

The mare snatched a final mouthful of grass before she trotted back to the herd. He grinned at the contrary horse. She had some feistiness and would make a good mount for someone. She would breed foals with that same independence, which would make them capable of enduring long days and hard work.

"Lucio. Look at me."

The cry came from behind him. He twisted in the saddle to see Maria seated in front of Ramón and trotting toward him. The child waved, and a moment of guilt shot through him. He'd wanted to teach her how to ride but had avoided the wagon. In doing so, he'd reneged on his promise. Children were so forgiving. He would make it up to the niños.

"I'm doing the reins." Maria lifted the leather straps to show him. The chestnut lifted into a quick canter. Maria would have fallen if Ramón hadn't grabbed her to steady her in the saddle. She squealed with laughter. Her mother's daughter.

Lucio marveled at the change in Maria. In all of Rosalinda's children. But he'd seen change in Maria more than the others. When she'd first come to the ranch, she didn't speak unless she was with Teo, and even then she seldom spoke loud enough to be heard. Now she chattered more than all his brother's children put together.

Ramón helped Maria slow the horse, leaning down to speak in her ear. He adjusted the reins in her hands before looking back up at Lucio. They pulled to walk beside him and followed along with the remuda.

Lucio glanced at his friend. He must have left Leya to drive the wagon while he took the niña for a riding lesson.

"That's some helper you have there, Ramón. She looks like quite the horsewoman." He winked at the young girl, and she straightened, her expression serious, as if she had the most important job in the world.

"Where are your siblings?"

"They are asleep in the wagon." Maria shook her head. "I will tell them about riding when I get back." Her mouth tilted in a smile so like her mother's that his breath caught. "They will be very jealous when I tell them how much I have learned."

Ramón's mustache quivered. His chest shook. Lucio tried to hold back the laughter at Maria's serious tone, but he had to chuckle.

Ramón nodded at the remuda. "How are the horses weathering the journey?"

"They think the grass along the trail was planted just for them to stop and eat." Lucio shook his head. "Like the vaqueros, all they want to do is eat." He grinned at his friend. So often, the men went from one meal to another talking about what food they hoped would be served next. Men lived to fill their bellies. His stomach growled, and he laughed again. His men weren't the only ones.

"I am hoping the weather holds. So far it hasn't been too cold at night, and the rains haven't come." Lucio glanced at the clear blue sky. Off to the north he caught a hint of a white cloud over the mountains but nothing on this side.

"How is the roan with the bruise? Is she walking all right today?" Ramón asked.

"I asked Ricardo to pony her on a lead this morning so she would be sure to walk on the softest ground. Her limp is almost gone. We'll pamper her for a few days." Lucio pointed to the man and horse off to the left of the trail making their way through the trees and brush.

"I want to go fast." Maria tried to lift the reins like she had a few minutes ago. Ramón had the sense to tighten his hold. She bounced in the saddle in a comical attempt to urge the chestnut to speed up. Her dark curls swayed around her shoulders, having come free of the braid she'd had this morning.

She twisted around to frown up at Ramón and pulled at his fingers. "Let go."

Ramón gave her a stern look. "If you want to ride my horse, you have to do what I say. ¿Entiendes?"

Her frown turned to a pout, and sudden tears swam in her eyes. Ramón gave Lucio a helpless glance, and Lucio almost laughed, but he didn't want the niña to think this situation was funny. She needed to understand the seriousness of life on the trail.

"Mija." Lucio schooled his expression. This niña could break hearts with her doe eyes and pixie face. "Mija, you must listen to Ramón and do as he says. Soon you will be able to ride a horse, but you can't gallop the caballos all over or they will get too tired. Just think if I made you run everywhere."

She turned solemn and nodded her head. "I would fall on the ground and not be able to get up. Mama would have to give me an extra tortilla."

"That's right." Lucio chuckled.

Ramón shook his head. "Some hombre is in big trouble with this one." He winked at Lucio and they both grinned.

The mare he'd corralled earlier drifted off to find another tastier patch of grass. Lucio left Ramón giving Maria a lesson on turning the chestnut and brought the recalcitrant beast back to the remuda.

He joined his friend again, watching as the young girl did a figure eight with the mare. He and Ramón both cheered her success.

"I want to go show mama." Maria turned the mare back toward the line of wagons.

"They will catch up when we stop for the evening. That will be soon." Ramón assured her. "We could practice another trick."

"Is Leya all right driving the wagon for this long?" Lucio couldn't see them from here. Too many turns in the road and other wagons in the way.

"Leya isn't driving." Ramón frowned at him. "Carlos is."

A chill skittered down Lucio's spine. He'd had such a hard time trusting his *mejor amigo* with the job, yet he knew Ramón to be trustworthy. The thought of the younger Carlos, who followed Rosalinda everywhere with his gaze, twisted his stomach.

"Why did you let him do that?" Lucio tried to rein in his temper as he swung the dun around.

"Because you sent him."

"I did not send him. I wouldn't have done that." Lucio wanted to shake Ramón. Carlos must have been very convincing to get Ramón to give up the job he'd been given.

Ramón urged the chestnut mare to match the dun's pace. "He said you told him to drive the wagon so I could give the niña a riding lesson. I knew you wanted me to do that, so I believed him. *Lo siento, amigo.* I'm sorry."

They passed the two wagons loaded with goods being taken to Yoana, keepsakes and furniture that belonged to her. In the distance, Lucio could see the wagon carrying the women and niños. How had they gotten so far behind?

Lucio's lips pressed together. Of course. Carlos wanted them to fall back so he could flirt with Rosalinda without the other vaqueros seeing him and reporting his activities.

Maria laughed as they raced down the road. The girl would be reckless on horseback if they didn't teach her to be responsible.

They rounded a curve. Lucio could see the wagon with three people on the bench seat. Leya sat on the outside with Rosalinda in the middle. Carlos had the lines in one hand and was reaching up to stroke Rosalinda's hair with the other. She leaned toward Leya but couldn't get away from him.

Lucio couldn't get there fast enough. The things he wanted to do to the man...

Before he could close the gap, Carlos looked up to see them racing toward them. He brought his hand down just as Rosalinda shoved him. The vaquero lost his hold on the reins, toppled off the seat, and landed face first in the dirt at the side of the road.

CHAPTER SIX

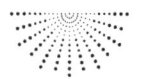

Don Francisco Armenta paced the floor of his study, doing his best to ignore the pain in his knees as he walked. In the past year, his joints had begun to ache, more so as the weather changed. Fall was coming now. Would he even be able to write his name when his fingers became as stiff as old leather in the cold?

The bang of the front door made him lengthen his pace to return to his desk before the vaquero he'd sent with a message entered the room. He wanted to exude calm control, not the demeanor of an impatient señorita waiting for her betrothed to arrive. He picked up a pen and bent over a paper as a knock sounded on the door to the study.

He waited a few breaths before calling out. "Enter." He didn't look up but followed the ring of spurs as the vaquero crossed to halt in front of the desk. Guilt prodded at him as he recognized old habits raising their ugly heads. He'd acted this way for years, and change came hard.

The pen clinked against the side of the ink bottle, the plume dipping in a graceful arc. He folded his hands and tried to still the hammering of his heart. There were things he had to do. People to see. Amends to make.

"Did you deliver my message?"

"Sí, señor." The vaquero twisted his hat in his hands. The brim would be ruined if he didn't stop.

Francisco gentled his tone. "Did you bring an answer?"

The man facing him relaxed a fraction, his incessant kneading slowed to a near halt. "Sí, señor."

Álonso, Alan… Why couldn't he recall the man's name? Lucio accused him of not caring about his men, but that wasn't true. Maybe he'd been that way once but not anymore. He just had trouble with names. Dratted things anyway. Names.

"Ángel." Francisco blurted the name out, startling both the vaquero and himself. He cleared his throat acting as if he'd almost yelled the name because of a problem, not because he'd suddenly remembered.

"Sí?" The man twisted his hat again.

"The message." Francisco held out his hand.

The vaquero shifted the sombrero to one hand and dug through his vest pocket with the other. The crinkle of paper sounded as he pulled out a rumpled page. He looked like he was going to try to smooth the paper, but Francisco cleared his throat, and the man passed him the missive.

"Thank you. You may go." He waited until the man clumped out of the room, trying not to be angry at the dusty footprints left on the dark hardwood floor. Floors could be cleaned. Leya had told him that many times, a reflection of the way her sister, his deceased wife, used to think.

His daughter-in-law had penned the note. Her precise writing made him smile. That same precision had her running her household with a determination that had everything going smoothly. Most of the time. She did have four rambunctious children. And a husband too hardheaded.

Like his father.

If only he'd been better about being a father and grandfather. He barely knew his grandchildren. He'd been too overcome with grief and too obstinate to see he was hurting himself and all those around him. Not at all what Josefa, his only love, would have wanted. Even after all these years, he sighed at the thought of her. She'd been the light of his life. His reason for living. The day she died, he wanted to die too. Part of him did die.

He bit his lip to bring his thoughts back from the abyss. He blinked to bring the paper back into focus.

Papá...

His heart warmed at the endearment. He'd mended enough bridges in the last few months that his daughter-in-law thought better of him. Now to repair the chasm between him and his sons. And Yoana. Especially Yoana.

Papá. We will gladly come and watch your hacienda for you. Emiliano will see to your stock since your head vaquero is away. We have good men at the ranch who will oversee here while we are there.

Please expect us to arrive later today. Packing up all sus nietos, *your grandchildren, is an exhausting task. I know from your letter you want to hurry. We will be there soon.*

CON DÍOS, *Papá,*
  Sofí

HIS THROAT TIGHTENED. Only last year, he would have been angry at her familiarity. He would have rebuffed any attempts sweet Sofí made to include him in their family gatherings or to make him feel welcome. He wanted to wipe away those horrible years. The years without Josefa. The years without compassion.

The years without God.

He folded the paper and placed it in a drawer, rose, and left the room. He needed to be ready to ride out as soon as possible. He stepped outside, then halted. So much of the day had passed. He'd been so busy getting paperwork in order and the work outlined for Emiliano, he hadn't realized how time had flown.

A cloud of dust in the distance heralded the arrival of his family. He waited, debating whether he should leave tonight or wait until early in the morning. The sight of his grandchildren peeking over the side of the wagon as they rolled through the gate made the decision for him. Tomorrow would be soon enough. He would spend tonight with Emiliano and his familia.

"*Abuelo.*" Elías, the four-year-old, stood up to wave. Sofí turned to say something to him, and he plopped back down in the wagon bed, only the top of his dark hair showing. Sofí faced forward and lifted one hand to wave. In her other arm she cradled Luana, their one-year-old daughter. Luana must have been asleep, but at the noise she started struggling to sit up, rubbing her eyes with a chubby fist.

"*¡Bienvenidos a mi casa!*" Francisco's smile felt more natural as he called the greeting. He guessed practice did help. He had prayed so often to see his family and others through God's eyes and to be blinded to the way he used to see everyone. Now he delighted in watching the grandchildren play. Their joy. Their innocence. Their laughter.

"Gracias." Sofí smiled as Emiliano helped her to the ground. The children jumped from the back of the wagon. Elías ended up tumbling in the dirt, but Aitana, his six-year-old sister, brushed him off and had him happy before anyone else could react.

Franco, the eight-year-old, retreated to the far side of the wagon. He would be the hardest one to convince. He reminded Francisco of himself, with his solemn demeanor and lack of trust in others. Franco no doubt remembered too well the stern *abuelo* who did not enjoy having children around. So far, the niño hadn't seen fit to trust Francisco's change. He stayed cautious as if expecting the angry *hombre* to return at any moment. Francisco wished with all his heart he could change the past, but he could only be a better person in the future.

"Abuelito." Elías pushed his sister away and raced toward Francisco. Emiliano tensed, his hand paused in a motion that would stop the boy.

"I missed you." Elías threw himself at Francisco, who caught him up in a hug. From behind the wagon, Franco's face had frozen. Francisco's heart ached a little more.

"Mijo." He hugged his grandson. "I have missed you too. I have a surprise for all of you. Can you guess what it is?"

"A surprise? For me?" Elías pushed away, looking up at Francisco with huge eyes.

"For you, Franco, Aitana, and Luana. A surprise for all of you." He smiled at the child's obvious delight.

"¿Qué es?" Elías wiggled to get down. Francisco leaned over until the niño's feet touched the ground. The boy turned a circle, looking around. Aitana came over, her curiosity evident.

"Ah, so you like surprises too, mija." Francisco held his arms open. After a moment of hesitation, Aitana stepped into his hug and squeezed him back. Her dark braids shone in the last of the sunlight. Hope warmed him. This was the first time Aitana had hugged him without Sofí urging her to do so. Progress.

"*La sorpresa.* The surprise." Elías danced around Francisco's feet, his hands clapping in time to his movements. "¿Qué es?"

"Why don't we invite your brother to join us. Then we can all go and see together." He had planned to send the niños to the barn while he, Emiliano, and Sofí went into the house, but now he wanted to witness their reactions. For too long he'd missed seeing joy on a child's face.

"*Ándale,* Franco. Hurry." Elías raced over to take his brother's hand and tug him toward his abuelo.

Franco dragged his feet. Sofí put her hand on Emiliano's arm and shook her head. Francisco knew his son wanted to intercede on behalf of Franco, but the boy needed to face his fear. He hoped once they interacted some, Franco wouldn't be afraid any more.

"He's here." Elías released Franco's hand and danced around

his abuelo again. His eagerness proved contagious. Aitana's eyes sparkled with excitement. Even Franco showed more interest than usual. Instead of a hug, he held out his hand for Francisco to shake. Without being told.

From the safety of her mother's arms, Luana watched them but didn't seem to want down. She was likely still tired from the long wagon ride.

"La sorpresa. ¿Qué es, Abuelito?" Elías tugged at his grandfather's pants.

"Elías. Patience." Sofí shook her head at her son, and his shoulders slumped. He dug his toe in the dirt.

"Why don't we head to the barn and see what we can find?" Francisco almost couldn't continue when Aitana slipped her small hand into his. He dragged in a breath and fought the burning in his eyes.

"Sofí, if you and Emiliano would like, you can stay at the house. We'll be right back."

Elías, who didn't like horses after being kicked last year, lagged back instead of racing forward as he might have. Francisco patted the boy's head as they walked along together.

"Luana and I would like to see the surprise too." Sofí smiled at him as she fell into step with them. Emiliano didn't say much but took the baby from his wife and walked beside her. Like Franco, Emiliano didn't trust the change in his father. Francisco had done much to ruin relationships. He couldn't expect to mend them overnight.

The barn door creaked when he pulled it open. Dust motes swirled in the air. Elías clung to Francisco's leg, hovering behind his grandfather.

"No caballos, Elías. La sorpresa is something you will like." Francisco smiled down at the little boy. Elías grinned back. Aitana's fingers tightened as they walked into the barn.

"Let's look in this first stall." Francisco led the way while the others followed, except for Elías who walked a step ahead. The stall door stood ajar. Snuffling noises came from the dim interior. He should have thought to bring a light.

"Emiliano, would you open the door farther so we can see, please?" He could feel Elías's little body pressed back against his knees. Francisco reached for the stall door and swung it wide, letting in more light.

Something wiggled at the back of the stall. The children stared, their expressions hesitant. As Emiliano pushed the big doors wide, a shaft of sunlight fell on the straw. A chorus of *Os* came from all the niños.

"Puppies!" Elías went forward and dropped to his knees. Aitana and Franco followed. Emiliano brought Luana and set her down so she could toddle toward her siblings.

"Puppies." Elías breathed the word again.

Six fat little black and brown mutts wiggled through the straw toward the children. Their tiny tails wagged, and their floppy ears almost dragged in the dirt. Elías giggled. The others followed suit. Luana tumbled to the ground, and a puppy licked her face. Her baby laughter warmed his heart.

Franco looked up at him. "Abuelito, what are you going to do with the puppies?"

The shock of having his grandson speak to him for the first time without being told to stole Francisco's thoughts. He knew he had to answer, but the words took a moment to come.

"Your father and mother are going to watch over the ranch while I am gone. I thought perhaps you niños would help by taking care of the puppies. Can you do that?"

As one, the older children nodded, each already holding a tiny quivering dog. Luana stared at him, her puppy's ear in her mouth.

"Luana, don't eat the dog." Sofí tried to sound stern but failed. They could all hear the laughter in her voice. She hurried to rescue the pup.

"Thank you." Emiliano clapped his father on the shoulder.

Francisco could see the gratitude in his son's eyes. Maybe they would begin to believe.

The rest of the evening sped by. Francisco climbed into bed ready for sleep. His supplies were ready for morning. He would have to get up, have some breakfast, and be off. He hoped to catch up to Lucio by tomorrow night since he could travel faster on a single horse than they could with wagons.

He closed his eyes, but sleep didn't come. Snippets of the evening drifted across his mind. The memories that hurt the most were of the love shown between Sofí and Emiliano. The way his son watched his wife as she cared for the children, love evident on his face. Sofí's smile for her husband. Her special glances at him from under her lashes, almost coquettish. The smile of promise.

He'd had that with Josefa. He hadn't allowed himself to remember those moments in so long. The pain was always too intense. Even now, his chest hurt at the memories. Maybe not as much as in the past, but still… He wanted his heart to just stop. For God to call him home. To see his Josefa again.

But he knew that wouldn't happen. God's plans were clear. Francisco needed to repair breaches in the relationships with his children. He had to go to Yoana. To his old friends. Then back here to his other children.

At least he'd made progress with Lucio.

Still, the thought of Josefa burned inside him. He missed that special relationship. A woman who looked up to him even though he was flawed. Who loved him. Sat with him on pleasant evenings. Read with him. Talked to him.

He would never have another relationship like he'd had with Josefa. But maybe God still planned something for a cantankerous abuelo whose heart had changed so much he didn't even recognize himself.

Maybe.

CHAPTER SEVEN

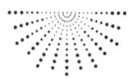

ROSALINDA TRIED to hold her breath to keep from bursting out laughing. She failed. As she snatched up the fallen reins, her laughter bubbled out. The sight of the odious vaquero landing on the ground made her want to howl. To preserve the moment.

She hugged herself. What she wouldn't give for a nearby stream so she could bathe. Her whole body felt dirty from the way he'd touched her. The way he'd looked at her. The filthy suggestions he'd whispered.

She should be immune to such behavior by now. These past few months, when she didn't have to worry about men, had been freeing. Yes, she'd flirted on occasion, but she'd had the option to say no...

She still could scarcely believe it. Sometimes, she'd flirted only to deny them. A new experience for her.

Lucio and Ramón thundered up on their horses, and Rosalinda pulled the wagon team to a halt. The horses snorted and swung their heads as Carlos scrambled up from the ground. She saw him swipe at his face, and she bit her lip. Beside her, Leya drew in a quick breath. Her shoulder shook the slightest bit where she brushed against Rosalinda's, meaning she must be trying to stop her laughter too.

"Mama, that man fell." Maria peered over the side of the wagon. The vaquero frowned at her before snatching up his sombrero and slapping it against his leg. Dust flew. Maria coughed.

Lucio and Ramón slid their mounts to a stop, and Lucio swung down. He flung his reins to Ramón, who still cradled Luis in front of him, and strode toward Carlos. All laughter fled from Rosalinda. Leya gripped her arm, her fingers trembling as if she too sensed the coming storm.

"What is going on?" Lucio's chin jutted forward. His tawny eyes were narrowed and appeared almost as dark as Ramón's. "What were you doing?"

Carlos slammed the hat on his head. He hooked his thumbs in the waistband of his pants and widened his stance. He looked every bit the cocky vaquero ready to take on the world.

"I was just having a little fun." He grinned at Lucio, his teeth flashing white in the sunshine. "No harm done."

"Did Rosalinda give you permission?" Lucio looked even angrier than when he first approached Carlos.

Rosalinda wanted to make this go away. She knew what Carlos would say. What any man would say.

"I don't need permission." Carlos leered up at her. She tried to hide her shivers.

"Rosalinda is a woman under my protection. She lives at my hacienda. You need permission before you touch her. Before you *speak* to her. Is that clear?" Lucio's hands fisted at his sides.

"She's a *puta*. They expect--"

Lucio's fist struck Carlos' jaw, sending him flying backward. The vaquero landed hard. He shook his head. Put his palms on the ground and pushed to his feet.

"You will apologize." Lucio's arm muscles bunched, as if he struggled to keep himself in control. "Now."

"To *her?*" Carlos swiped the back of his hand across his mouth, wiping away a dribble of blood. "Never. She is just a--"

Before he could finish, Lucio sent him to the ground again. This time blood poured from the cowboy's nose. He rolled to the side, letting the blood run onto the ground. He shook his head. Red droplets spattered in the dirt.

"You will apologize." Lucio's stance didn't change. He didn't glance at Rosalinda, and she was glad. Her face burned. Carlos spoke truth. She'd been bought for one thing and treated one way for almost as long as she could remember. She deserved what Carlos did to her.

Leya's fingers squeezed. The older woman leaned close. "No, you don't."

Rosalinda startled. She turned to meet Leya's gaze as the woman lifted her mantilla. The compassion in her friend's eyes nearly did her in.

"I can see your thoughts." Leya spoke so low Rosalinda knew the others couldn't hear. Her children were riveted on the drama beside the wagon.

"You are thinking he spoke truth in what he said, but you are wrong. Did you choose that way of living?" Leya's question burned down into Rosalinda's soul.

"No, but..." She didn't know what to say. She hadn't run away. Ever. Not as a child. Not when she grew older. Not when the man who bought her beat her until she could barely walk.

"*No.*" Determination in her eyes, Leya gave Rosalinda's arm a firm shake. "You did not go willingly. You are not to blame."

"Mama, why are they so mad?" Maria came up behind the seat and stuck her head between Leya and her mother. "That man is bleeding."

Leya released her hold and dropped the mantilla back over her face. She straightened on the bench. Through the veil, Rosalinda could see the shadow of her features. Leya still watched her.

They would talk later.

"Señor Armenta is upset because…the vaquero wasn't being nice to me." Rosalinda didn't want to tell her daughter what the man had been trying to do. A motion behind Maria caught Rosalinda's eye. Isabel cowered on the blankets under the seat, her face a mask of fear. "Maria, why don't you and Isabel play a guessing game so she won't be afraid."

Thank heaven Maria didn't argue but plopped down and put her arm around Isabel. Rosalinda allowed the low drone of Maria's voice to fade to the background as she focused once again on Lucio and Carlos. Ramón still sat with Luis on the chestnut mare. Luis rested back against the vaquero, his eyes heavy.

How the child could be sleepy right now was beyond her.

Up ahead of them, the wagons carrying goods, and the horses, continued to put distance between them. They needed to catch up. To be away from this uncomfortable situation. How could she ever change if people continued to judge her by her past?

From the corner of her eye, she could see rage darkening Lucio's face. The thought of him defending her sent much needed warmth through her chilled soul, and yet…

This just showed how wide the chasm was between her and Lucio. He could never be with a woman his vaqueros felt they could disrespect.

Her fingers burned, and she realized she'd tightened her grip on the reins so they were digging into her palms. She forced her muscles to relax but couldn't ease the ache inside.

She would never amount to anything. Would never be wanted by any man for more than one thing. Would never know what it felt like to be part of a family. A real family.

Leya had told her about God and his son, Jesus. Well, God might be love, but He would never love her. Would never look past her bravado to the frightened child hiding deep inside. Besides, God had the whole world to watch over. All the good people. Why would he want a soiled person like her?

"Rosalinda." The slight command in Lucio's voice startled her.

She looked sideways at him. How was she to hide the hurt and turmoil roiling inside her? Silence hung heavy. Had he called her name before and she hadn't heard him, lost in her own musings?

"Yes." She cleared her throat. Tried again. "¿Sí?"

"Can you drive the wagon? If not, give the reins to Leya. You will go on and we will catch up. ¿Entiendes?"

"Sí." She sat for a minute trying to process what he'd said. Realizing she hadn't the experience needed to drive the team, she started to pass the reins to Leya. Luis sat on Leya's lap. Rosalinda blinked. She hadn't even noticed Ramón bring her son over to her friend. How had she missed that?

Somehow, Luis still slept. Leya transferred him to Rosalinda's arms and clicked for the horses to go. Her niño's tiny lips were parted, his breath soft on her cheek as she held him close. The sweet scent of flowers floated in the air. Rosalinda closed her eyes. Oh, to run away. To be free of her past. But that was impossible.

There was no escaping who--or what--she was.

Lucio waited until the women were far enough away that Rosalinda wouldn't hear any more of Carlos' venomous words. He wanted to throttle the man. To wipe his face in the dirt.

Ramón cleared his throat. Lucio glanced over at him, and the compassion in his friend's eyes spoke volumes. Lucio struggled to curb his temper. He wanted to protect Rosalinda and defend her honor, but all the vaqueros probably thought of her the way Carlos did. They only knew where she came from. That she had three children, not all from the same father. That she had never been married. That she had belonged to the worst bandolero they'd ever heard about.

Anger bubbled up from his gut. He watched Carlos struggle up from the ground. Blood covered the man's chin, his cheek, and the front of his shirt. He was a mess. Satisfaction almost made Lucio smile. Now to see if the vaquero had learned anything.

"I want you to work with the horses and stay away from Rosalinda and from Tía Leya." He'd never heard any of the *vaqueros* say anything about his tía, but Lucio didn't want to allow that chance. His tía had been hurt enough by what happened to her as a young woman, when she was kidnapped and nearly killed by outlaws.

Carlos swiped his sleeve across his face. He stared at Lucio, his gaze still defiant. "You can make me do that, boss, but she will come to me. That's the type of woman she is. She likes men. You'll see."

The cowboy leaned down to retrieve his sombrero, and Lucio wanted to land him in the dirt again. He caught the shake of Ramón's head and forced his fists to unknot.

He thought of all the times his father had answered his questions with anger, always humiliating him. Had he learned anything from it? No. He hadn't learned anything until an old vaquero working for his father befriended him and talked to him, showing him why something was wrong or how his view might not be the correct one.

Carlos turned to retrieve his horse. Lucio held up his hand.

"Wait, Carlos. Give me a minute more." *God, give me wisdom. A way to make Carlos understand something even I had trouble understanding.* A glimmer of an idea formed. "Carlos, you have a sister, right?"

"Sí." Carlos frowned.

"How old is she?" Lucio didn't know much about Rosalinda's past. He didn't think it his business unless she chose to share. But maybe what he did know would help.

"She is eight years old." Carlos pushed his hat back on his head. "*¿Por qué?*"

"I've heard you talk about her. You mentioned how pretty she is and how well she sings. Isn't that right?"

One of the horses jangled its bridle and then nudged Ramón's ear. The head vaquero bumped his head against the chestnut's head in an affectionate gesture.

"She sings like a bird." Carlos's eyes lit up. His whole demeanor changed. This man loved his sister.

"Eight years old." Lucio reached for the reins of his dun, taking them from Ramón. The horse came close to nudge at him. He drew in the scent of horse and sweat, one of the most comforting smells to him.

"¿Por qué?" Carlos shifted, his expression turning wary again.

"Your sister is one year older than Rosalinda was when her mother sold her." He paused to swallow down the horror of what he'd just said. Understanding and loathing dawned in Carlos's eyes.

"Sold her to a man who used her, destroyed her innocence, then sold her to someone else until he tired of her. And sold her to someone else." Bile tasted bitter in the back of Lucio's throat. He could picture his little nieces, their innocence and sweetness. Rosalinda must have been that way before she endured all that cruelty. What would she be like today if she hadn't been bartered? What monster of a mother would do such a thing?

Lucio met Carlos's gaze. "Do you think if your sister were sold today, she would want to go with a man? A man who would hurt her or use her?".

"My parents would never do that to her!" Anger darkened Carlos's eyes.

"That is good. But what happened to Rosalinda as a little child was done *to* her. She didn't choose it. She did not want to go with *any* of those men. When you treat her like you did on the wagon, you tell her she is right to never trust men. That they are as evil and brutal as she was taught when she was a child. When you look at Rosalinda, don't see her beauty as a woman. See the child, the girl like your sister, who had degradation forced on her."

Silence hung between them. In a nearby tree, birds twittered a complete conversation while Carlos pondered, his brow furrowed. "You are right." He scuffed his boot against the ground. "I didn't know. I thought she wanted to be there. She often flaunts her...um, her attributes. That makes it hard for a man to think otherwise."

"Seven. Years. Old." Lucio understood what Carlos was saying. He truly did. But he had to make Carlos see, because if he did, the truth would get around to the other vaqueros. And that might make Rosalinda's life a little easier.

"From childhood she's been taught to behave the way she does. And now? Can you not see that her behavior may be a way to protect herself? If she acts flirtatious before men disrespect her, then she feels she is in control. At least one of the men treated her with violence. A woman trapped in that life will do almost anything, learn to act in whatever manner it takes to survive. ¿Entiendés?"

"Sí." Carlos nodded. "I am sorry. If you would like, I will apologize to the señora and to your tía."

"Maybe tomorrow." Lucio nodded. "Thank you."

He watched as Carlos mounted his horse and rode off toward the remuda. By this time, the wagon bearing Leya, Rosalinda, and the children was almost out of sight.

Ramón clapped him on the back. "Well done, mí amigo. I thought you would not be able to control that temper, but you made him see reason. That was a bit of wisdom comparing the señora to his sister."

"That was God's wisdom, not mine." Lucio gave him a slight smile. "I wanted to rub Carlos's face in the ground."

"Shall we catch up to the ladies and see how they are faring? I'm not sure how long Leya can handle the team before she tires." Ramón swung up on his mare. Lucio leaped astride his dun.

Maria and Isabel saw them coming and jumped up and down in the wagon bed. Lucio had to grin. They were so cute, with their curls bouncing in wild disarray and their eyes sparkling. They both looked so much like their mother.

Luis stood on Rosalinda's lap and waved over her shoulder at him and Ramón. He probably wanted to get down and run. All the niños needed time to get out of the wagon.

"I want to ride now!" Maria yelled at him as soon as he was close enough. "I need another lesson. I'm ready."

Lucio laughed. "I think you need to run first. If I put you on my caballo right now, you will bounce off instead of sitting still."

"I can sit still." Maria put her hands on her hips, her mouth in a pout.

Rosalinda swiveled around on the seat. "Maria, sit down." Her eyes were red, and she kept them downcast. Had Leya said something to her, or was she still upset from what Carlos said?

He could see from the slump of Leya's shoulders that she was weary. "Ramón, why don't you take over driving. Leya, do you want to walk for a while with the niños?"

She tugged the reins, stopping the team, and nodded at him. "I would love to stretch my legs."

He dismounted to help the women down while Ramón tied his mare to the wagon and lifted the children out.

Leya took a minute to steady, and he waited until she got her footing before he reached up for Rosalinda. She started to put her hands on his shoulders--then straightened back up and put her hand up to shade her eyes as she stared down the trail behind them.

"Who is that?" Rosalinda's full lips pursed.

Ramón clambered up onto the bench seat from the other side, dipping the buckboard. He stared back the way they had come.

Lucio lifted onto his toes in the stirrups, narrowing his eyes to try to close the distance. His heart thudded. Only one man sat a horse like that.

Only one.

CHAPTER EIGHT

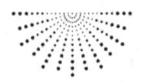

AT THE SIGHT of Lucio standing by the wagon with Ramón, the women, and the children, Francisco's heart pounded. Was he doing the right thing?

A snort escaped him. Don Armenta, uncertain? He'd always been so decisive and focused on what needed to be done.

Yes, at the expense of everyone around you.

This was new. A sense that other people mattered, and he should be aware of what they lacked as well as his own needs. That he was even supposed to consider them first. Such a concept was foreign to the way he'd lived for most of his life. Since Josefa died.

How could he have lost sight of her ideals? How had he gone so far from her loving ways to a place of filling his children with dread at the very sight of him?

From what he could see in the distance of Lucio's stance, his son wasn't happy to see him. He probably thought—and rightly so —that the overbearing Don Armenta had come to check up on him or to take the lead on the trek to the Santiago hacienda. If Francisco weren't careful, that might well happen.

Even now, he could feel the desire rising up inside to question all that had happened. He'd been close enough to see Lucio hit a man and knock him into the dirt. Twice. Why? What did the vaquero do that needed such swift and violent action?

Why were the women and children so far behind the rest of the group? Didn't he worry about wild animals? Bandoleros? One never knew when they would strike or where they would come from. What if they swooped down and carried off Leya, or Rosalinda, or those little niños?

Questions and doubts swirled through his mind. Why were they getting the women and children out of the wagon? Did Lucio intend to make them walk the whole way? Why hadn't he brought a more comfortable conveyance for them instead of this buckboard?

He slowed his black to a walk, reining in his thoughts, a far more difficult proposition than reining in the antsy stallion. Lucio could be trusted. He had a reason for everything he did, and Francisco had come to trust him with the daily running of the ranch. But––he now realized––his trust in his son still wasn't complete. Every day he questioned his son on details.

No wonder Lucio preferred to eat with the men. They probably let him consume his meal in peace.

The black's sides heaved as he whickered a greeting to the horses ahead. He tossed his head, and his long mane gleamed in the sunshine. Francisco kept a tight hold on the reins as the beast pranced sideways down the trail, his neck arched, his tail sweeping high behind him. He seemed to know he was a showpiece of the Armenta stock.

"Don Armenta." Lucio held himself stiff as a board. His eyes were hard, although he'd pushed his mouth into a half-hearted smile.

Hiding his regret over his son's formal address, Francisco tipped his sombrero to the ladies as the children clustered around their legs. He nodded at Ramón, who nodded back.

"Lucio." Francisco swung down, trying to hide the grimace of pain as his joints objected. A moment's respite from the saddle would be good. He rode every day, but only short distances. Getting older made him feel every bump in the road.

"What brings you here?"

Lucio stood close to Rosalinda. Why? Yes, Francisco had noticed his son watching her when he thought no one would notice. Did he think to woo a woman such as this? Part of Francisco wanted to yank his son away from her and give him a talking to. The new, more reasonable part of him let it go. A barely remembered voice whispered it would be all right.

"I would like to accompany you to visit my friend, Don Santiago. It has been a long time since I've seen him and his familia." Why couldn't he soften his tone when he spoke to his son? And why the need to lie? Why couldn't he just admit he wanted to make amends to Yoana?

Perhaps because he hadn't yet finished healing the rift between Lucio and himself.

He sagged mentally but stiffened his stance. They would have another week to ten days on the trail, depending on the weather and the road. During that time, he would do his best to apologize to Lucio. Also to Leya.

All he had to do was figure out how.

Something tugged at his pants leg. He glanced down to see Rosalinda's boy looking up at him. Tiny curls covered the boy's head. His full cheeks rounded in a smile, and his dark eyes sparkled.

"Wie." He pointed to the stallion. "Wie."

Someone gasped. Perhaps, Leya. He couldn't be sure. All of the adults were strung tight as a new fence. The two girls clutched their mother's skirt. The smaller one had her thumb in her mouth. As happened often to him, regret stabbed deep. What had he missed with his own children? Especially with Yoana.

Francisco ignored the complaining of his knees and knelt in

front of the child. "I don't understand what you're saying. What do you want?"

"Luis, come here." Rosalinda's sharp tone dimmed the sparkle in the child's eyes. Who could blame her? He hadn't been gracious even in more recent days. He held up his hand to her, palm out, while he kept his focus on Luis.

"Do you want to pet the horse?" he asked.

Luis smiled. Held up his arms. "Wie."

"You want to ride?" Francisco nodded. He eased upright, ignoring the creak of his knees. "Señorita, por favor. May I take your son for a ride when I am ready to go?"

She glanced from Leya to Lucio, as if wanting to ask them. He could only imagine the horror stories she'd heard. After all, she had spent time with Yoana. What had his daughter related about the monster who raised her?

"No, señor." Rosalinda hurried forward and swept the child into her arms. "He needs to walk."

Disappointment arced through him, but he kept his expression passive. He didn't want this woman to know she had wounded him with her lack of trust and her fear, as if he would hurt a little child. He didn't want Lucio to see his vulnerability either.

"You are welcome to join us." Lucio gestured to Ramón, and the *vaquero* settled on the bench seat.

"The women and children are walking. You can walk with them, ride with Ramón, or accompany me to check on the remuda." Lucio ran his hand down his dun's neck and gathered the reins. He swung up and waited, staring at Francisco, his face expressionless.

"If Ramón doesn't mind, I'll ride with him." Francisco tied his stallion to the opposite side of the wagon from Ramón's chestnut. Leya and Rosalinda herded the children to the side of the road and started off. Lucio nodded at Ramón and reined his dun around to head for the remuda. The wagon creaked as Francisco climbed aboard.

He and Ramón rode in silence. He watched his son until he went through a copse of trees and disappeared from sight. Twisting in the seat, he looked back at Leya, Rosalinda, and the children. The oldest girl skipped along and chattered, her shining curls bouncing on her shoulders. The younger girl tried to skip like her sister but ended up looking more like an awkward, galloping foal.

"Why did you come?" Ramón had been at the ranch for several years, was always respectful, but never cowed like many of the people who worked there. Francisco appreciated the man's honesty.

"You saw Don Santiago not three months ago when Lucio rescued Yoana from the bandoleros and you nearly hanged Gabrio, the don's son. Why do you need to see him again?" Ramón leaned forward, his elbows resting on his knees. His droopy mustache quivered. He didn't so much as glance at Francisco.

"He is a friend. I have not been to his hacienda in a long time. Why do you doubt that is why I want to go?" Francisco reached to the side of the wagon and plucked a leaf from a tree growing close to the road.

"There is more." Ramón squinted toward him. "I can tell. I've known you too long." The vaquero glanced back over his shoulder. Francisco turned to see the women far enough back they wouldn't hear anything. "I've seen changes in you since Yoana came home. I know there is more to this trip for you. Is it about Yoana?"

Francisco turned his back on the women. He didn't want Leya to see his face or try to figure out what he said. Rosalinda didn't know him, but Leya did, even though she'd been hidden away most of the time.

"If I talk to you, I would appreciate your discretion." He waited until Ramón gave a stiff nod. "I...have changed. God has changed me."

Ramón's eyebrows lifted, and he tipped his sombrero back. "I heard some rumors. Lucio seemed to think…" He snapped his mouth shut and shook his head.

"Lucio thought I was putting on a front for my friends." Francisco blew out a heavy breath. "I understand. I have committed many sins. Most of them hurt my familia. I can't go back and undo twenty years of meanness, but I have to try to atone."

Now that he'd started talking, he couldn't seem to stop. Ramón didn't glance his way. His face kept the same expression, neither judgmental or accepting. He simply listened.

"The problem is I don't know where or how to start. When Emiliano and Sofí came to stay, I tried to show the change by my behavior. I wanted to tell Lucio why I came, but when I tried, the story about visiting Don Santiago slipped out before I realized I would say the words.

"Besides, how do I tell him I want to get to know Yoana, his sister, when I treated him almost as poorly as I did her? He would resent me even more than he does now." He tugged the sombrero off . A breeze cooled the sweat from his head. He closed his eyes to relish the touch of the wind.

"Lucio has noted some of the ways you've trusted him with the working of the rancho. He also told me you question everything he does. It's as if you want to trust him but don't know how to let go." Ramón sat up and turned to Francisco. "Your son is a good man. He works hard. He is capable. You should believe in his abilities."

"It's so hard to let go." He slapped the hat back on, hating the feel of the damp sweatband on his forehead. "When you have been one way for so long, being someone different is like climbing a tall mountain on a rainy day. You go up, hit a slippery patch, and slide part way back. I keep slipping back even when I don't want to."

"Keep in mind, Lucio is trying to find his way too. He stayed under your thumb for years, doing only what you demanded." Ramón winced as if he'd said more than he meant to.

"You're right. I don't know who was more surprised when he

stood up to me and defied my order to quit looking for Yoana. We haven't talked much at all other than discussing the business of the ranch, but I need to tell him how thankful I am that he kept looking for her and for Leya. Without him"--he met the vaquero's gaze—"without you, they might not be back home."

They rounded a curve in the road. Up ahead, Francisco could see the remuda being corralled for the night and that the wagons had stopped. The men would be getting ready to prepare the camp. He didn't see his son but knew he would be working right along with all the vaqueros. Like a true ranchero should.

From behind them he heard a child's wail. Ramón pulled the team to a halt. They both turned to look. Rosalinda knelt in the road beside one of the children. Leya bent over too, but he couldn't see what had happened.

"Go ahead with the wagon. One of the niños probably twisted an ankle or got a scrape. I'll ride back and see if I can help." Francisco climbed down from the wagon, his muscles protesting every move. He swung onto his stallion as Ramón drove on. A squirrel skittered across the road giving the black cause to snort and prance.

He spurred the horse, then pulled to a halt beside the group and swung down. "What happened?"

They were huddled around the two girls. The younger one sobbed as if her heart had been broken. The older one had tears but didn't seem as prone to cry aloud.

"Maria wanted to teach Isabel the proper way to skip." Leya's soft voice had a melodic tone he loved. He leaned closer to hear her better over the caterwauling.

"They ended up getting their legs tangled somehow. One of them tripped the other, and they both went down." She touched her mantilla, a gesture he'd seen hundreds of times before. She always made sure her scars were hidden away where no one would see them. The physical scars as well as the emotional ones.

"But she tripped me." Isabel renewed her wailing as she looked at Francisco. He pressed his lips together to keep from smiling. He didn't want to encourage her dramatics.

"Isabel, that is enough." Rosalinda didn't seem to know what to do with her daughters. He recalled her story and knew the only training she'd remember would be that of violence and pain. He hadn't been a good parent, but maybe he could show how redirecting an upset child could help. He recalled Josefa doing that with their niños when they were young.

"The vaqueros are making camp up ahead. Why don't I put the niños on my horse, and they can ride the rest of the way?"

Tears vanished. The girls beamed at him. The oldest leaped to her feet. The younger one scrambled up a little slower. Luis pushed away from Leya.

"Now you have three niños ready to ride." Rosalinda shook her head. "That will never work. You will have to choose one, and the rest will cry." At her words, all the smiles disappeared.

"I have a very strong stallion." Francisco rose from where he'd crouched down. "I believe he can carry three niños without too much trouble."

"I can do the reins." The oldest girl clapped her hands.

"Oh, no. I will have you hold your brother in front of you." He lifted the girl to the saddle and placed her sister behind her. Then he lifted Luis in front. "I will hold the reins." He winked at them, and they all laughed.

The black swung his head around and nudged Francisco. He patted the horse's neck and turned. Lucio sat astride his dun a few feet away, his face set in a frown.

CHAPTER NINE

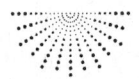

HE COULDN'T BELIEVE the sight in front of him. His eyes must be deceiving him. Don Armenta, the authoritarian patriarch who never showed compassion, had three children sitting on his prize stallion. Three children who belonged to a woman he would think of in the same way Carlos did. Three children not even related to him.

Lucio almost forgot to breathe. The sweet airborne scent of some flower he'd been enjoying moments before faded. The song of the birds around them ceased to sound like a melody. A light breeze could blow him out of the saddle.

Don Armenta gave a command that came out more a suggestion than his usual fail-to-do-this-and-die command. "Rosalinda, if you walk along on the other side and keep your hand on Maria's knee, I will be on this side. They will be fine."

His father noticed him as he faced back around. His expression turned sheepish. *Sheepish.* Lucio couldn't even process the thought. What had happened to this man? Did he only look like the don?

"The niñas fell down. I offered them a ride since they hurt their knees." Don Armenta patted the black's neck.

"On your prize stallion?" Lucio couldn't keep disbelief from coloring his words. His father winced.

"Vámanos, caballo." Maria bounced in the saddle. The stallion snorted and tossed his head. Luis laughed and clapped his tiny hands.

"The caballo will be fine." Don Armenta clicked his tongue. The black started to dance away from him. Rosalinda gasped, her hand still on Maria's leg, and she leaned at an awkward angle to keep her feet from being stepped on.

Before he could dismount, his father said something in a low tone that Lucio couldn't hear. The stallion settled. Snorted. Nudged Don Armenta. His father rubbed the horse's neck and ears with more affection than he'd ever shown any of his children. Lucio tried to tamp down the jealousy.

Who would be jealous of a horse?

"Lucio, walk with us." The don clicked his tongue again, and they started off. Lucio reined his dun to the side of the road out of their way. He wanted to argue that he had other duties, but his father would sense the lie.

He could feel his tía's gaze on him as he dismounted. She walked slightly behind and to the side of Rosalinda. She tilted her head to the other side, indicating she thought he should cross over and be beside his father. He frowned at her. She tilted her head again.

They continued this silent conversation for several yards before he gave in. She'd always hoped he and his father would restore their relationship. Leya talked to him several times since his sister moved up north with her new husband, Gabrio Santiago. She insisted the don was a different person, even though she still avoided him. Her eternal hope wore him down, but he still didn't believe his father would ever truly change, even though he let the children ride his stallion.

"I need the reins." Maria called to Lucio as he rounded to walk alongside his father. She frowned at him as she let go of her brother to hold out her hand. "He won't give me the reins."

"Wie." Luis flung himself forward with his arms raised overhead, almost tumbling off the black. Don Armenta kept the niño from falling, his hand nearly covering the little one's chest. Luis laughed. Lucio shook his head at the boy's fearlessness.

"You see what happened, Maria. Hold onto your brother." Rosalinda's voice drifted from the other side of the horse.

"He won't fall." Maria's tone climbed into the whine range. "See?" She let go of Luis and leaned back so she wasn't touching him. She bumped against Isabel, who lost her grip on the saddle.

The smaller girl wavered. Her eyes grew wide. Lucio took a long stride toward her. The stallion startled and leaped sideways. Isabel toppled toward him.

He flung himself forward, releasing the dun's reins. He caught Isabel in his outstretched arms before she hit the ground. The stallion hit Rosalinda, and she hit the dirt hard. He heard the breath whoosh out of her. Leya dropped down out of the way as the black went over the top of Rosalinda and pranced around to the far side of Don Armenta.

Lucio leaped to his feet. He flung Isabel in his tía's direction making sure she had the child. Maria and Luis were still in the saddle, and his father had the horse under control.

He dropped down beside Rosalinda. She lay face down at the edge of the road, so still he couldn't tell if she was breathing. He'd seen the large hoof land in the middle of her back.

"Rosalinda." He brushed the hair back from her temple. Her eyes were closed. His heart thudded in his chest. His hand shook as he felt for a pulse in her neck. She moaned. Intense relief flooded through him. His shoulders bowed. He closed his eyes and gave thanks.

"Is she…" Leya stood beside him, her hand resting on his shoulder. Isabel sobbed into her neck.

"She moved." He kept his tone even, not wanting to frighten

the children. "Please take the *niños* and Don Armenta on to the camp. Send Ramón back to help me."

When he looked up, she lifted her mantilla and met his gaze. He knew she understood the seriousness of this type of injury. If Rosalinda died, he didn't want the children present. She nodded, dropped the mantilla again, and moved off to where Don Armenta waited, his face a mask of concern. Maria clutched her brother, her eyes wide with fear. And, maybe, regret.

Leya and Don Armenta spoke in low tones as they moved away. Lucio focused on Rosalinda. He could see her eyes slitted open. Had she regained consciousness? One of their vaqueros had been trampled by a horse. He'd never awakened but died a few days later. They could do nothing for him.

He sank down onto the dirt beside her. He thought about lying down so they were eye to eye in case she woke up. He didn't want her to try to move too soon.

"Rosalinda." He brushed his fingers across her cheek. The satin skin still held warmth. She didn't react.

"Rosalinda. Wake up." He let his fingers caress her temple, tuck silky strands of hair back behind her ear. Such small ears. He ran his thumb around the delicate shell, an intimacy his *tía* wouldn't approve.

His pulse thrummed. He bent lower until his forehead touched hers. Why did this woman matter so much to him--?

She moaned. Her eyes closed. Opened again. She blinked, looked at him. This time he could see her focusing.

"Don't try to move." He glanced up the road to see if Ramón was coming. The don and Leya were still within sight.

"What--" She took a breath. Her lips stood out against the paleness of her face. Tears glittered in her eyes and traced a path across her nose. Her breaths came in quick pants, pain reflected in her eyes.

"You were knocked down. By my father's horse. And stepped

on." He hated this feeling of helplessness. Why couldn't he take away the pain? Help her somehow? "Try to relax."

He brushed his fingers across her cheek and wiped the tears away. She closed her eyes. He'd never realized how beautiful teardrops on eyelashes could be. Like tiny diamonds, they shimmered in the westering sun. "Breathe easy. As soon as you can, tell me where you hurt." It was so hard to be patient as he watched her. She swallowed. Slowed her breathing.

"Está bien." She attempted what she probably meant as a smile but turned out to be a grimace. Her hands moved closer to her head, and she put her palms to the ground.

"Don't try to sit up." He grasped her fingers. "Let me touch your back, and you can tell me where it hurts. We need to know if you have any broken bones."

She gave him an unreadable look. Did she want him to do as he said or not? He waited. In the distance he heard the pound of hooves. Ramón must be on his way at last.

Indeed, his friend approached with Leya on the horse in front of him. She must have come back to see if she could help. Who was watching the children?

Rosalinda made a noise. He turned to see her swiveling around, her face set in a mask of pain, her legs drawn up under her. He reached out. The look in her eyes stopped him. Her fierce frown told him to keep his hands off.

ROSALINDA COULD BARELY RESTRAIN A SCREAM. Everything felt as if it was shattered. If Lucio touched her, she would not be able to keep from crying. She'd always been strong and able to take whatever men dished out to her. But this. This hurt beyond anything she remembered.

Every breath sent agony through her chest and down her back. Something must be broken inside… What should she do? Nausea swirled in her stomach and burned up her throat. She fought it.

She would pass out if she vomited right now.

"Rosalinda." Lucio knelt in front of her. He wanted to touch her. She could see it in his eyes. The way his hands flexed. The set of his shoulders.

"Rosalinda. Tell me where you hurt. What can I do for you?" The compassion in his voice made her want to weep. Most of the men she'd known would have backhanded her—or kicked her—and told her to get up. For the first time in her life, she'd met a man who cared more about her, and her welfare, than about what she could do for him.

And he could never be hers.

He held his hand out, palm up. She took a few more sips of air. The agony eased enough for her to extend her fingers to touch his. He didn't grip her hand but let their fingertips rest against each other. She blinked back tears. Such remarkable compassion. And it was for her.

"I will" she drew in another breath—"be all right."

Leya knelt on the ground next to Lucio. She pushed the mantilla back over her head. Her dark eyes were filled with worry. "Take your time, amiga."

She and Lucio sat with Rosalinda until she could manage to talk and move without feeling the world go fuzzy. The sun had dropped below the horizon by the time she could get to her feet with Lucio's help.

"I can lift you onto Ramón's horse." Lucio's palm rested below her elbow, as if he feared she would fall over in a dead faint. For a moment she thought she might do that too.

"No." It came out too harsh. Her world swayed. Or maybe *she* swayed. With her eyes closed, she heard Leya's indrawn breath. She caught her balance, steadied by Lucio's grip on her arm.

"I think it would be easier if I walk. Slowly. The wagons aren't far." She took a step to show them she could do this. The memory of Cisto helping her walk to camp after he'd beaten her swirled through her mind. She'd managed then, and she would manage now.

"Lucio and I will walk with you." Leya took her other hand and put it in the crook of her elbow. Rosalinda tried to smile, but even that hurt.

"Where are my niños?" Every step jarred up through her spine. She could feel an area that hurt more than the rest and tried to step so that part of her wouldn't be jarred as much.

"Don Armenta is watching them," Ramón said.

The three of them stopped and stared up at him as he sat on his chestnut. He grinned. "He is. He said he would teach them to throw a rope. They were all clamoring to be the first to try." Ramón's grin faded. "He didn't want them to worry about you, Rosalinda. If they are busy, they will have less time to wonder what happened."

She snapped her mouth closed. Never would she have imagined the authoritarian Don Armenta would watch her niños. They could be such a handful, and she hadn't figured out yet how to corral them and keep them from getting into trouble. Would she ever?

Maybe that was why her mother had been so eager to get rid of her. Rosalinda had always been the one to explore where she shouldn't and to ask questions about things that were not her business. Her sister had been the sweet one. The shy, quiet one. Like Isabel.

Mother kept her sister.

"Maybe you could see if he needs help, Ramón." Leya's directive was so unusual the men both looked at her. Lucio nodded, and Ramón wheeled his mare around and trotted toward the campsite.

Leya patted Rosalinda's arm. "When we have some privacy, I will look at your back. I'll see if anyone has some salve that will help with the pain and bruising. If that brute stepped on you, there will be marks."

Warmth threaded through her as everyone helped with her and with her children. She couldn't express her gratitude.

The walk proved bearable, albeit interminable. When they reached their wagon, Rosalinda saw her children across the way trying to twirl a rope. Their laughter floated to her, a balm to her nerves. She settled onto a log someone had set on end for her.

Lucio and one of the vaqueros put up some branches and lay blankets across them so she and Leya had some privacy. Then Leya eased open Rosalinda's blouse to look at her injuries.

"Oh, Rosalinda." Leya's horror came through loud and clear. "The horse stepped on you twice. I see two clear hoof prints. The bruises are very dark."

She hurried to retrieve a pan of water and a rag to cleanse the area. The cool water felt good, but even though Leya tried to be gentle, each touch reverberated through Rosalinda.

"There are no cuts. Only bruises." Leya dropped the cloth into the basin. "I don't know if I would be able to tell about broken ribs or other bones. May I ask Ramón to look? He is very knowledgeable about such things."

"No." She didn't want *any* man looking at her bare skin. To see her like this. Not even if he only meant to help her.

"Está bien." Leya applied the salve she'd found and then helped Rosalinda adjust her blouse. "I will check you again in the morning. And I will keep the niños with me so they don't bother you."

Rosalinda got little sleep that night. The next morning her body had stiffened, so getting up and moving was hard. Lucio declared a day to rest and do some repairs on the wagons. She knew he made excuses for her to gain strength, and she appreciated the gesture.

"Mama." Isabel came running toward her. The other two children looked up from the rope they were playing with and came barreling toward her too. Rosalinda braced herself.

"*Stop.*" Don Armenta's command rang through the camp. Her

children froze. Even the vaqueros halted their work. Everyone turned to stare. At her.

Rosalinda's face warmed.

"Isabel. Maria. Luis." Don Armenta stood, hands on hips, legs apart, waiting. The two girls gave a longing look in Rosalinda's direction before dragging their feet through the grass as they approached the don. Luis ran straight for the stern man as if he didn't care about his demeanor. The don swung the boy in the air making him laugh.

"Yo también. Me too." Both girls bounced on their toes and demanded a turn.

"In a minute." Don Armenta set Luis down beside his sisters. "Remember what we talked about last night? About your mama?" He waited until they all nodded. "When you go to see her, remember to hug her as if what?"

"As if she is a *gatito pequeñito*." Maria spoke up first.

A tiny kitten. Rosalinda couldn't hold back a smile. She felt about as strong as one.

"That's right." The don squatted down in front of them. "Be very gentle with her. ¿Está bien?"

"Sí." Maria turned and led the way to her mother. Rosalinda watched a miracle in progress. Who were these obedient niños? How had the don made them listen? Did he threaten them? No, not even such a threat had stopped her children in the bandolero camp.

She sat down on the log to hug each of her niños. They chattered about learning to throw a rope and riding the black stallion. They were so happy. Even quiet, fearful Isabel brought out a piece from a lariat and twirled it as she danced for her mother.

Oh, how much her children had changed!

Rosalinda laughed, clamping her arms across her middle to ease the pain it caused. Across the way, she saw Lucio watching the children's antics. Watching her. Her heart warmed.

Do not be a fool! He treats you with respect because of his station and because he is a better class of man than you have ever known. He has no interest in you and never will. Do not equate kindness with interest.

One day he would meet a young woman from one of the other important familias. He would court her, marry her, and be happy. That girl would not be a saucy flirt. She would be able to control the children they would have. She would be able to read and write. This woman would be everything Rosalinda could never be. The perfect woman for Lucio.

Don Armenta squatted beside her. "My son seems to think you are something special."

She stared open-mouthed at him. At his stern visage.

And steeled herself for the harsh words that were coming.

CHAPTER TEN

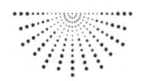

THE JOUNCE of the wagon on the rutted road sent shards of pain through Rosalinda. Not as much as the previous day or even the day before that. They'd been back on the road two days now. Leya determined that Rosalinda didn't have broken ribs but wrapped her torso with a cloth just in case they were cracked. The purple bruises had darkened. Leya showed her the imprints on her back with a mirror.

She had to admit the support helped, but nothing took away the constant ache. As with all of her previous injuries, time would be the best healer.

Luis snuggled back against her as she sat in the wagon bed, her back supported by the seat and rolled blankets behind her. Leya sat next to her, Isabel on her lap, and Maria on the other side of her. Maria chattered like a squirrel. She still couldn't believe her once shy daughter would talk so much.

"I want to hear more about Joseph and his brothers." Maria looked up at Leya, her gaze intense. "What happened to them?"

Leya glanced at Rosalinda as if to ask permission. "Your mother may want to nap instead of listening to a story."

"No. Go ahead. I can rest while you talk, and then we can walk when you are done." Rosalinda's smile turned to a grimace as the wagon hit another rut.

"¿Está bien, Rosalinda?" Don Armenta drove the wagon today. He turned to look down at her. "I am trying to avoid the worst of the holes, but there are so many. This area must have had a lot of rain."

"Está bien." Rosalinda tried for another smile and must have succeeded because he nodded and turned back around.

"The story." Maria tugged on Leya's arm.

Rosalinda clucked her tongue at her daughter. "Patience, mija."

Leya settled in with the children. "Remember how Joseph forgave his brothers for what they did to him? And, remember how he was the second most powerful man in Egypt?"

Maria nodded. "I thought he would be mean to them, but he wasn't."

"No, he forgave them because he was a godly man and had learned a lot." Leya brushed a bit of dust from Maria's cheek. "I want to tell you what happened afterwards. The pharaoh loved Joseph. Remember pharaoh was the ruler in Egypt."

Maria nodded. Isabel leaned against Leya's chest, her thumb in her mouth. Luis played with a piece of rope as he sat on his mother's lap.

"The Egyptians should have thought highly of Joseph and his people, but they forgot about all the good he had done for them. The story in the Bible doesn't tell us all that happened, but says that after four hundred years, the people forgot about Joseph and made the Israelites, God's people, slaves."

"Four hundred years." Maria's brow furrowed. Her lips formed a pout. "Is that older than my mama is?"

Rosalinda gasped. Leya bit her lip. From behind them they heard a low chuckle.

"Yes, that is much older than your mother."

"More than Don Armenta?" Maria looked at Leya wide-eyed.

Rosalinda put her forehead against the top of Luis' head, her cheeks burning.

Leya chuckled. "Mija, four hundred years is more than all of us put together."

Maria's mouth fell open. She stared up at Leya as if trying to process so large a number.

"So, let me tell you what happened after all those years." Leya put her arm around Maria and pulled her close. Rosalinda watched. Was this how to be the mother her children needed and longed for?

"The Egyptians were afraid of the Israelites and made them slaves. The new pharaoh feared the slaves would rise up and take over the land. He heard about their God sending a man to save them, so he gave an order that all the Israelite baby boys would be killed when they were born."

"Killed?" Maria's eyes rounded. "Babies?"

"Yes, but the midwives who helped birth the babies knew God didn't want that, so they tried to save them."

"Good." Maria crossed her arms. "You shouldn't kill babies."

"That's right. But the babies were still in danger if they were found." Leya shifted Isabel on her lap. "Then a woman named Jochabed had a baby boy named Moses, and she refused to let him be killed. She hid him for three months, but then his cries became too loud, and she knew the soldiers of pharaoh would find him and kill him."

"What did she do?" Maria asked. "Did she put a rag in his mouth?"

Rosalinda closed her eyes. What her little niña had learned in her short life...

"No, mija, she made a waterproof basket and put the baby in it. Then she put him in the water at the edge of the river. She put him in God's hands." Leya didn't sound at all put out at Maria's questions.

"Did God let him go over a waterfall? Did he drown?" Maria

asked in a hushed tone. "If we went to the stream in the mountain, we would fall in and drown or be washed away."

"God takes care of his people, and He had special plans for Moses. He caused the pharaoh's daughter to find Moses, and she thought he was such a beautiful baby she kept him."

"Pharaoh's daughter? Did Pharaoh let her keep him?"

"Yes, he did. Pharaoh's daughter asked Moses' mother to help take care of him and then Moses grew up in Pharaoh's household."

The wagon hit a deep rut. The jolt stole Rosalinda's breath. She groaned and dropped Luis onto the wagon bed. He began to cry. Isabel, almost asleep against Leya, started to wail too. Don Armenta slowed the wagon to a stop.

Rosalinda couldn't think. Couldn't hear. Couldn't breathe. Her vision wavered to blackness. She heard someone talking but couldn't make out the words.

After what seemed an eternity, the agony eased. She drew in a wisp of jasmine-scented air. Another breath.

"Rosalinda, lie down." Leya knelt next to her. The children had stopped crying. She didn't even know where they were. She eased back onto the blankets. The prone position eased the agony even more. She relaxed a little. Closed her eyes and drifted for a time.

She must have slept. When she awoke, she heard voices from a distance. She couldn't make out the words and descended into sleep again.

The movement of the wagon brought her around. She squinted her eyes open. She couldn't see anyone else in the wagon bed with her. Above, she noted Lucio's sombrero as he sat on the bench.

Drawing in a deeper breath, Rosalinda realized the pain had receded and she could breathe again without discomfort. She pushed against the bed to sit up, working through the agony.

Lucio must have heard her. He pulled back on the reins and eased the team to a halt. "How are you?" He turned on the seat to look down at her.

"Está bien. Much better." She glanced around. "Where are my niños?"

"Luis is riding with Don Armenta. Isabel is with Ramón, and Maria is walking with Leya. Under protest though. Maria thought she should have her own horse."

His smile warmed her.

"I am sorry to be so much trouble." Her eyes burned, and she looked down so he wouldn't see the tears gathering. "This is why you wanted me to stay at the hacienda. I should have listened."

"No." She felt him touch her hair, the sensation electric. When she lifted her head, his fingers trailed down the side of her face. He cupped her chin. "I am happy to have you with us. Your children have helped me see a side of my father I have not seen since my mother died."

He blinked his eyes closed for a moment. "It's almost as if he died that day too and is only now coming back to us." He pulled his hand away.

She wanted to ask him to touch her again. All the times men had touched her she never wanted them to. Revulsion or acceptance would fill her, but never interest. Never the things she felt when Lucio touched her.

"Would you like to come up here and sit?"

She started at his question, then glanced at the trees lining this section of road. Actually, she had a more pressing need. He must have understood, for he wrapped the reins and hopped down to help her from the wagon.

"I'll wait here for you." He squeezed her arm as she gained her footing. She barely noticed the discomfort as she walked. Instead, she absorbed the foreign sensations she'd been experiencing.

Anticipation thrummed through her, but she didn't even understand what she looked forward to. Lucio's attention? Over the years she'd had plenty of male attention, more than she ever wanted. Handsomer men. More powerful men.

Crude men.

They all wanted her body, but none ever cared about *her*, or her feelings, like Lucio did.

When she exited the trees, he was leaning back against the wagon. He glanced up, and his smile lit his eyes in a way that warmed her clear through.

LUCIO HELPED Rosalinda onto the wagon seat and swung up to sit beside her. She moved with a little more ease than she had in the past couple of days. Her color had come back. She'd been so pale earlier, and he feared the jolt had hurt her inside. Laying her flat in the bed and giving her time to rest had done wonders for her.

The sleeve of her dress brushed against his arm. He liked that she sat close even when Leya wasn't with them. He liked the way she took in the countryside and enjoyed the sights.

Who was he kidding? He liked *her*.

What would his father say? Rosalinda was not the type of woman a don's son should be interested in.

She put her hand on the seat between them as they hit a rough patch. He slowed the team to make the jouncing easier on her.

"Don Armenta feels terrible about driving into that rut." He glanced at her but didn't want to take his focus from the road. "The grass covered the divot, and he didn't see it until one of the horses stumbled. By then it was too late to do anything."

"I don't fault him." Her full lips tipped in a slight smile. "We were all distracted by the story. Leya's storytelling is almost as captivating as your sister's. Yoana used to keep the whole bandolero camp enthralled."

"I'll bet she did." He smiled at the memories. "She often told stories to my nieces and nephews when the little ones came over with my brothers." He guided the team around a rough patch.

Silence fell between them. Not strained, like with his father, but companionable. He liked being with her. Too much.

"Do you mind me asking how you came to be in the bandolero

camp?" He didn't want to lose the camaraderie they had developed, but he needed to know more about her. He couldn't erase the thought of her at the hands of the desperado Gabrio had described to him.

Her face flushed. She turned from him as though looking at the hills to the side of them.

"I don't know how much you know about my background." She hesitated, her fingers twisting the material of her skirt. "When I was a young girl, I got in trouble often. I dragged my sister into trouble too." She laughed, a hollow sound.

"I tried to deny my guilt, but my mother always knew. Mother and I did not get along. She loved my sister very much, and my sister deserved her love. Elena was so sweet and compliant, the opposite of me."

He wanted to tell her she still deserved her mother's love, but he stayed quiet and let her continue.

"My mother had very little. My uncle, her brother, lived with us. I believe he fell in with a bad crowd, although I don't remember much." She swallowed hard. Stayed silent so long he thought she wouldn't continue.

"One day some bandoleros came to our casita. We lived in a little house. My mother had a tiny garden that helped to feed us, but we were always hungry. Maybe that is why my uncle fell in with the wrong people. Perhaps he wanted a way to provide more for us or enough food that we wouldn't starve."

She wiped at her cheeks with the back of her hand. Sniffed. Her breath shuddered out.

"What about your father?" Lucio had to ask. Why hadn't she mentioned him?

She looked at him for the first time since their conversation started. Her eyes were greener today than brown. This close he could see the yellow highlights.

"I have no memory of a father." She shook her head. "I've wondered since then if my mother was even married. My sister and I looked nothing alike. She had a round face, obsidian eyes, darker skin, and hair as straight as sticks laid in row. I'm not sure we had the same father."

He could see what she meant. Her hair didn't have the curls like her children's, but the waves were beautiful. Her skin tone, fair with a hint of tan, was much lighter than his. Her hazel eyes captivated every person, as did her heart-shaped face. He could look on her for hours—days…forever—and never grow tired.

"When the men came that day, my mother sent my sister and me to hide out in the small shed that housed our chickens. She told us not to make a sound." Rosalinda twisted her fingers together, the knuckles turning white.

"Elena obeyed, of course." She huffed a sound. "Me, not so much. We peered out through the cracks in the shed. There were four men, but the loudest one had to be the leader. Elena started to cry because he scared her. I called her names because nothing scared me."

He longed to put his arm around her and pull her close. He could see how much she hated telling what had happened.

"I taunted her. Poking her. Berating her. All things I did all the time. I guess out of jealousy because she was mama's favorite." She looked down at her whitened fingers, untwined them, and rubbed her palms on her skirt.

"We stopped watching through the cracks in the walls. I made Elena cry, and she never cried softly. She'd learned to cry loud so our mother would run to her rescue. This time her sobs brought the awful men." She shivered. "They dragged us out from the shed, killing the chickens to take with them." She closed her eyes.

Why had he ever asked her to relive this? Had she ever talked with anyone about that horrible day?

"The outlaws threw us at the feet of their leader. My mother cried and begged for them to leave us with her. The leader, a horrible man who smelled like rotten meat and had a voice like the thunder in the sky, gave her a choice. He said they would take one of us for payment, and she could choose which one. He would even throw in a little coin since his men killed her chickens. And I knew." She wrapped a wave tight around her finger, her voice fading to a whisper. "I knew who she would choose." A tear leaked from her eye to roll down her cheek.

She shuddered. "Stop the wagon!" Anger darkened her face. Her mouth pulled to a thin line. "Stop, or I will jump!"

He'd been going slowly, caught up in her story. With a light tug, the horses halted. "Wait--" He started to get down and help her, but she was off the wagon almost before he could move.

"Go." She nodded her head toward the rest of the party, her arms crossed over her chest. "Leave me alone. Just leave me alone." Her chin tilted up. Only the trembling of her lower lip hinted at her vulnerability.

There was no way he could talk her into joining him on the seat again because he didn't know why she'd gotten down. Had his expression revealed his horror over what her mother chose to do? He didn't think so, but something set her off.

He clicked his tongue and lifted the reins. The team ambled off at a slow walk. He kept the pace languid so she wouldn't fall too far behind, so he could keep an eye on her in case she tired.

Memories of the early years when his mother still lived ran through his mind. Did she have a favorite among him and his siblings? He couldn't imagine it. She'd been so full of love and life. She sang. She danced with them. Played games and laughed. Even their father would join them in the gaiety sometimes. She would have fought to the death before she sold one of her children. In fact, she died saving Yoana.

Heaviness weighed him down. How could he show Rosalinda that her mother should have loved her enough to fight for her? Did she even know where her mother and sister lived now? Probably not. That one so young would have experienced so much horror...

He glanced back to see Rosalinda trudging not far behind him, her gaze on the road, her shoulders slumped. The very picture of dejection.

The cadence of a cantering horse drew his attention. His father approached on his stallion, a fierce frown on his face. He slid to a halt by the wagon.

"Lucio, what have you done to Rosalinda?"

CHAPTER ELEVEN

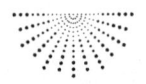

"I WILL BE SO glad to be done today." Leya handled the lead lines for the team like a pro now. "My sitting parts are so tired of sitting." She made a face at Rosalinda. They laughed.

They had been traveling steadily, pushing the teams to try to get to the Santiago hacienda before any rains would come to bog them down in the road. A few sprinkles threatened more, but the biggest rains were in the mountains behind them, which didn't affect the roads they traveled.

Since her embarrassing revelation to Lucio and her humiliating retreat, Rosalinda refused to ride in the wagon if he was driving. Refused. Leya tried to talk to her, but she wouldn't budge. She didn't want to be around him. He would soon learn he needed to look for a woman who would be accepted among his peers. She would never fit that standard.

"I could try to get Ramón's attention and see if he would take over driving. Then we could walk." She glanced behind her. All three children were curled up on a blanket, careful to not touch one another. They had reached their limit of getting along, and the fighting this morning sounded like a couple of cats on the outs with one another. Such screeching!

Leya glanced back too before turning around to watch the road. "I don't want to disturb the peace." She winked at Rosalinda. "If we stop to walk, they will all want to go too, and the fighting will start again."

Rosalinda opened her mouth to apologize for her niños but didn't know what to say. Leya patted her on the knee.

"Don't worry. They are children. Children who are tired of traveling this bumpy road. What started as a fun adventure has become a chore. A tiresome one at that." She guided the team around a large rock at the edge of the trail.

"Have you forgiven Lucio?" Leya asked.

"I don't need to. He did nothing wrong." Rosalinda stiffened. Why did everyone want to tell her how to live her life? They didn't understand her reasons for her actions but wanted to give her advice anyway.

"I didn't say either of you did anything wrong, but at least one of you has hurt feelings. If there is anything wrong between you two, then you need to figure out what." Leya started to say more but then snapped her mouth shut.

In the bandolero camp, Rosalinda had been a strong woman. She knew her place, but she let everyone around her know the boundaries. No one crossed her. Well, almost no one. Cisto, the outlaw who owned her, did as he pleased.

Still, she always knew what she wanted and how to get it. Now, with Lucio stirring unfamiliar feelings, she didn't know what to do or how to act. Flirting used to be her normal. All the men understood she didn't mean anything when she smiled at them in a come-hither manner or swayed her hips enough to make them drool. They didn't mess with her because Cisto would have killed them. Without question.

These vaqueros thought if she looked their direction it was an invitation. She had no barriers these men respected. No protector. Only Lucio and Ramón were different. And she didn't know how to respond. Their kindness would kill her.

"Why is he coming here?" Leya tugged the mantilla down over her face, but not before Rosalinda saw the flash of anger in her eyes. Leya. Calm, controlled Leya never showed anger.

As she followed Leya's gaze, Rosalinda heard the clomp of the horse before she saw the rider. Carlos. Coming their way. His broad face creased in a grin, he tipped his hat toward them. His pinto pranced in place as he stopped to watch them pass.

She decided to test her theory. To see if these men knew the difference between a woman who wanted their attention and one who only meant to be friendly. Rosalinda tipped her head to the side and smiled at Carlos.

His smile faltered. Broadened. His whole countenance beamed. The pinto whirled in place, causing him to swivel in the saddle to keep her in sight. She feared he might fall from the steed.

"*Buenos tardes*, señoritas." He started to ride closer, glanced over his shoulder, and backed his horse away. He doffed his hat and bowed before turning to canter away.

"I wish you wouldn't do that." Leya flung her mantilla back over her head. Her dark eyes sparked with ire as she narrowed them at Rosalinda.

"What? What did I do?" Rosalinda pulled her skirt away from Leya. She knew what the older woman would say, but she didn't want to hear.

"It's not a conscious action." Leya's lips thinned. "You have a way of speaking without words that makes these men crazy. They forget who they are and how they are supposed to act. You need to stop."

"How can I stop something I don't know I'm doing? I smiled at him. That's all." She did her best to ignore the prick of her conscience. She knew all right.

Since she'd been a very young girl, she'd discovered the power she wielded with her looks and her physical appearance. She hadn't been away from home for long when she learned that manipulating men worked better than cowering from them. By now the actions were ingrained, and she did them without thought. In fact, she didn't know how to smile at a man without doing what she'd just done with Carlos.

"Rosalinda." Leya's voice softened. She wrapped her hand around Rosalinda's fingers, which were twisting her skirt in a knot without her realizing what she'd done.

"This is important. Your little niñas watch everything you do. They will begin to mimic the way you walk. The way you flash your eyes. The way you smile." Leya squeezed her fingers and then let go to focus on driving. "Maria and Isabel are beautiful girls. You don't want men to get the wrong idea about them, do you?"

Revulsion stole her speech. Her greatest fear involved her daughters and how they might be treated by men. They were so young. But Maria was almost as old as Rosalinda had been that fateful day. She knew the number of men who liked little girls. A shudder chased through her, leaving her chilled.

She pressed her fingers to her eyelids to stop the burning. Her chest ached. Memories of her early years after being sold flashed through her mind. Images she tried to block. The depravity. She wanted to erase them forever.

Leya rubbed circles on her back. Rosalinda rocked back and forth and fought the sobs that would startle her niños. She didn't want to have to explain to them why their mother was crying. She never wanted them to know the atrocities she'd experienced as a young girl. They needed to have the fun and enjoy the innocence every child deserved. She might not understand how a family worked, but she did know she wanted to be the best mother she could be, and she would protect her children with her life.

"I didn't mean to be harsh." Leya's concern brought Rosalinda back from the brink of despair. "I'm sorry, Rosalinda. ¿Está bien?" Leya must have stopped the team. The horses stood at rest in the middle of the road, tails swishing, ears flicking. Rosalinda called on a calm she didn't know she possessed to rid her mind of the reprehensible images. Leya pressed a cloth into her hand. Rosalinda wiped her eyes and blew her nose. She closed her eyes and drew in a few deep breaths before facing her friend.

"I did not think of how my actions would hurt my niñas. Thank you for bringing that to my attention." She wiped her eyes again. "Leya, I smiled at him. I know the way I did so held an invitation, but to tell you the truth, I have no idea how to show friendliness to a man without making him think inappropriate thoughts about me. This is all I know." She pressed the damp cloth to her eyes.

"Perhaps, you need to not smile at all until you can learn." Leya's seriousness softened her words. "It is better to be thought cold and unfeeling than to have the vaqueros think they are free to take advantage of you. Don't you agree?"

"But how will I learn to smile again? Or to talk to a man? Or to walk without having them all watch me?" Rosalinda shook her head thinking she would have to relearn everything she knew.

"I will help you," Leya said. "The Bible says there is great value in a woman who is beautiful on the inside. You are lovely, outside and in, but the men don't see both. They get distracted. We need to emphasize your inner beauty." She smiled and clicked her tongue to start the team moving while Rosalinda digested this new idea.

THE HILLS they were passing through gave way to some familiar landmarks. Lucio couldn't suppress his excitement. By evening they would be at his sister's new home. The Santiago hacienda. He would see Yoana and Gabrio. The difficulty of this trip would be over soon, and he refused to think of their return.

Maybe Rosalinda would choose to stay here. After all, her *compadre*, Delores, from the bandolero camp, lived here. Maria and Delores's son, Teo, were best friends. If Rosalinda chose to stay here, he would be free of her and could forget this woman who rattled him so much.

"Lucio." Ramón's call broke into his reverie. He swung his dun around and cantered back to see what his amigo wanted.

"The wagon carrying the furniture for Yoana slid off the road and one of the pieces fell off and broke. The writing desk." Ramón gestured back to the conveyance in question, which had halted by the side of the road.

"Tell everyone we'll take a break for lunch and repairs." Lucio watched Ramón ride away and reined the dun around to see if the piece could be fixed. His mother's writing desk. Yoana would be upset. He remembered his mother seated at the desk with the table folded down and the drawers that held all manner of paper and pens. So fascinating to him as a child.

He swung down and knelt with the man who had been driving the wagon. Two of the legs had broken off, but the folded-up desk seemed to still be intact. He clapped the man on the shoulder. "This can be repaired. Help me get it back on the wagon and secured. We'll fix it when we arrive. Don Santiago has a carpenter whose skill is well-known."

They loaded the broken piece and tightened the ropes again. Lucio knew he should have been checking to see if the goods were still secure after the rough roads they'd traveled. He assured the hombre again and told him to get some food. Then he headed for the group of vaqueros who were eating and talking.

As he approached, he heard Carlos bragging about something. A good worker, but that man had to be best at everything. Or, to hear him tell the story, he was the best. He wondered what the braggart had done now.

"She smiled at me so sweet." Carlos stood with his back to Lucio and must not have noticed the glances of the other vaqueros. "The boss thinks she likes him, but I'm telling you, it's me she's sweet on. I'll meet her somewhere tonight, and we'll see what happens."

Silence met his proclamation. Carlos fell quiet for a moment before he swiveled to look behind him. His eyes widened a fraction before he pulled his mask of bravado back down and grinned at Lucio.

"Lo siento, señor. You have lost the *mujer*. The woman likes me the best." Carlos glanced around at the other men, obviously hoping to get some support from his compadres. They were silent. Unsmiling.

Carlos didn't back down. He swaggered toward Lucio, his thumbs in his waistband. "I rode past the mujeres a little while ago. Rosalinda smiled at me in a way that invited me to meet with her tonight. I am sorry for you, boss, but she likes me." His flat nose wrinkled as he grinned. The smile didn't reach his eyes.

Lucio wanted to ignore this man and his challenge. He wanted to walk away. Instead, he took a step until he was almost nose to nose with the vaquero. They stared at one another for a long moment.

"You are to stay away from Rosalinda. We had this discussion already."

"You said I couldn't talk to her the rest of the trip." Carlos' eyes took on a triumphant shine. "Our trip is over tonight. If the señora wants to meet me, then we are free to have a good time."

A heavy hand fell on Lucio's shoulder. He knew it must be Ramón, but when he glanced to the side, he saw Don Armenta standing beside him. Carlos ducked his head.

"Lucio, Ramón and I need to speak with you." His father left little choice when he gave a directive. Too many years of obedience and respect kept Lucio from continuing with Carlos. The interchange would not end well anyway.

He walked beside his father to where Ramón waited with the horses. He had Lucio's dun as well as the chestnut and Don Armenta's stallion. His father mounted and waited for them to join him. "I think we should retrieve the children and give the women a break."

He focused on Lucio, his visage stern. "I recall hearing that Maria wants to see her friend at the Santiagos's. I propose you take her and ride on ahead to let them know we will be there by evening. The last thing you need is to start a war with one of the hands over who will win the right to court the señora."

He wanted to protest. How could he walk away when one of the men challenged him? Plus, he didn't want to see Carlos making advances on Rosalinda. She wouldn't have flirted with the man on purpose, would she? His mind swirled with thoughts and conflict.

Confusion. He didn't want to court Rosalinda. But he didn't want anyone else to be interested in her. He didn't want her to be sweet on him, but he couldn't stand the thought of her being with any other man.

Lucio dropped behind Ramón and his father. He bowed his head, knowing he needed to pray about this situation and his confusing emotions.

"Lord, help me." He had no idea what else to say. The request came from his heart, but his mind had no more words. He groaned with frustration. A verse he'd heard Tía Leya say popped in his head. Something about God not being the author of confusion but giving peace to his people.

Understanding swept over him. These feelings weren't from God, and he shouldn't trust them. Instead, he would pray every day for God to make it clear what he wanted him to do. He would pray for Rosalinda, that she would know God and act accordingly. He didn't want to see her hurt anymore. She'd suffered enough.

He took too much time. Ramón and his father already had the niños on their horses and were riding his way. Ramón had Isabel in front of him and Maria behind. He sidled his horse next to Lucio's so Maria could slip over onto the dun.

"We will see to the wagons and remuda." Don Armenta nodded at Lucio. "You go on ahead."

He started to say something more but closed his mouth and

frowned into the distance. Lucio had an idea that his father wanted to ask him not to tell Yoana he had joined their party.

"Why don't you come with me?" At Lucio's request his father raised his eyebrows. Not much surprised the don, but this must have.

"You could leave Luis and ride with Maria and me." As much as he'd avoided his father since he arrived, Lucio knew he needed to extend the courtesy of asking him along. He had no idea how Yoana would react to having the don arrive unexpected. He wished he could give her advance warning, but that wasn't to be.

"I appreciate the offer." Don Armenta's stallion pranced in a circle, his dark hooves lifting high. He snorted, flinging his head up and down before settling under the don's firm hand.

"Your sister may prefer to greet you first." The don twisted his mouth into a semblance of a smile. "Besides, this little niña is wanting to see her friend. Right mija?"

Lucio twisted around to see his father tug one of Maria's curls. Maria bounced behind him, her excitement apparent. Lucio wondered what his sister would say when she saw their father interacting with Rosalinda's children. Would she see this as positive? Or would she resent all the years he'd treated her like a leper and refused even to talk with her? All the years he blamed Yoana for something that wasn't her fault.

"Maria and I will see you tonight." Lucio nodded at Ramón as he lifted the reins and urged the dun into a slow canter. Now that the decision had been made, he couldn't wait to get to the Santiago hacienda and see his sister. He could trust his father and his best friend to bring the others safely through the hills. They only had a few miles left to go.

"Are we there?" Maria leaned around him and almost fell. Lucio felt her slip and put his hand back to set her upright.

They topped a brown hill and looked down at the buildings below them. Activity swirled. Vaqueros. Horses. Dogs.

"Is this where Teo lives?" Maria stood up behind him on the dun's wide rump.

"Sit down before you fall and break your neck." Lucio shook his head as she slid back down and clamped her arms around his waist.

Below, in the yard of the hacienda, he watched a young woman with a long braid come out of the house. She stood in the yard, her hand over her eyes looking in their direction. She waved as she raced toward them. Lucio grinned and kicked the dun into motion.

CHAPTER TWELVE

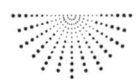

"I don't see Teo." Maria almost choked Lucio as she pulled on his collar to stand and peer over his shoulder. Again. He drew on his patience as the dun shied to the left.

"Maria, sit down." He reached back to tug her down without both of them ending up in the dirt. "We can't move until you do."

She kept a tight hold on his arm as she pulled the opposite side of his shirt. When he felt her straighten, he guided the dun around to descend to the hacienda. He could understand Maria's excitement. Seeing Yoana running to meet them made him want to race downhill without regard to safety.

Yoana turned to call something over her shoulder. A door opened in a *casita* to the side of the main hacienda. A young woman stepped out. She motioned to the barn, then lifted her skirt and hurried that way.

"Lucio!" Yoana stopped by the gate into the rancho and put her hand to her chest.

The road flattened, and he lifted the dun into a canter.

"Where's Teo?" Maria shoved his elbow up and stuck her head through, her arms tight around his waist. "Do you see him?"

"Not yet. Sit back before you land in the dirt." Lucio slowed his horse and trotted up to Yoana.

She held up her hands and Maria leaped off into her arms. Yoana hugged the niña tight to her and kissed her on the cheek.

"I've missed you, mija."

Lucio swung down, his chest near to bursting. His sister glowed with a contentment and joy he'd never seen before. She'd always been beautiful, but this woman was radiant. He knew the years she'd spent under their father's oppressive rule had been hard, but he hadn't realized what had been stolen from her. What would she say when she realized the don traveled with them? He hoped she didn't slip back into that shell of a woman she'd been before.

"Lucio." Yoana held out her free arm and dragged him into a hug, with Maria squeezed between them. The girl giggled and squirmed.

"I want to see Teo." Maria pushed at Lucio and then patted Yoana's cheek to get her attention. "Where is he?"

"Who is this you've brought, Lucio?" Yoana's eyes twinkled as she glanced from him to Maria. "I don't recall the Maria I knew talking this much."

"She has chattered the whole trip." Lucio gave an exaggerated sigh. "The horses thought she would talk their ears off."

"They didn't." Maria put her hand over her mouth and giggled. Yoana smiled at Lucio, and he could see her joy at how the young girl had changed since she'd last seen her. Maria wiggled again, pushing at Yoana, wanting down.

"Maria." Footsteps pounded across the yard. Lucio looked over to see Teo tearing toward them. The woman who had fetched him followed at a more sedate pace. Lucio almost didn't recognize her. She wasn't Delores, Teo's mother. Then her slim frame and her shy dip of her head struck a memory. Feliciana. She'd come to the Santiago hacienda along with Delores and Yoana.

"Lucio, you remember Feliciana." Yoana smiled at the girl, who nodded with a dip of her head. Yoana patted her shoulder. "She works in the kitchen with our cook, Carmen."

Yoana set the niña down. Maria, at first eager to see her best friend, now hesitated. She grasped Lucio's leg as if afraid of what to say to Teo.

Teo showed no hesitation. He raced up to Maria and hugged her, lifting her off the ground. Even though he was only a year or so older, he'd grown since he moved up north. Not only had he grown taller, but he was no longer the skinny waif he'd once been. From the smell drifting off of him, he must have been cleaning stalls in the barn.

"I've missed you." Teo set Maria back down. His round face creased with a wide grin. He brushed a hank of dark hair from his eyes. "Want to see the barn? I work there." His chest puffed out. Maria nodded, and the pair raced away as if they couldn't wait to see the stinking piles of manure that needed to be cleaned up.

Lucio chuckled. "She has been so anxious to get here."

"She's come out of her shyness, except for the moment with Teo."

"She'll be talking his leg off by the time they reach the barn. She not only talks, but she wants to be in charge of everything. Wait until I tell you about her stealing my horse." Lucio could chuckle about that now. "The others will be here before nightfall." He smiled at his sister's delight. "Rosalinda, Isabel, and Luis came, as well as Tía Leya."

"Leya is with you?" Yoana's hands flew to her mouth. Her eyes widened. She must have missed her tía more than all the rest of them. Should he tell her their father was coming too? Telling her would spoil the joy of seeing Leya.

"Where is Gabrio? Is he out working?"

Yoana turned to look out past the barn. "He went to check on some of the grapes. He should be back any time. Come in while you wait. I'll get you something to drink. Are you hungry? I will fix you something to eat too."

Lucio tried not to grimace. He really tried. And failed. Feliciana snickered, and Yoana glared at him, her hands on her hips.

"Señor, I will see that you have something refreshing from the kitchen." Feliciana whistled, and Teo stuck his head out from the barn. She motioned to him, and he raced toward them. "Teo, see to Señor Lucio's horse before you play with Maria."

Feliciana preceded them into the hacienda. Lucio smirked down at his sister. "So, some things don't change. They still keep you from the kitchen, right?"

"Don't be mean when you are staying in my home." She swatted him on his arm. "I have other duties, but, yes, they are smart not to let me cook." They both chuckled. The stories of her attempt to cook in the bandolero camp had been told and retold, along with the tales of her sewing skills. Or, rather, the lack of sewing skills.

"Married life agrees with you." Lucio reached around her to hold open the door. "You are happy?"

She smiled at him. "Very happy. I have never been so accepted. Don Santiago has me helping keep his books for the ranchero, and I teach the children too. There are several who live here, including Teo. They are all eager to learn."

"I am glad." Lucio gave her a quick hug.

"How is everyone? Is Leya well?" Yoana led him to a comfortable room with a small table. Feliciana came in with glasses of *horchata* and a plate of meat and beans. A warm wrapped tortilla sat at the edge of his plate. He thanked her. A shy smile brightened her face as she left the room.

After saying a prayer, Lucio took a bite. Delicious! He hadn't realized how hungry he was for food that hadn't been fixed on the trail. He looked at his sister. "Leya misses you. I did not want Rosalinda or Leya to come, but Rosalinda is an unrelenting force and doesn't back down. In her quiet way, so is our tía."

Yoana chuckled. "I remember that."

"She insisted on coming, and Leya insisted on accompanying

her. I sometimes wonder if Leya is the one who came up with the plan." He took another bite, savoring the taste of the fresh tortilla.

"The trip must have been slower with three children along." Yoana sipped her horchata.

"Rosalinda's children have stolen the hearts of the men. Maria insists she must learn to ride a horse. Ramón has taken on the task of making sure the niños get to ride every day."

The door to the hacienda opened and shut with a bang. Gabrio, Yoana's husband, strode into the room. Lucio pushed up from the table to greet his friend.

"I see you have invaded my house and are eating all my food." Gabrio grabbed him, pulled him close, and pounded him on the back. "Welcome, hermano. Where are the others?"

Lucio explained the trip as Gabrio joined them at the table. Yoana left to bring her husband a glass of horchata. By the time she returned, Lucio had filled Gabrio in on most of the conversation he'd had with Yoana. He then told them about Maria trying to steal his dun, which made Yoana clap her hands at the bravery of the little niña.

"Does Ramón spend his whole day taking children for rides then? I will have to tease him about that." Yoana's eyes gleamed.

"No, the three of us take turns with them. Our father takes Luis most of the time--" Lucio stopped, but it was too late.

The blood drained from Yoana's face.

EVERY PART of her body ached. Her feet from walking. Her bottom from sitting. Her skin from too much sun. And her head from the constant whining of her children. The younger niños demanded to know where their sister went, even though she'd told them over and over. Rosalinda gathered the shreds of her patience and fought not to snap at Isabel. At least Don Armenta had Luis with him, so she only had Isabel now.

"Mija, you will see Maria before bedtime tonight." She closed her eyes and hoped she'd told Isabel the truth. What if they had another delay? She shuddered at the thought of one more night sleeping in the hard wagon with bugs crawling around and the noise of unknown creatures in the brush.

"I want Luis. I want Maria." Isabel's wail squealed across her nerves.

"Would you like to hear a story?" Leya's question sent relief spiraling through Rosalinda. A story almost always settled the children down.

"I want Maria." Isabel's demand hit a higher note. She wiggled on the seat between them. "I want Luis." She sobbed, her wails loud enough to make a flock of birds in a nearby grove of trees take flight.

"Maybe I should get down and walk with her. We could kick some rocks or practice skipping." Rosalinda looked over her daughter's head at Leya. She could see the same exhaustion she felt in Leya's drawn features.

"Would you like to drive while I walk with her?" Leya asked. "You walked a long time this afternoon."

Rosalinda shook her head. "I don't like driving the team. Besides, the road is getting hillier, which takes more skill than I possess. Maybe Don Armenta or Ramón will be back soon, and we can both walk." She peered ahead but didn't see the don or the head vaquero.

"I want my sister." Isabel tilted her head back to pour out her misery.

"*Hush.*" Rosalinda's sharp tone shocked her daughter but not enough to quiet her. By this point, Rosalinda wanted to turn her over her knee and spank her, but she'd discovered after coming to the Armenta hacienda she had no control or common sense when punishing her children. At first, she'd used too much force and horrified everyone at the ranch.

Of course, her own memories of punishment involved severe pain and deprivation. How else did one punish a child? She hadn't had any idea until Leya befriended her and taught her how to love her niños as well as discipline them.

"Whoa." Leya pulled back on the reins and stopped the team. Isabel ceased her loud wailing to look up at the older woman.

"You are going in the back by yourself." Leya didn't smile or soften her expression as she lifted her mantilla to study Isabel. "It is a privilege to sit up here with your mother and me. You only get to do so because Maria and Luis aren't here. If you want to cry, you will sit in the back. If you quit crying, you can stay up here with us. What is your choice?"

Isabel gaped at Leya. Rosalinda snapped her own mouth shut. She'd never heard her amiga give such an ultimatum. Why hadn't she thought to give her daughter a choice like this? Would she never learn?

"Well? We're waiting."

Isabel's lower lip trembled. She rubbed at her face with the sleeve of her dress. Sniffed. "I want to sit here." She shuddered a tiny sob but didn't start crying again.

"Está bien." Leya faced forward and clicked her tongue. The team leaned into the harness. The wagon gave a jerk and then rolled along.

They chatted for a bit, able to talk now with a subdued Isabel between them. Rosalinda kept an eye out for Luis. Don Armenta kept the boy with him more and more of the time. She loved her son receiving attention from a man who would be a good example, but what would happen when she had to leave the ranch? They had given her a home, but she didn't fit in, and they didn't need her. Wouldn't they get tired of having her there?

THE SUN HUNG low in the western sky when they wound through the hills that Don Armenta, who'd taken over driving the team, said led to the Santiago hacienda. Rosalinda wanted to be excited, but she'd grown too tired of the journey to muster much emotion. Why was she so exhausted?

She sat on the bench next to Don Armenta. Leya rested in the wagon bed with Luis and Isabel curled up on either side of her. They all looked to be asleep. Relief gave her a slight boost in energy but not much. Her head pounded a steady drumbeat.

"You are so good with my niños. Thank you." Rosalinda needed to talk to distract herself from all her discomfort.

"You have wonderful children." Don Armenta didn't even glance her way. She studied his stern visage. In profile, his hooked nose gave him a patrician air. Dark hair brushed against heavy eyebrows. He must have been a very handsome man when he was young. He still attracted attention from women at his age, but she heard he never returned any interest.

"I think your daughter, Yoana, will be very excited when she finds out you are visiting. You must have been a good father when she was a little girl like Maria and Isabel." She pictured all the ways she would have liked her father to be. Him talking with her, making her laugh. Teaching her all the ways to work and make life easier. Maybe even showing her how to find the right man for a husband.

Certainly not disappearing and leaving her to a loathsome mother and a heinous fate.

The don remained silent, and she had to fill the quiet. "I wanted so much to have a father like you. One who would care about me and put me first." Anger tightened her chest and choked off her next words.

"Maybe your expectations were set too high for your father." He glanced at her, a flick of the eyes she almost missed. "How old were you when you left your home? When you last saw your father?"

"I didn't leave my home." She hated the bitterness in her words. Pushed years of anger and hatred back inside and spoke in a lighter tone. "I never knew my father. He left before I was born."

"So, you had no father to set an example? What about an uncle? A grandfather?"

"I had an uncle. He is the reason my mother sold me when I was seven-years-old. To pay his debts." Why had she even started talking? What would he think of her now? Did he want to toss her out of the wagon and leave her here to die?

But she couldn't seem to stop the flow of words. "My mother and uncle cared so little for me that they sold me to a man who hurt me and abused me. Then he sold me to another man." She stared unseeing at the bushes by the wagon. Her eyes burned like she'd gotten soap in them. "This is the first time in my life I don't belong to a man who cares nothing for me."

She wanted to shut up and not say anymore, but his silence seemed to pull the words from her mouth. She told him the story of what her mother had done. "I don't even know what to do when I don't have a man to slap me and give me orders." She pressed her fingertips to her mouth to stop the flow. What must this man, this important don, think of her?

The horses strained to pull the wagon up a hill. Don Armenta sighed. "Did you ever consider your mother might have had no choice? Maybe she chose you to go with the men because she had the hope you would survive." His gaze held compassion, not condemnation.

She didn't know what to say.

He slowed the team and halted the wagon. They sat at the crest of a hill. Below them sat a beautiful ranch with a sprawling hacienda.

Rosalinda could see the shaded courtyard in the center of the hacienda. Behind the barn, the vaqueros were putting the remuda into a pasture. The wagons they'd brought were pulled up to the house, and men were untying the ropes holding the goods secure.

She drew in a shuddering sigh. "Your children are so lucky they have you, that you didn't abandon them to unmentionable horrors." She waited for him to flick the reins and start them down the hill, where he could reunite with his daughter and visit his friend.

"Rosalinda." Don Armenta cleared his throat. He stared down into the busy yard, his cheeks drawn. "There are different types of abandonment." This time he looked at her.

Such pain in his eyes! It cut through her own self-pity and made her hurt for him.

"I didn't sell my daughter, but what I did to her was nearly as bad as what your mother and uncle did to you. I don't think she will be glad to see me."

His words grew hoarse. She had never imagined such a powerful man could hurt so deeply.

His grief-filled eyes met hers. "The truth is I'm not even sure I will be welcome here."

CHAPTER THIRTEEN

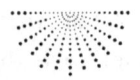

THE WAGON CREAKED as they headed down the hill leading to the ranch. Rosalinda thought about what Don Armenta said. Yoana had said, back in the bandolero camp, that her father didn't care about her. In fact, he refused to pay the ransom to get his daughter back. He paid a ransom for Leya, his sister-in-law, but not for his daughter.

At the time Rosalinda had been glad to see the haughty Yoana suffer the degradation of being rejected. But once she got to know her, she realized Yoana wasn't pretentious. She only acted the way she did to keep from being frightened of the situation.

Something Rosalinda understood only too well.

Why had Don Armenta treated his daughter with such disregard? She considered asking him, but the set of his shoulders and his tight grip on the reins told her he struggled for control. What would he do when he came face-to-face with his daughter? Would he beg forgiveness or revert to the autocratic head of the family who didn't care what anyone thought?

What would Yoana do? Reject her father? Disregard the changes in him? Or would she extend the same forgiveness to her father that Joseph extended to his brothers in the story Leya had told them?

Rosalinda shifted on the seat. Perhaps... should she forgive *her* mother? She pushed the thought away.

Don Armenta had been a haughty man when she first came to his home. She'd been intimidated by him then. But on this trip, he seemed different. What made him change?

As they approached the gates, people poured out of the house. Word must have spread of their arrival. Rosalinda glanced behind her to see Leya rousing Isabel and Luis. A twist of nerves shivered through her. What if Dolores, Feliciana, and Yoana didn't want to see her? She hadn't been the easiest person to get along with. Bossy. Haughty. Confrontational.

Why would any of them want to be around her?

She could see the same doubts, or similar ones, in Don Armenta's pensive expression. She touched his arm. He started.

"I don't know what made you change, señor, but Yoana will see you are different. She will welcome you." She couldn't find a smile, but she tried to encourage him anyway.

He slowed the team. "I don't even know how to explain what happened to me. We don't have time for that. I only know God can work miracles, and I'm hoping for one while I'm here."

"Mama!" Maria raced toward the wagon, Teo beside her. At least Rosalinda thought the boy must be Teo. He'd grown taller and developed more muscle. When he grinned at her, she had no doubt. He still had that crooked tooth and a smile that lit his whole face.

Maria jumped up and down as they drew close. The horses snorted. If the team hadn't been so tired, they might have shied and tried to run. They were probably as glad for this trip to end as she was.

"Don't get stepped on." She called out to her daughter and Teo, but at the same time, Isabel and Luis called out to them, and her caution got lost in the melee. Thankfully, everyone's toes were safe.

Amado, no, *Gabrio*, strode toward them. She still had trouble thinking of him as Gabrio. He used the name *Amado* when he infiltrated the bandolero camp. Behind him, Yoana stayed in the doorway of the house. The shadows hid her face, but from her stance, Rosalinda could see she was not happy.

"Don Armenta, welcome." Gabrio nodded to Yoana's father and reached up to Rosalinda. "May I help you down?"

As her feet reached the ground, her legs nearly buckled, and she grabbed the side of the wagon for support.

Once he had steadied her, Gabrio moved to the end of the wagon to lift the children down, swinging Isabel and Luis in the air before setting them on the ground. Leya he pulled into a tight hug as he steadied her.

"We have rooms made up for you inside. Yoana can show you where you'll be staying. Supper should be ready in about an hour, so you have time to rest."

Gabrio turned to Don Armenta, who had climbed down from the bench seat. The two men clasped hands. Don Armenta pulled the younger man into a hug. Rosalinda saw Gabrio's eyes widen.

"My father is very glad you have come." Gabrio held out one hand to usher the other man toward the house. He nodded at Rosalinda, and her face warmed at being caught watching such an intimate exchange. She hurried to catch up with Leya.

"Tía." Yoana's eyes teared up as she embraced the older woman. The two had been so close. How hard it must have been for Yoana to leave her tía and move so far away where she only knew her husband.

"Rosalinda, beinvenido." Yoana's embrace held no animosity, and Rosalinda relaxed a fraction and hugged her back.

The house held the cool of the day. The scent of roasting meat and peppers drifted down the hallway. Rosalinda's stomach rumbled. Her mouth watered. Oh, to have a meal that didn't come with a helping of grit.

"Rosalinda, the children have grown. Maria has changed so much." Yoana smiled at her. She'd forgotten how pretty Yoana was. Her long braid still hung over one shoulder. She hadn't chosen to wear her hair in a more matronly fashion, even though she'd married. But then, Yoana rarely followed what everyone else did or bowed to what others thought she should do.

"Maria is talking so much. She told me all about your trip and the stories Leya told. I do think there were a few exaggerations." Yoana led them into a beautiful bedroom. "I was surprised to hear that Joseph made his brothers do dishes for a year since they were bad to him." Her lips twitched. "I don't remember reading that in the Bible, Leya."

Leya gasped. "I didn't tell her that."

They all snickered.

"I told her that must have been a very fitting punishment." Yoana gestured to the room that had one large bed and a small bed. "Rosalinda, I hope this will work for you and your children. The girls can sleep in the small bed and you and Luis can use the larger bed."

"This is lovely. I don't need anything this grand." Rosalinda stared around. Even her room at the Armenta hacienda didn't have this much space. She had a fine room there to share with her niños but nothing like this.

"Please, rest a while. I'll let you know when the meal is ready. I know you are tired from the trail. I remember when I first came here." Yoana touched Leya's back. "Come, Tía. I have you in a room closer to mine."

They left, and Rosalinda reveled in the quiet. She went over and sat on the bed, fell back across the covers, and sighed. No hard boards under her. Tonight, she would sleep so well. Except for Luis, who liked to kick when he dreamed.

She closed her eyes for a moment. Perhaps she should find out what happened to her niños. Someone would need to watch them and that someone should be her...

"Rosalinda."

Someone touched her. She started upright to come face-to-face with Yoana. She blinked. Why was Yoana standing beside her bed?

"What? Why are you here?" She closed her eyes, and the past few days came flooding back. She surged up off the rumpled bed and brushed her hair back, glad she'd been lying on her back instead of imprinting the covers on her face. "I'm sorry. I didn't mean to fall asleep. Are the niños all right?"

"Your niños are having fun playing outside." Yoana shook her head. "I don't know how children can take the same trip we do and still have such energy when they arrive. I came to tell you the meal is almost ready."

"Oh, I should be helping with the cooking." Rosalinda smoothed her dress, trying to gather her thoughts. When was the last time she'd slept so hard?

"No. You are here as a guest, not as a worker." Yoana waited while Rosalinda scrubbed the sleep from her eyes and fixed her hair. She hooked her arm through Rosalinda's. "Come, I'll take you out where everyone is gathering."

"I can't." Rosalinda pulled back, but Yoana didn't let go.

"Can't what?"

"I have never been a guest anywhere." Rosalinda tried to pull on her aura of haughtiness to cover her discomfort. "I've always been.... I've always worked."

Yoana's smile faded. Moisture shone in her eyes. "This time you are my guest. You, and your children, are part of my family." She shook her finger at Rosalinda. "I don't want to hear any argument."

Lucio watched his father as he talked with Don Santiago. The men had grown up together, and their families both migrated to the Americas from Spain. They kept in touch even when they were so far apart.

Don Armenta had chosen to raise horses, his first love. His herd was known to be the finest anywhere around. Don Santiago raised grapes, his wines gaining notoriety even in Europe and Spain. When these two old friends got together, they spent hours talking with one another about their holdings and their businesses. Lucio suspected Don Santiago's friendship was the only reason his father had survived after his mother's death.

He hoped Yoana and his father would get along tonight. They would both be in the same room, eating at the same table. In the days after Yoana's rescue, and before she left their hacienda to move with her husband, the don and Yoana hadn't interacted much. They had been civil, but no more than that.

Señora Santiago swept into the room. A true lady, she had a soft smile for her husband that turned into a welcoming smile for the others in the room. She spoke to Don Santiago, who announced they were to go to the dining room.

As they left the room, Leya, Yoana, and Rosalinda came down the hallway. Lucio's heart gave a thud at the sight of Rosalinda. Even after two weeks on the trail and only an hour or so to freshen up, she glowed. His sister's beauty made him smile, but Rosalinda made him catch his breath.

"Lucio, there you are." Leya hugged him. "I haven't seen you since we arrived."

"I was helping get the horses settled and the wagons unloaded and missed your arrival. Did you get some rest?" He focused his attention on his tía, but he could feel Rosalinda's presence.

"Lucio." Yoana slipped her arm around his waist. "I still can't get over seeing everyone again." She might seem relaxed to everyone who didn't know her, but Lucio could see the tension in the set of her shoulders and the lift of her chin.

"It will be all right." He hugged her close and put his mouth close to her ear. "He has changed."

"There you are." Gabrio strode up to them. He swept Yoana away from Lucio and hugged her close. "We'd better get in before our fathers eat all the food. Leya." Gabrio held out his free arm and Leya hooked her hand through the bend of his elbow. He ushered the women toward the dining room.

Rosalinda twisted her hands in her skirt. Lucio could see she didn't want to look at him. What troubled her? She'd never seemed so uncomfortable. His heart went out to her.

"I believe that is our cue." He held out his arm for her to take. Did she know how to be escorted into a room? She turned her hazel eyes on him, confusion confirming his thoughts. He lifted her hand and placed her fingers on his arm, then patted her hand.

"I should check on my niños." She started to pull away, but he kept a gentle grip on her fingers and shook his head.

"Señora Santiago has Feliciana watching them. They are eating with some of the other children who live here. You don't have to worry about them."

She hesitated as he started off, and he stopped to wait. She opened her mouth. Closed it. Opened again.

This uncertainty was something he'd never seen in her.

"Why?" She stared at him. "Why am I being treated like family? I am not familia."

"Because my sister said you are to be treated this way." He wanted to touch her. To brush her cheek. To smooth her silken hair.

"But I was so hateful and mean to her in the camp." Moisture brightened the green in her eyes. "Why would she be nice when I wasn't?"

He patted her fingers and urged her to walk with him. "I believe Yoana has gone through some transformations in the past few months. She's seen another side of life and of people. I am guessing she wants to show you what kindness feels like." He stopped in the door of the dining room. People were finding their places, and he took a moment to note that he and Rosalinda were seated together.

He glanced down at her. She had regained some of her composure.

"Ready?"

She nodded, and he led her around to their seats and held hers for her while she sat down. Perhaps no one had ever done that for her either? She frowned up at him as if she thought he might pull the chair away. He winked at her. She blushed and turned back around.

As the servants carried in the meal, conversation flowed. Rosalinda sat statue-stiff in her chair. Lucio studied her. How could he help put her at ease?

He leaned close to her. "Relax. No one here bites."

She turned wide eyes on him. Her face had paled. Her cheekbones stood out. The woman must be almost paralyzed from fear.

"If you watch what I do, you will be fine." Lucio took the napkin from beside his plate, flipped it open and placed the cloth on his lap. Rosalinda picked up hers, flicked it--and the napkin flew from her fingers, landing in the middle of the table. Conversation halted. Rosalinda reddened.

Lucio stood up and retrieved the cloth. "Slippery." He nodded at Yoana. She caught the cue and asked a question. In no time, the low murmur of voices filled the room again.

"Here you go." Lucio handed the cloth to Rosalinda, who looked like she would rather run all the way back to their hacienda. "Next time will be easier."

Her blush deepened.

As the meal progressed, he showed her which utensil to use with each dish. "If you would like, when the meal is finished, I will take you for a walk and show you around the Santiago ranch. We can check on your niños too." He loved the relief that finally relaxed her. She nodded, a genuine smile lighting her face. Not her usual come-hither smile. He wondered at the change.

Gabrio's brother, seated on the other side of Rosalinda, claimed her attention. She warmed to the conversation, and Lucio took the chance to glance around for his sister and Leya. They were seated farther down the table. Yoana wasn't close to their father. Had she planned that on purpose? Had she arranged the seating or had Señora Santiago? Either way, Yoana had a brief respite while she adjusted to the don's presence.

She'd been so upset when he let the news about their father's coming slip out earlier. Gabrio said she refused to go to the wagon to greet Leya and Rosalinda because her father was there.

He'd told her of the differences he'd noticed in Don Armenta on the trip. Instead of being excited that he interacted with Rosalinda's niños, she'd been upset. He now understood jealousy had overcome her. She'd longed all her life for a father who cared about her, but he'd been so distant. That he'd befriended children who didn't belong to him must have been hard for her.

The meal ended, and Lucio escorted Rosalinda outside, telling Yoana she wanted to see her niños. The night air carried a chill now that the sun had set. The fresh ocean breeze had him breathing deep.

"Would you like me to bring you a shawl?"

"I don't think we will be out long." She tilted her head back to gaze up at the stars spread across the night sky. "It is beautiful here and a lovely night. I like being able to see the stars. In the mountains, we only had trees to look at."

"I love the stars. With no moon, they are very bright." He took her hand on his arm again to keep her from stumbling on the uneven ground. "Would you like to see the corrals first or your children?"

"Maybe a little walk first. I like the night air. I've missed the smell of the ocean."

He led her toward the barn. The structure towered over them. Around the side, his father's stallion snorted at them from one of the corrals. A silhouette moved at the rails.

Carlos turned to face them. *"Que bonita.* You are beautiful, Rosalinda. Did you come to visit me?"

CHAPTER FOURTEEN

His daughter avoided him like he was a disease. He'd seen her standing in the doorway when he pulled the wagon into the yard. Her face almost hidden. Her arms crossed over her chest. Her shoulders hunched forward as if she could hide from him.

He'd ignored her for years. Hidden her. Kept her from his sight. But that hadn't done any good. He would still see her around the yard on occasion or hear her voice from down the hallway. He used to go, when no one would be around, to stand outside the room where she taught her nieces and nephews, just to hear the melodic sound when she talked.

She sounded...looked...acted. Like her mother. The spitting image. As if Josefa stepped through time to be her daughter.

He tried not to stare at her as she sat beside her husband at the other end of the table. He attempted to carry on a conversation with Augustín Santiago, but the way Yoana gestured with her hands distracted him. Now and then, the sweet tones of her voice would drift his way, and a wave of nostalgia would sweep over him. How he missed Josefa.

But you no longer want to die so you can be with her.

The realization hit him. When had that changed?

"Tomorrow I will take you to look at my vineyards." Augustín leaned forward to push his plate away and put his elbows on the table. Juana, his wife, frowned at him, but he either ignored her or didn't notice.

"I have some new vines that came on a ship from *España*. They are said to be the best, and I'm hoping they do well in my soil."

"Have you been able to make wine from them yet?" Francisco had no heart for this small talk tonight. Talk of the vineyard usually fascinated him, but this time he had too much on his mind.

"This is the first year they have produced. The crop turned out small. I am hoping to have plenty of grapes for next year." Augustín pushed back from the table and stood. "Let's retire to my den and share a glass of my newest success. I would like to hear your opinion, mi amigo."

Francisco rose, bowed to Juana, thanked her for the meal, and followed his friend from the room. Don Santiago's sons would stop by for a few minutes, but usually they left the men to talk while they saw to their families.

An hour later, he still swirled the wine in his glass, entranced with the deep red in the lamplight. He'd taken a couple of sips. Augustín produced some of the best wine Francisco had ever tasted, but tonight the flavor fell flat.

"My friend, you seem troubled. Is there a problem with your rancho? Your sons?" Augustín sat back in his chair, glass in hand. "I have never seen you so quiet when we are together."

Francisco could talk to his oldest friend, and what they said would stay between them. Augustín would not judge. He would offer sound advice, even godly advice. Still, admitting wrong twisted something inside him.

He took a sip of wine, savoring the mix of flavors. "I have made such a grave mistake, Augustín. I don't know how to rectify what I've done." He leaned forward and set the glass on the low table in front of him. Stood and walked closer to the burning coals.

"What is this mistake? Anything can be fixed."

"You know what I've done. You talked to me often enough." Francisco rubbed his palms over his face. "You told me I would lose my daughter if I didn't treat her right, but I was so blinded by grief, I didn't want to listen. Now I've lost her. She wouldn't even look at me during our meal tonight."

"Yoana." Augustín's voice softened. "I have come to love your daughter, Francisco. She is a fine woman and a good wife to Gabrio. Her quick intelligence makes talking with her a joy. I'm sorry you have missed so much with your pigheadedness."

Francisco glared at his friend. How could Augustín accuse him so unjustly in the face of his grief?

Before he could speak, Augustín held up his hand. "One moment, mi amigo. Don't be angry. Hear me out."

Francisco gave a brisk nod.

"I remember your Josefa. She loved you as if you were the only other person on the planet. She loved her children with all her heart, but you, my friend, you were her sunrise and sunset. I know you blamed Yoana for her mother's death at first. But the child didn't understand the dangers and had no idea her mother might die to save her life." Augustín fell silent when Francisco began to pace the room.

"Then, about four years after the tragedy, when I came to see you, do you remember what you said to me?" Augustín emphasized the question with an arched eyebrow.

Why did they have to talk about his past? Why should he look back on the most painful time in his life? He trusted Augustin. And he didn't want to lose Yoana completely.

He returned to the chair beside Augustín's.

His friend studied the wine in his glass. "You told me Josefa warned you to get rid of that bull because Yoana had become so interested in the beast. And because Yoana never knew danger.

She would try anything. Josefa had to be on her toes all the time watching her." He poured them both a little more wine. The burgundy liquid gleamed in the light as it splashed into the glass.

"You knew Yoana wasn't at fault. You knew." Augustín shook his head, his eyes sad. "Yet you persisted in making her stay away from you and out of your sight. That poor girl grew up thinking you hated her for killing her mother. She carried the guilt for many years. She still does."

He couldn't say anything in his defense. His best friend knew him too well. "Then what do I do? How do I repair the wrong I've done?"

"What have you tried so far?"

Silence thickened the air. What had he done? Nothing. No spoken apology. No letter begging her forgiveness. He'd let her go without remorse when she left with her new husband. Oh, he had spoken to her when he first allowed Gabrio to live and agreed Yoana could marry him, but then he'd backed away. He didn't understand why, but he had.

"The things I do I don't want to do, and the things I don't do I want to do. I believe there is a Bible verse about that." Francisco couldn't meet Augustín's gaze. "I want to do what is right, but at the same time I make so many mistakes. Before Yoana and Gabrio came here, I shut her out again. I want to be a good father. To make up for what I did wrong." His throat tightened, and he had to fight for the words to say.

"Every time I look at her, I see Josefa. I get sad for all I've missed. I get angry. Not at Yoana." He shook his head. "You are right. I get angry at my stubbornness. At how I didn't get rid of a dangerous animal. Any one of the children, or even the vaqueros, could have been gored and killed. All because I wanted to keep what I saw as beautiful, when the creature was all ugliness on the inside." Not unlike he had been after his wife was killed. "What do I do, Augustín? I can't lose her. I want her back."

"Mi amigo, you have always loved animals, especially horses.

Do you remember when we were almost of an age to go out on our own and you found that mare? She'd been beaten and abused for so long, she trembled anytime someone came near. If you tried to touch her, she went wild and fought the rope like a crazy thing. The owner claimed her to be worthless and planned to shoot her. Remember?" Augustín swirled the liquid in his glass and took a sip.

"I do. I had forgotten about her until now. Took me several months to get her to trust me--" Francisco paused. Oh. He sighed. "I've changed, but Yoana, my sons, and their wives have to learn they can trust me. Like always, I want this to happen overnight."

"But this will take time." Augustín saluted him with the glass and drained the last mouthful of wine. "Yoana is intelligent. She is also forgiving. Be who you are now, and she will come around."

His friend pushed up from his chair. "Now, I will leave you. This has been a long day, and my bed is calling to me. I will see you in the morning."

Augustín closed the door on the way out, leaving Francisco in the quiet den, surrounded by mementos from the vineyard, the Santiago children, and the past he shared with Augustín.

Francisco closed his eyes, contemplating the mare Augustín mentioned. His father called him daft for buying the *loco* caballo, but he had to. The mare had something in her eyes that cried out to him. He spent hours sitting outside her stall or beside the corral when she was outdoors. Months passed before he felt the soft touch of her breath on the back of his neck as he sat working on a ledger with his back to her. He knew then he'd won the battle, but she still took time to tame.

When he finally won her heart, and her trust, that mare would take him anywhere and do anything for him. She never let another person touch her or sit on her back, but she would fall asleep with her nose over his shoulder, her forelock falling across his ear. He'd been heartbroken the day she died.

"Time. And kindness. I need to give her those." He tapped his fingers against his knee. "And space." He closed his eyes, tilting his head back. This would be hard. He would have to be there but let Yoana make the first move. Patience.

How he hated being patient. "God, please help me."

He left the room and stepped outside. Perhaps a short walk would help him clear his mind for sleep. He almost stumbled over a slight figure on the path leading from the house. In the light of the rising moon, he saw her as she jerked her mantilla down to cover her face.

Leya.

"I am sorry. I didn't mean to stumble over you." He realized he'd grabbed her arm to steady her. He quickly let go. She stepped back.

"It's a beautiful night. I thought I would take a short walk. Would you like to go with me?"

She startled. Didn't answer. He remembered now. He had more than Yoana and his children to apologize to. He'd offended Leya as well. Perhaps his short plea to God had been answered this way. Leya and Yoana were close. If he showed Leya he'd changed, maybe she would encourage Yoana to work on forgiving him.

While he'd spent time talking with Rosalinda on the trip here, he only now realized Leya hadn't interacted with him much at all. She'd been polite but distant. His focus had been on Lucio and Yoana. How could he have missed that he needed to apologize to her too? Yet he doubted she would trust his words. He tucked his regret down and held out his arm.

She hesitated, then placed her palm on his arm. She didn't tuck her hand in the crook of his elbow, as many would. Maybe she wanted the option to escape should he revert to the overbearing monster she'd known so long.

He walked toward the road leading from the ranch. The trail shone in the moonlight. The sounds of night pressed in around them. Crickets. The chirp of a gecko. The distant howl of a coyote.

He wanted to talk with her, but his mind had gone blank. What should he say?

"Thank you for being so kind to Rosalinda and her niños." Leya's dulcet voice, so much like Yoana's, brushed across his ears. His heart beat faster.

"They are a delight. The children." He paused, uncertain what to say next.

"Who is in charge at the hacienda?"

Relief rushed through him. This he could talk about. He told her about Emiliano and Sofí coming with their children. He told about surprising the niños with the puppies and their delight. He reveled in the sound of her low laughter as he described the puppies' antics and his grandchildren's joy.

"I wish I could have seen them. I have missed having the niños around. Maybe they will visit more." She didn't mention his different attitude, but he knew what she meant.

"I hope so. I have missed so much with them. With my children. With my whole family." The words seemed to stumble from his mouth in an awkward rush. He didn't talk like this. He only gave orders and usually barked them at people, expecting to have them obey or be banished.

They stopped to gaze up at the myriad stars overhead. One broke free and dashed across the sky in a shower of light. Leya let out a cry of delight.

"*Mi madre* used to say you could make a wish on a falling star." She pressed her fingertips to her mantilla. He could see the outline of her lips. "If I believed in wishes, I would do that."

"Maybe there is something you could do instead." Why was he prattling on with this woman?

"I will say a prayer. Prayer is always good, whether there is a falling star or not." She tilted her head to look up at him. Her features were obscured by the veil, but he could feel the weight of her gaze. "Do you pray for what you need, Francisco?"

His mouth fell open. He couldn't recall the last time someone other than Augustín called him by his given name and not his title.

"I do." He swallowed hard around the lump in his throat. "I recently started after years of silence."

He could sense her smile. "Years of silence on your part. I'm sure God tried to talk to you."

"He did. All He found were closed ears and a hardened heart. I'm sorry to say that, but it is true." He looked up at the twinkling sky again, not wanting her to read the pain in his eyes.

She nudged his arm, and he turned back toward the hacienda. They walked in silence until the house loomed before them. He didn't want this time to end. He had so much he wanted to say to her. To ask her. But the words would not form in his head.

Out in the hills a coyote howled. Another joined in, and soon a chorus of yowls cried to the heavens. He paused to listen. Were they singing of their happiness or sorrow?

"Thank you for the walk." Leya took her hand from his arm and stepped up on the doorstep. "I will tell Yoana of our talk."

His heart hammered in his chest. He couldn't speak as she disappeared inside. He could only send God the thanks in his heart.

CHAPTER FIFTEEN

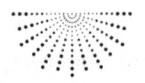

LUCIO CIRCLED to stand between Carlos and Rosalinda. He didn't have the authority to tell the man to stay away from her forever. She wasn't his wife or his sister. By interfering, he would suggest his intent to wed her, and he couldn't do that. He heard the murmur of voices from Gabrio and Yoana talking behind them, but they weren't close enough to see Carlos. Plus, he hadn't mentioned anything to them about the problems on the trail. If he had, Yoana would have had more questions than a four-year-old.

"I am taking the lady for a walk, Carlos."

The vaquero stepped to the side, trying to get closer to Rosalinda. She edged into Lucio, and he knew she didn't like the young man, no matter what her prior smiles and coquetry had suggested.

"Perhaps we should find your niños now." He turned, putting his body once more between Rosalinda and Carlos. The vaquero shoved around him, not being gentle this time.

"Rosalinda, my sweet." Carlos grabbed her free hand and brought her fingers to his lips.

Lucio's blood heated.

"Come with me." Carlos's teeth gleamed in the low light. "I will show you a good time. And we can talk business."

"What business would you have with her?" Lucio took another step to block the man. Rosalinda yanked her hand free and half hid behind Lucio.

"I have a great business venture that will make us both a lot of money." Carlos's grin took on a leering quality.

Rosalinda made a sound, half disgust, half fear, and pressed closer to his back.

Realization dawned at what Carlos was suggesting. Lucio's fists clenched. He wanted to wipe the ground with this vaquero. To keep him from ever leering at another woman again.

Carlos leaned around Lucio, and he grabbed the hombre by the shirt front and yanked him close. "You will stay away from Rosalinda. She does not want to have anything to do with you or your business. Now get out of here" His voice rose as he spoke.

Quick footsteps approached.

"What is going on?" Gabrio hurried to them, Yoana on his heels.

Lucio fought to get his temper in check. He didn't want his sister, or Rosalinda, involved if a fight broke out.

"Carlos is just on his way to his bunk." Lucio released his hold, satisfied to hear Carlos suck in a gulp of air. He shoved him away. The vaquero stumbled back, wiped his mouth with the sleeve of his shirt.

"I will talk with you later, *dulcita*." He tipped his hat toward Rosalinda and sauntered away, not looking back.

Everything in Lucio wanted to go after him and beat some sense into him. To make him leave now and never return.

"Rosalinda, come." Yoana took her hand and pulled her away from Lucio. He didn't want her to leave but understood the logic in her going with Yoana.

"Let's go see your niños," Yoana said.

The two women disappeared into the shadows in the direction opposite of where Carlos had gone.

"Is something wrong?" Gabrio stared into the darkness where his wife and Rosalinda went before turning to face Lucio. "Is there something I should know?"

"No. Yes." Lucio didn't know what to say. He didn't like the way Carlos treated Rosalinda, but sometimes she flirted. Who was at fault?

"Why were you upset with that vaquero? If he is a danger to my people or my familia, I need to know." Gabrio wouldn't back down.

"I didn't like the way he talked to Rosalinda." Lucio wanted to walk away, but that would raise more questions. "I think he suggested something to her she didn't want."

"Rosalinda." Gabrio rubbed the back of his neck and stayed quiet so long Lucio thought he'd dropped the matter.

Wrong.

"Rosalinda can take care of herself. She is a force to be reckoned with and doesn't take anything from a man unless she wants to." Gabrio put his hands on his hips and faced Lucio. "I know her pretty well from the bandolero camp. She is conniving and self-serving. You'd best not get between her and anyone. She will throw you to the wolves."

If he and Gabrio hadn't been good friends, Lucio would have punched him. Instead, he glared, which probably didn't matter in the low light. Besides, what Gabrio said could be true. How did he know Rosalinda had changed? She'd learned to manipulate men at an early age. Maybe he was her new venture.

How was he to know if she wanted to be respectable? Or if she wanted the attention of men like Carlos? He didn't know her.

"Are you interested in her?" Gabrio's tone held a note of surprise. He leaned a bit closer as if trying to see through the darkness. "As a woman? You do know her—and her past—don't you?"

Lucio huffed out a breath. "No. I am not interested in her. She is my responsibility in part because she and her niños live at the ranch."

"But your reaction with the vaquero shows more interest than in a worker. I'm assuming she works there, right?" Gabrio stepped over to stroke the stallion as he poked his head over the rails. Lucio followed him even though part of him wanted to walk away.

The black lipped at Lucio's fingers, wanting a treat. He rubbed the horse's cheek while he contemplated how much to say to Gabrio. They had been friends since they were young. Anytime their fathers got together, Lucio and Gabrio would spend time playing and talking. While Don Santiago hadn't come to the Armenta rancho after Lucio's mother's death, they often met partway between the two to deliver horses or a shipment of wine. Each time Lucio begged to go.

He'd told Gabrio of his secrets, and Gabrio often pelted him with questions about Yoana, his betrothed. But this secret was harder to reveal. His attraction to Rosalinda was a weakness on his part. Would Gabrio see it that way as well?

"Do you remember my mother?" Lucio's face warmed as he realized he'd avoided the real issue.

"I have vague memories from when I was a boy and we visited your rancho. I remember her laugh. Maybe not a true memory but something I liked about her. And that she was kind to me." Gabrio rubbed the black's ears. "Why?"

"I think you hit on something." Lucio shook his head. "I have memories of my mother that may not be true memories, but how I saw her as a young boy. I have always wanted to find a woman just like her. One who liked to laugh. One who would be kind. One who cared about me without question."

"Do you think Rosalinda is that woman?" Even in the dim light, Lucio could see the white of Gabrio's eyes and the surprise on his face.

"No. I don't. She does have some good qualities. I don't mean to say she doesn't." Lucio drew in a breath and held it, trying to gather his scattered thoughts. "What I'm saying is she is not at all like my mother or the memories I've carried of her. She is not the woman I've been waiting for at all."

The stallion snorted a breath into his ear, and he shook his head at the tickle.

"I don't know what to do though, because as much as she is not what I want, my heart doesn't seem to be listening. I try to avoid her, but then find I'm watching to see her when she walks with the children. I ride close when she doesn't see just so I can hear her voice or maybe catch a bit of her laughter." He put his forehead against the rough board of the corral so he wouldn't see the shock that must be on his friend's face.

"If I never see her again, I think my heart will still remember her when I am old and ready to die." Lucio squeezed his eyes shut. He should have kept quiet and not said anything to Gabrio. What if Yoana found out? He jerked upright. "You can't tell Yoana. Or anyone else. Please."

The corners of Gabrio's mouth turned up. His eyes narrowed. "I will pray about this, mi amigo. Matters of the heart are very hard to figure out. She might not be accepted in our circle of acquaintances. Maybe by us and by your family, but others?" He frowned and shook his head. "What about your father? Does he know how you feel?"

"No. I haven't said anything to anyone but you. I can't imagine how Don Armenta will respond. Well, I can, but I don't want to consider his reaction."

Gabrio stiffened. "He would disown you."

SHE COULDN'T SLEEP. For the first time in weeks, she was in a comfortable bed, exhausted beyond reason, warm and safe. And her eyes were wide open.

Beside her, Luis breathed in soft snores. The girls were in the other bed, fast asleep after the excitement of the day.

Rosalinda sat up, easing Luis away from her. She padded to the window and gazed out at the night sky. The moon hung overhead now, brightening the landscape. Shadows vied with moonlight, creating an eerie picture to some. But she loved the play of light and shadow. Always had. When she was younger, nighttime became a place of refuge. Sometimes she could hide in the dark and couldn't be found easily.

At least, she'd tried.

Leaning against the window casement, she couldn't stop the questions. Why had her mother sold her? Why couldn't Rosalinda have grown up to meet a man like Lucio Armenta? A man who cared about whether a woman would be cold on a walk and not so concerned with what liberties he could take.

Your life is what it is.

She'd heard those words somewhere before. But were they true? Hadn't Leya talked to her about allowing God to change the course of her life? What about Joseph, the story Leya had told? He could have remained a lowly slave, but he trusted God and accomplished great things.

She didn't want to accomplish anything great, but she wanted a different life than she'd led up to now. She didn't want to belong to any man again. To be treated like chattel or something that could be thrown away when he finished with her. Yet maybe that was her only value.

She pressed her forehead to the cool glass. Outside, a coyote trotted out of the shadows by the cookhouse. He lifted his nose and tested the scent of the air. Took a tentative step. Cocked his head. Trotted out of sight.

What gave a creature like that coyote the freedom to come and go as he wanted when she had no freedom? She was at the mercy of whoever owned her. Now she had to listen to her employer. Because where would she go if the Armentas made her leave? How would she survive, let alone care for her children?

Another movement caught her attention. Larger than a coyote, a shadow moved along the side of the cookhouse. Her pulse thumped. She edged back from the window. Fear prickled across her skin. She strained to see what was moving.

A low shape scuttled toward the house. Something hunched over. Moving awkwardly. A man? But why would a man be moving with such stealth?

Sounds faded. She couldn't breathe. Her vision swam, and she sank to the floor. Memory assaulted her... The time when her first owner paraded her in front of some of his friends. One of them wanted her. Offered a lot of money. Her owner refused. That night, the friend crept into her room and stole her away. She'd seen him creeping across the street much like the shadow moved across the Santiagos's yard.

She shoved her fists against her mouth to keep the screams from bursting out. She had to be quiet. To protect her children. No one would do to her niñas what had been done to her. No one.

Rosalinda didn't know how much time passed as she huddled on the floor. By the time her panic ceased, her energy fled. She didn't even know if she could drag herself back to bed. The house had been silent, so no one had come inside.

Lifting up until her head cleared the windowsill enough to look outside, she studied the moonlit yard. No bandoleros were waiting for her. No leering men. Nothing.

She released a breath she hadn't realized she'd been holding and used the windowsill to pull up and stand. All was quiet. The stars still shone overhead, playing their feeble light on the earth below.

Maria moaned in her sleep. Rosalinda went to her and stroked the hair from her forehead. Her niña quieted.

She wanted so much to be a good mother. How could she when she had no idea how to be a good person?

Her throat dry, she slipped from the room to search for a drink. Maybe the inside kitchen had a bucket of water. Just a sip was all she needed.

Shadows were thick in the room. Rosalinda wove around the table and past the counter where the large bowls for the morning cooking were waiting. In the corner sat a stool with a bucket on it. A ladle for drinking hung on the wall behind the bucket.

The cool liquid tasted sweet and soothed her throat. She slipped the ladle back on the nail and turned to go back to bed. A strong arm grabbed her and yanked her into a hard body. A hand covered her mouth, taming her shriek to more of a squeak.

Carlos grinned at her like he was the coyote and she the rabbit.

"I knew you would come." He spoke low. She twisted and tried to break free. He wouldn't release her but held her even tighter. She struggled to draw in a breath.

"Quit fighting. We need to talk." His breath feathered across her ear. She shuddered.

"I told you on the trail I would find some business for you. There are many hombres here who would like to meet you. We can make a lot of money, you and I."

She closed her eyes. *God, please, no...*

"I am going to take my hand from your mouth so we can talk. Keep your voice down. If the familia hears you, you will be sorry. ¿Entiendes?"

What did he mean he would make her sorry? What could he possibly do to her that hadn't been done before? She should not be afraid of him. But she was. Terrified.

The pressure against her mouth eased. His eyes were black in the shadows as he stared down at her. "Don't scream. Remember your little niños."

Terror blurred her vision. Her *bambinos*? Her niños? He would threaten her babies? How could he? If he wanted to hurt her, that was one thing, but to harm her *niños*? She would not allow that.

"What do you want? I am not interested in any business with

you." She hissed the words at him. One thing she knew--she could not let him see her fear. If he knew he had a way to keep a hold over her, he would never let up. She would belong to him as surely as she had belonged to Cisto.

"These hombres want to meet you. All you have to do is entertain them each night after the familia is in bed." He grinned. "They will be very appreciative and very generous."

"I do not work for you." She shoved at him, wanting to break free and get back to her room where she could lock the door.

"Yes, you do." He chucked her under the chin. "Because if you don't work for me, I will tell Lucio you have done this on your own. Or I will make your niños disappear. The hombres will back me up just to get the chance to be with you. In fact, I think we will not go back to the Armenta rancho. I will take you to Los Angeles and we can start a business there."

He ran his hand down her arm. She jerked away and bumped the bucket on the stool.

The bucket rattled and almost fell, but Carlos grabbed it first. "Be careful, dulcita." He grabbed her arms with both hands. His fingers dug deep.

She would have bruises tomorrow.

"I know what kind of woman you are. Lucio may say some sad story about you not having a choice because you were only a little girl, but I know better. You are missing the life you had."

"I'm missing having some man hurt me nearly every night? I miss being beaten? I miss having to do despicable things? I miss having my niños threatened if I don't behave?" Tears burned her eyes, but she refused to cry. "Go away and leave me alone! Find some other woman who will do what you want. That woman is not me."

She tried to pull away and go around him, but he didn't release her.

"You will do as I say." Carlos's grin faded, his expression turning hard.

She couldn't show fear. Couldn't.

"What is going on?" Lucio stood in the doorway to the kitchen. The dim glow of his lantern wavered in the dark. Rosalinda hadn't even noticed the light approach and, by his surprise, neither had Carlos.

"We were just having a little talk." Carlos eased his grip on her arm. Before he released her, he leaned close. "Remember your niñas. They are beautiful girls."

CHAPTER SIXTEEN

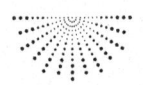

SHE SHOVED AT CARLOS AGAIN, fear and anger giving her strength. This time he didn't push back. He turned and strode toward the door leading outside.

"Carlos." The command in Lucio's tone halted the vaquero. "Why are you in the hacienda? You don't belong in here."

Lucio strode across the room to stand in front of Carlos. Lucio had height on Carlos, but the vaquero made up for that in sheer mass. His stocky build made him appear the size of a grizzly.

"I came to meet Rosalinda." Carlos's gaze roved over her.

Rosalinda gaped at him. She started to object to his statement, but the words he'd spoken, combined with the warning glare he sent her, caused her to snap her mouth shut. What would he do to her niñas? Cold chills skittered down her spine.

"Later." Carlos nodded at her. "We will finish this later." He yanked the door open and disappeared outside.

Lucio faced Rosalinda. She could see the questions he wanted to ask. She didn't want to talk about this. She had to go to her room and consider what to do. Would she never be free?

"I thought you didn't want to have anything to do with him. Now I find you made plans to meet him by the corral and here in the middle of the night." Lucio dug his fingers into his hair before lifting his head to gaze at her again. She couldn't look at him. The lies ate at her soul, but fear kept her silent.

"Why are you doing this? You need to think of your niños." Lucio held out a hand as if pleading with her. Her heart ached. This wonderful man cared enough to try to intervene. Cared for her. For her children. For her family's future.

Forcing away her fear, she pulled on her covering of bravado. "You know nothing about me." Head high, she sauntered toward the hallway, swaying her hips when she wanted to run.

Lucio caught her before she reached her room. He whirled her around, his face angry, his mouth open, probably to berate her for being the worst mother in the history of mankind.

He must have seen the desperation in her eyes, because his whole demeanor changed. Instead of shaking sense into her, he dragged her into his arms. Held her against his strong chest. Leaned his cheek against the top of her head.

Bravado failed. The tears she'd been fighting would be denied no longer. The torrent gushed from her eyes. She tried to be quiet, not wanting to wake the whole house. Her near silent sobs shook her as a storm of shame and vulnerability swept through her.

When the tumult slowed, she heard Lucio murmuring to her, his hand rubbed slow circles on her back. She'd never felt anything so tender. So comforting. So wonderful.

She almost cried again from the beauty of the moment.

"Rosalinda, you need sleep. And being together like this isn't appropriate. Can we talk in the morning?" Lucio cupped her shoulders as he stepped back. She swiped at her face, embarrassed to be seen with reddened eyes.

"Yes. I need to get back to my niños." She pulled away from him, turned and fled to her room. She'd lied to him. Guilt tore at her. She couldn't talk to him in the morning or any other time. She had to put the safety of her children before anything else.

Carlos would follow through with his threat.

Back in her room she leaned against the closed door. Her heart hammered a painful rhythm in her chest. What to do? What? To? Do?

Luis whimpered and rolled over in the bed. She climbed in beside him and pulled his small body into hers. He quieted. She held him much as Lucio had held and comforted her. Is this what family did? Offered support without condemnation simply because they loved one another?

The glow of moonlight coming in the window dimmed. She raised up to look. A man stood outside in the dark. She couldn't see his face in the shadows, but she knew his broad shoulders and massive chest.

Carlos.

She froze. She didn't know if the light allowed him to make out anything in the room. She hoped not. If she stayed very still, perhaps he would leave. If he wasn't sure this was her room, he wouldn't dare tap on the window, would he?

She trembled as she huddled with her son, hoping the girls would stay asleep and none of them would make a sound. Moments stretched out like hours, but Carlos finally left the window. She thought she heard the fading crunch of his footsteps as he moved away.

Little by little she relaxed. She intended to stay vigilant. To watch over her little family. The next thing she knew, dawn lightened the sky, and Luis pulled up her eyelid.

"Is morning. Day morning." He grinned at her. Although her head pounded from stress and lack of sleep, she couldn't help smiling at his enthusiasm.

By the time she had all the niños up and dressed, she could smell the food cooking. How would she keep her children in her sight at all times without telling anyone they were in danger? Leya and Yoana would be quick to catch on. She had a feeling Lucio and Gabrio would be the same. No matter what plan she thought of, they would see through it and ask questions. Questions she couldn't answer.

Someone pounded on the door.

"Maria. Come on." Teo's loud call could probably be heard as far south as Los Angeles.

Rosalinda winced at the spike of pain in her head.

"Maria, you can help me clean stalls today. It is a lot of fun."

Rosalinda almost snorted a laugh. Maria jumped up and clapped her hands. "Can I go? ¿Por favor?"

"Teo, come in here." Rosalinda frowned at her daughter's eagerness. The door swung open, and Teo barreled in. He hugged Maria and grabbed her hand, preparing to dash out the door.

"Wait." Rosalinda's order halted the eager pair. "Teo, who watches over you while you clean the stalls?"

Teo's chest puffed out. "I am so good, I can do it on my own."

"I know you are a good worker." Rosalinda softened her tone. "Who else is working in the barn with you?"

"Sometimes Gabrio is there when he works with the horses. One of the Santiago vaqueros works in the stalls too. Manuel is his name. His *esposa*, Carmen, works in the kitchen. She is a very good cook." He gave a lopsided grin and lowered his voice to a whisper. "Sometimes she gives me special treats. If we hurry, Maria and I can get some this morning before we work."

"I want to go too." Isabel stood before Rosalinda, her hands held up palms together as if she were praying.

"Me. Me." Luis echoed.

Rosalinda held up her hand when she saw Teo about to voice his objections. "Isabel and Luis, you will stay with me." The crestfallen looks on their faces plucked at her heart, but that couldn't be helped.

"Teo, promise me you will watch over Maria and not let her out of your sight." She fixed him with a firm stare.

He straitened to his full height--how he had grown in the last few months!--and pressed his palm to his heart. "I will be with her all day."

His nose wrinkled. He leaned closer to Rosalinda, but his words could be heard by everyone. "Except the *baño*. I will not watch her there."

Maria slugged his arm. Isabel giggled. Rosalinda pressed her lips together to keep from smiling. "Thank you. I trust you to watch over her. You may go." She watched as the pair raced away hand-in-hand down the hallway and hoped she'd made the right decision.

Now she would guard Isabel and Luis.

She met Leya and Yoana in the hallway outside the kitchen. Isabel and Luis ran to Leya and hugged her knees. She bent down to kiss their heads before greeting Rosalinda.

"Did you sleep well?" Yoana asked.

Rosalinda nodded, once more feeling a twinge for lying. How their God must hate her for all these lies. How could she begin to tell them all that transpired last night?

She lifted her head and met Lucio's gaze. He stood on the far side of Leya, and she hadn't heard him approach. Her face warmed, and she bent down to pick Luis up, hoping no one noticed her reaction to Lucio's presence.

HE DIDN'T HAVE to wait for her to answer his sister's question. Lucio could see the dark circles under Rosalinda's eyes and the fatigue that pulled at her. He wanted to demand answers from her. Why had Carlos been in the house? What did those looks he'd given Rosalinda mean? Why had she sobbed so hard when Lucio held her?

Had Carlos spoken the truth when he said she fancied him? Or was there something else going on? He knew Rosalinda lied last night about meeting Carlos. He just didn't know why. And he wanted to know.

"I'm sorry for asking." Yoana reached out to touch Rosalinda's arm. "You look a little tired. Did the niños keep you awake last night? Sometimes a new bed or different place has sounds that make it hard to rest."

"They slept through the night." Rosalinda's smile looked strained and didn't reach her eyes. "I'm afraid I had more trouble relaxing than they did."

"Well, if you are like me, by tonight you'll be so tired nothing will keep you awake." Yoana's smile brightened the room and discharged the tension. "Shall we get some breakfast and talk about our plans for today?"

Yoana swept Isabel into her arms. She and Leya led the way to the dining room, leaving Lucio to follow with Rosalinda.

"Here, let me take him." He held out his arms, and Luis leaped in his direction. Lucio couldn't help but laugh as he caught the niño midair. "In a few months, mijo, you will be so big I will drop you if you do that." He swung the boy over his head. Luis held out his arms, his giggles filling the air.

"You will get him too excited, and he won't eat his breakfast." Rosalinda frowned at Lucio, her lower lip out a fraction more than her upper lip. He stared, and his breathing sped up. How could she be tired and angry and still so beautiful?

"You coming?" Yoana called.

Lucio gestured for Rosalinda to precede him and Luis. He needed the few minutes to get his breath back and his thoughts in order.

One of the kitchen servants came to take Isabel and Luis to another room for their food. Rosalinda started to object but fell silent. She watched the children leave, and Lucio frowned. Was that fear in her expression? Why would she be afraid of the women who worked in the kitchen?

Gabrio strode in, lifted Yoana off her feet, and gave her a loud kiss. She squealed and shoved at his shoulders. She laughed when he set her down, but Lucio noted she didn't scold him. She had settled into marriage. Where she would have been impulsive before, now she considered others and their needs. Her happiness shone in her face and posture and made him long to have the same in his life.

"What do you ladies have planned for today?" Gabrio asked as they sat at the table eating the best food Lucio had tasted in a long time. He must compliment the cook when he had the chance.

"I thought we all might ride out to look at the vineyard with you." Yoana smiled at her husband.

He frowned. "Our fathers are going with Lucio, Ramón, and me today. If you would like to go along, you are welcome." Gabrio ran a finger down the side of Yoana's face. At his words, her happiness dimmed. She shook her head.

"In that case, we will ride into the hills to my favorite spot. I have wanted to show Leya the view. I'm sure Rosalinda would love it too." Yoana smiled at the women. Leya nodded. Rosalinda looked hesitant.

"What about the children?" Rosalinda plucked at the table cloth. "I should stay here and watch over them."

"No need." Yoana waved her hand in the air. "Manuel is in the barn with Teo and Maria. I will ask Carmen, his wife and our cook, or Feliciana, to make sure Isabel and Luis are taken care of."

"But they are so busy. I don't want to add to their work." Rosalinda's eyes widened.

What was she so afraid of?

"They have plenty of help. Don't worry about your niños. Nothing will happen to them here." Yoana turned to Gabrio as he spoke to her.

Rosalinda poked at her food. She hadn't eaten much at all.

Gabrio folded his napkin and placed it beside his plate before pushing his chair back from the table. "Luis will go with the men today. We can keep an eye on him, and he will have fun running through the rows of vines."

He leaned down to plant a kiss on Yoana's head. "Teo and

Maria will be safe with Manuel. You ladies will take Isabel with you." He smiled as if the whole matter was decided. Rosalinda relaxed a little and picked up a bite of egg to put in her mouth.

"I don't want you ladies riding alone." Gabrio paused at the doorway. Lucio stopped beside him. "I asked for a volunteer to watch over you. Carlos agreed to go with you."

Rosalinda choked. Her bite of egg flew across the table and landed on Gabrio's empty plate. She coughed. Grabbed a glass of water to take a drink.

Lucio started to go back around the table.

Leya waved him off. "She will be fine. She probably swallowed wrong. You go on."

He followed Gabrio from the room to the sounds of Yoana and Leya asking if Rosalinda would be all right. She hadn't swallowed a bite the wrong way. She'd been upset to hear that Carlos would accompany them.

She did *not* favor him.

His heart lifted. But if she didn't favor Carlos, why had the vaquero lied to him? A thousand questions raced through his head. He didn't want Carlos around Rosalinda, but could that be jealousy, not practicality?

"Gabrio, I wonder if we could send two men with the women today. Maybe another of my vaqueros or one of yours."

His brother-in-law frowned at him. "Why do you think another man needs to go along? You said I shouldn't worry about Carlos."

Lucio shook his head, feeling a little foolish when he had nothing to back up the allegations in his head. "I think there might be a problem between Carlos and Rosalinda. I don't know what. I think she would be more comfortable if he weren't the only man along."

"If he is a danger, I don't want him around my wife or Leya either. Nor any of the women on the rancho." Gabrio paused on the path, his hands on his hips.

"I have nothing to base this on, mi amigo. I don't think the women are in danger from Carlos. I just think there is something off between Carlos and Rosalinda." He hated making insinuations like this. He clapped Gabrio on the shoulder. "Besides, he may be big, but Yoana could whip him with one hand behind her back, right?"

Gabrio laughed. "That's my wife."

They continued to the barn where their fathers were waiting. Manuel had their mounts saddled and ready to go. Gabrio talked to him about the horses for the women. Then he asked Manuel's brother, Arturo, to go with Carlos and Yoana and her company.

As they walked toward their fathers and the waiting horses, Gabrio explained that Arturo would be a good choice. Nothing swayed the man from doing what was right. He would make sure the mujeres were well protected, and he would keep an eye on Carlos, too, since Gabrio had asked him to do so.

Lucio had to be content with that.

THE DAY STRETCHED on forever but proved productive. Luis rode with Don Armenta most of the day. His father taught the little boy songs and rhymes as they rode. Lucio hadn't known his father remembered any rhymes or could sing.

Would he ever understand this man?

The vineyards stretched across hillsides in beautiful rows. The orderliness appealed to Lucio. The season of harvest had passed, but the leaves were still green, and the plants were beautiful. Gabrio explained the pruning process and the differences in vines and fruit.

"I even think the soil and sunshine have much to do with finding the right taste for the wine." Gabrio gestured at a hillside as he and Lucio rode behind their fathers on the way home.

"This vine, for instance. The vines are all the same, but the grapes are different. The ones at the bottom get less sun and more shade than the ones higher on the hill. There is a difference, even though the vines are the same type."

They continued to discuss the problems and benefits of different plantings and grapes as they rode home. The stable boys came running to meet them and take their horses. Lucio frowned. Why wasn't Teo among them?

"I wonder if the women have returned." Lucio peered into the barn to see if their horses were there but couldn't see much in the dim light.

He reached up to take a sleeping Luis from his father. The boy woke, but his eyes were still heavy as Lucio took him in his arms.

Manuel came running from the back of the barn. "Señor Gabrio." The man panted, his face a mask of panic. "Teo is injured, and the little girl, Maria, is missing!"

CHAPTER SEVENTEEN

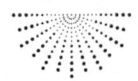

Relief flooded Rosalinda when she rode into the yard with Yoana and Leya. The sight of Luis, and knowing he was all right, made her sigh. Now to find Maria.

For the whole ride she'd made certain to stay near either Yoana or Leya. Carlos would never dare to bother her or say anything around them.

But his predatory gaze followed her the whole time.

Had Lucio said something to Gabrio to make him send one of his men along with them? Arturo, a young man with a boyish grin that endeared him to all the women, stayed close. He entertained them with stories and took Isabel on the horse with him several times. Her shy daughter loved the hombre.

A man came rushing from the barn and ran up to Lucio and Gabrio. He looked distraught, but they were too far away to hear what he said. Unease skittered across Rosalinda's nerves. Had something dreadful happened?

She nudged her horse to a trot.

Lucio must have heard their approach. He turned, and when his gaze met Rosalinda's, her stomach dropped. Maria. It had to be. Luis and Isabel were both in sight. Fear put a choke hold on her throat.

"What is wrong?" She reined in the horse and accepted Lucio's arms as he lifted her down. Her legs wobbled.

"Maria is missing." His tightened hold kept her from falling. "We will find her."

He explained that Teo had been injured, but he didn't know more than that. By that time, Leya and Yoana had gathered around. Yoana had Isabel in her arms. Gabrio stood beside her, his arm around her shoulders.

"Rosalinda, go with Lucio. We'll take care of Isabel." Yoana hugged the niña tight. "We will go in the house and see if Maria is there."

Lucio nodded and took Rosalinda's arm, but she yanked away from him. She held her body rigid, trying not to show her fear. Carlos had been with her group all day, so he couldn't have done anything to Maria. But what if he had a partner. He mentioned last night that many of the men were interested. Had he only been bragging, or had he told the truth? She had no way of knowing.

"I need to talk to Teo. Where is he?" Rosalinda glanced around for the man who'd run up to Lucio, but he had disappeared. He'd come from the barn, and Maria and Teo were working there, so she took off at a run for the open doors of the building. "Please, God, if you are there, if you care at all about my children, please keep Maria safe."

She heard footsteps pounding behind her. Voices calling. She didn't stop until she got inside but didn't know which way to go. She'd never been in this structure before. To her right and left, short passageways led to a few stalls. The way she faced looked down a long row of stalls. In the middle of the right side ahead of her was a door, probably to a tack room. She headed that way before Lucio could catch her and stop her.

She reached the door to the room when she heard Gabrio call out behind her. "Manuel, where are you?"

A man's voice echoed from farther down the aisle. Rosalinda bypassed the tack room and raced toward the end of the passage. Manuel, the man who'd run up to Lucio outside, poked his head out of the end stall. His eyes widened when he saw her barreling toward him, but he stepped aside.

She hurried into the stall, squinting to see better. Along the side, a small form sat with his back against the wall, his head in his hands. She dropped to the straw beside Teo, almost afraid to touch him. She hated the thought of hurting him.

"Let me see, Teo." She pulled his hand away from the cut on his temple. She nudged a rake out of the way to scoot closer. Blood dripped down the side of his face. His swarthy skin had turned pale. He pinched his lips together, always the brave one.

Lucio knelt behind her and handed her a cloth, which she pressed to the bleeding cut. Teo winced and started to pull away but stopped.

"I see you are still strong enough to fight bears, mijo." She smiled as his eyes jerked up to meet hers. A smile trembled at the corners of his mouth.

She dabbed the cut again, glad to see the blood slowing. "I remember when you waved that burning branch at the bear and scared him away. You protected us all."

Calm had replaced her panic, but why? Had Leya's God truly heard her prayer? Was this His way of saying He'd keep her daughter safe?

"Can you tell me what happened, Teo?" A few moments earlier, she would have been shaking him to get answers. But now she waited for him to speak as peace washed over her.

"We were working hard." Teo's gaze slanted up to where Manuel and Gabrio hovered behind her.

"I'm sure you were working hard." She kept her tone as soothing as possible.

Teo's lip quivered the tiniest bit.

"We wanted to take a break and play." He sniffed. The blood flow slowed to a seep. She kept the cloth pressed to the wound.

"I had some toy weapons. I made them out of pieces that were thrown away." He kicked at something in the straw.

Rosalinda reached down to find a stick with a long piece of metal tied to it. Blood was drying on the metal. She swallowed hard. What if Maria had been hurt by this, too?

"We were just playing." Teo's lip quivered even more.

"Teo, you are not in trouble." Gabrio knelt beside Lucio. "We want to know where Maria is. Did she get hurt too?"

Teo frowned. His face scrunched as he thought. "I don't think so. She was right here with me the last I remember."

"Was anyone else here?" Rosalinda's center of calm seemed to be slipping. She needed to find her daughter.

"No. Just Maria and me." The boy gave Gabrio a pleading look. "We did work hard."

"I'm sure you did. Teo, you are not in trouble. We just need to find Maria and see if she is all right. We don't want her to be bleeding too." Gabrio's words seemed to reassure Teo.

"Maria swung her sword at me. We were playing swords and fighting. She hit my sword, but then hers slipped off of mine and hit me. It hurt." He lifted his hand to touch the cloth Rosalinda still held to his temple. "I don't remember any more until Manuel was talking to me. I don't know where Maria went."

"Rosalinda, would you take Teo to the house and help Carmen get him cleaned up?" Gabrio stood. "We will gather the men and have them start searching for Maria. We will find her."

Lucio squeezed Rosalinda's shoulder when she started to object. She wanted to find her daughter and let someone else care for Teo. She realized how selfish that was. These men knew the grounds of the ranch, and she didn't. They would find her daughter much faster than she would.

"Come, Teo." She helped him to his feet. He wobbled a little and then did his best to stand without her help.

They stepped out of the stall and turned toward the house. Yoana raced into the barn. "Rosalinda. Where are you?" Her call echoed in the rafters.

"Here." Rosalinda led Teo toward Yoana. "What is it?"

"She's in the house. Maria is in the house." Yoana pressed her hand to her side, breathing hard. "She went to get help for Teo right before we rode in. She's safe."

Yoana reached for Teo. "Here, I'll walk with him. You go on ahead. She's in the kitchen with Leya and Carmen."

As soon as Yoana had Teo, Rosalinda lifted her skirt and raced from the barn. Carlos stood just outside by the horses they were cooling down. His hawklike gaze chilled her blood. She didn't realize she'd stopped until Lucio came up behind her and put his hand in the small of her back.

"Come. I'll walk with you." He spoke quietly, but she noted the scowl he sent toward Carlos. She slowed to a more sedate pace, her heart still hammering.

They were almost to the back door of the house when Lucio put his hand on her arm to stop her. He turned her to face him, his hands cupping her arms. "Rosalinda, I don't know what Carlos has said to you or done to you, but I need to know. If you or your niños are in danger, I want to protect you. Please don't shut me out."

INDECISION TRAVELED ACROSS HER FACE. He waited, hoping, praying. He ached to pull her close as he had last night but knew he couldn't. There were too many factors to consider, and he couldn't give her a promise of something that couldn't be.

She pulled away. "I have to see Maria."

Bereft, he tried to keep his expression even so she wouldn't know how much she'd hurt him. He followed her into the kitchen.

Leya sat with Maria cradled on her lap. Maria's cheeks were

tear streaked, her eyes luminous. Her hair, matted with sweat and bits of straw, clung to her scalp.

She lit up when she saw Rosalinda. "Mama." She leaped off Leya's lap and ran to Rosalinda, who knelt down and swept her daughter into her arms. Moisture glittered in her eyes.

She'd never looked more beautiful.

"Mama, I hurt Teo." Tears tracked down Maria's cheeks. "I think I hurt him bad." She sobbed. Rosalinda struggled to talk.

Lucio knelt down beside them and put his hand on Maria's back. He could feel her shuddering. "Maria, we just spoke with Teo."

The niña jerked back from her mother. "He's alive?"

"Very much so." He smiled at her obvious relief. "Yoana is bringing him inside to get the cut on his head tended. They should be here any minute."

"I'm going to meet him." Maria pushed away from her mother and raced for the door. She jerked it open to find Yoana and Teo standing on the doorstep. Yoana had her hand out toward the doorknob.

"Teo." Maria burst into tears again. "I'm so sorry I hurt you."

The boy grinned and puffed his chest out. "Yoana says I might have a scar, and girls like scars. I can tell them I was wounded in a battle."

Maria giggled, her tears drying in an instant.

"Let's go in and get you cleaned up." Yoana ushered him through the door. Carmen clucked her tongue and hurried to fetch a basin of water and a clean rag.

"You sit right there at the table." Carmen nodded toward an empty chair. "I told you children to behave, and now look what happened. You think I wait all day to wipe up blood and sew up cuts when I have so much work to do?" She continued to scold as she gathered the items she needed to tend Teo.

Lucio had to work not to smile. He could see Yoana had the same problem. He figured they were both thinking of the woman who worked in their familia's kitchen and pretty much ran the hacienda. She had the kindest heart and the angriest scolding, just like Carmen. He could see her tenderness from her touch as she washed Teo's wound.

Rosalinda swayed on her feet. Lucio cupped her elbow and leaned close. "Let's step outside and talk." She turned, her eyes wide, her face pale. He could see she didn't want to, but he needed to know what was bothering her. Even if they never had anything between them, he still had to protect her.

The sun had warmed the day so much that he sought out shade for them. They stood near the house, the coolness of the walls comforting.

"Rosalinda, why are you afraid of Carlos?" He watched the stubbornness rise up in her features. There had to be a way to keep her from shutting him out. Part of him wanted to force her to tell him, but she'd been forced to do too many things in her life. He needed her to choose to talk to him.

"I am not afraid of him." The subtle sag of her shoulders as she spoke told him she was lying.

"He has upset you. Why was he in the house last night? He said he was there to meet you, but I don't believe that." He prayed she would answer with honesty this time.

"He...maybe he wanted a drink."

"No. He stays in the bunkhouse with the others. He had no reason to be in the house. If he wanted a drink, he could have gotten one out there." He clenched his fists to keep from reaching for her.

"You will have to ask him then." She studied the ground.

"He said he was there to meet you. Why?"

She flipped her hair across her shoulder and gave him that saucy smile. "Many men want to meet with me."

He gritted his teeth. "But how did he know you would be in the kitchen at that time of night? That isn't the usual time for someone to be up and about."

"Perhaps I told him that time." She cocked her hip and put her hand there in a provocative motion designed to distract him. It almost worked.

Almost.

"Did you? Did you tell him that time?" He waited, watching the play of emotions in her eyes and her body language.

"I could have." She shook her hair back across her shoulder, where the mass fell almost to her waist.

"But *did* you?" He would stand here and ask until she told him the truth. Or he finally got angry and left.

"I...I need to go see if Carmen needs help with Teo." She edged around him, along the side of the house.

He had to let her go. Maybe he could talk to Yoana and Leya. See if they would try to find out what was happening between Rosalinda and Carlos. What had her so afraid?

When the door clicked shut, he glanced around and saw no one. He leaned against the coolness of the house and closed his eyes. "Lord, You know what is going on with Rosalinda. You know what she needs and what I can do to help her." He sighed and shook his head. "Father, I know You are our protector, and You can take care of Rosalinda. Let me know if You need me to do anything. I want to help."

He pushed off the wall and strode toward the barn. He needed to find Carlos and see what he could learn from the man. Maybe he should get Gabrio to go with him so he didn't do something he'd regret. Gabrio had a calming effect on him. Ramón steadied him too, but he was at the vineyard with the don's men learning more about the vines and soil.

He found Gabrio giving some instructions to Manuel. They were examining the pretend weapons Teo had made and shaking their heads. He glanced up as Lucio approached. "It's a wonder the niños weren't hurt more than a cut on the head. Look how sharp these are." He held one out to Lucio, who tested the heft in his hand.

"I can't believe little Maria was able to lift this and hit anyone. She must be stronger than she looks." The metal wasn't knife-blade sharp, but it did have an edge.

Lucio waited as Gabrio gave Manuel some instructions about talking to Teo and warning him not to make something like this again. "Maybe I will help you make some toy swords for them. Something that won't hurt them more than a bruise or two."

When Manuel walked away, carrying the weapons to dispose of them, Gabrio turned to Lucio. "What is wrong, my friend. You look troubled."

Lucio told him of his observations with Rosalinda and their conversation. "I need to find Carlos and speak to him, but I would like you to go along so I don't end up knocking him on his backside again."

"I could assist you." Gabrio's low laugh held derision. Lucio grinned and Gabrio shook his head. "With knocking him silly or preventing you from doing that. I don't much care for men who think they can frighten women into doing what they want them to do. I saw that too much in the bandolero camp."

"Do whatever you feel is needed."

They left the barn and headed for the bunkhouse. Lucio wasn't sure if his men were there or if they were out with Ramón. He didn't know what assignments Ramón had given them. After this, he would check with Ramón at the beginning of the day. This morning he'd been too concerned with Rosalinda and hadn't thought to check.

None of the men were in the bunkhouse. Lucio and Gabrio circled the grounds without finding Carlos. They were approaching the house from the back when they saw him. With another man.

Outside Rosalinda's window.

Prying the window open.

CHAPTER EIGHTEEN

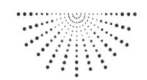

Rosalinda herded her children down the hall to their room. Should she take them and go? Or leave the niños here without her? Yoana or Leya would be much better mothers to her children than she could ever be. They wouldn't have men trying to make them do something horrible. They wouldn't have men thinking such despicable thoughts about them.

They didn't have a past they could never escape.

"Mama, I don't want to go to bed. I want to see Teo first." Maria dragged her feet along the floor. The sound scraped across Rosalinda's already frayed nerves.

"I think you need time apart from Teo. You could have killed him today." The instant the words left her mouth, she knew they were a mistake. The stricken look on Maria's face almost made her cry out.

"Mija." She reached out to her daughter, but Maria dodged away. "Maria, I know it was an accident. I'm sorry for what I said."

Maria nodded but trudged ahead of them to the room, her shoulders bowed as if she carried the weight of the world on her fragile frame. Isabel let go of Rosalinda's hand and ran forward to slip her fingers around her sister's. Maria's slumped form straightened. The weight that had bowed her settled firmly on Rosalinda.

Maria stopped inside the bedroom, staring at the tub filled with water. "Do we have to take a bath tonight?"

"You cleaned stalls today. What do you think?" She set Luis in a chair by the window and turned to undress Isabel. The girls could bathe first and then Luis. She missed the mountain stream. The cold water made for quick bathing and was much simpler than hauling pails, filling a tub, and then having to dip the water out. The Santiago servants helped, but she still disliked doing this.

By the time she had the three done with baths, she shivered in her damp dress. "Come here, Maria. I'll finish brushing your hair and then do Isabel's."

"I'll do my own." Maria's lower lip jutted out.

"No. You won't." Rosalinda sat on the bed with her back to the window and held out her hand for the brush. Maria trudged over, her face twisted in a mask of defiance. The niña might want to rebel, but she knew better. She slapped the brush into Rosalinda's palm. Rosalinda stared at her daughter, waiting. She watched the realization of what she'd done wash across Maria's face. Tears welled in her eyes. She looked down.

"I'm sorry, Mama." She turned around and backed up to Rosalinda.

Maria had always been a compliant child. Maybe a little wild when she'd been allowed to run free, but she always obeyed. Did this new defiance have to do with all the uncertainty in their life now?

Rosalinda worked at the tangles in Maria's hair as Isabel and Luis played on the floor with some blocks Yoana had brought for them earlier. She smiled as the pair stacked the blocks, giggling as their tower toppled to the floor. The laughter of her children did something deep inside her. All those feelings of inadequacy seemed to melt away. Her desire to run and leave her niños behind—protected—faded. She wanted to make this family work...

But how?

"Isabel, your turn." Rosalinda ran the brush one last time through Maria's curls. She pulled her back into a hug and kissed the top of her head before releasing her. Maria whirled around and threw her arms around Rosalinda's neck for a tight hug. Rosalinda blinked fast to keep tears at bay. She didn't deserve any love from her niños. Not after what she'd allowed.

Maria joined Luis at the pile of blocks. The clink of wood faded into the background, and Rosalinda's thoughts wandered in the rhythm of the brush through shiny dark curls. Maria, ever the chatterbox now, kept a running conversation with Luis. Rosalinda wished she knew how to bring Isabel out of her shell enough to start talking more and interacting with others. Her quieter niña rarely said anything, not even with her siblings.

"Did you have fun riding with Yoana today?" She leaned around to see her daughter smile as she nodded.

"Did she tell you a story?" This prompted a very enthusiastic nod from Isabel, causing Rosalinda to lose her hold on the brush. It clattered across the floor. Luis scrambled to pick up the brush and return it to her.

"Can you tell me about the story?" Rosalinda slowed her brushing, holding her breath in the hope Isabel would comply.

"A story about Babab."

"Who?" Rosalinda leaned closer again.

"Babab." Isabel spoke a little louder.

"I've never heard of anyone by that name." Rosalinda tried to recall Yoana or Leya mentioning that person. She didn't even know if the name was for a male or female.

"Can you tell me the story?"

Isabel shrugged. "Babab was a hart."

Rosalinda blinked. "A heart? Like a nice person?" This had to be the most confusing tale ever, but Isabel was talking, and she didn't want to stop her."

"What happened with Babab?"

"She hid spies." Isabel's voice dropped to an exaggerated whisper. "Izerlite spies."

"Ah, from the stories about the Israelites." Rosalinda worked at a difficult tangle.

"She hid them and helped them escape. She put a red rope around their neck and threw them out her window. She and her family lived when the Izerlites came back. Ouch!" Isabel rubbed her head as Rosalinda freed the last of the tangle.

"Mama." Maria's fear-filled voice caught her attention. Maria sat with Luis on her lap. Both of them had their attention riveted on the window. Rosalinda realized she'd been hearing scratching noises in the background, but she'd been so focused on Isabel talking, she hadn't paid attention.

She turned to look. The blood in her veins turned to ice. Carlos stood outside her window prying at the glass. When he saw her looking at him, his broad face split into a lecherous grin. His dark eyes promised grief.

"Maria." Rosalinda forced her voice to remain calm as she waited for her eldest to look at her. "Maria, I want you to take Isabel and Luis and find Yoana and Leya."

"Why?" Maria's eyes were huge as she stared at her mother. "What are those men doing? I want to stay with you."

Isabel hid her face against Rosalinda's skirt and trembled like a leaf in the wind. Luis clung to Maria's hand, his dark eyes wide as he stared at the men framed in the window.

"Maria." Rosalinda grappled for some excuse that would make sense and not frighten her niños more than they already were. "I want you to ask Yoana to tell you the story about Babab. It sounds fascinating, and I want to hear more."

"Then come with us." Maria glanced toward the men again.

"No." She took a calming breath, not meaning for her tone to be so harsh. "I need to see what is wrong with the window and if these men need help fixing it." Her knees went wobbly as the fabrication tumbled out. Maria seemed to accept the lie and led her siblings from the room.

As soon as the door closed behind them, she faced the window, anger surging through her. She stalked toward the men, her gaze locked on Carlos.

"What are you doing?" She hissed through her teeth, trying not to yell. She didn't want to frighten her niños if they were still within hearing distance.

"We are coming for a visit." Carlos's teeth gleamed. She wanted to wipe the smile from his face. Her fingernails dug into her palms as she fought for control.

"Go away. Leave me alone. Leave my *children* alone." She tried to maintain her facade as she searched for a way to block the window and keep them from gaining access. There wasn't a way to lock the window. She couldn't move any of the heavier furniture on her own.

Carlos and his friend continued to pry at the base of the glass. She thought she saw a weakening as the pane moved.

"Stop. Now! Leave us alone." Anger gave way to fear as the men persisted. She didn't have to ask what they would do if they entered the room. Experience had taught her more than she wanted to know. The best she could do now was sacrifice herself and save her children.

"Wait, amigo. Lucio."

He ignored Gabrio and raced toward the hacienda. His vision narrowed until all he saw were the two vaqueros trying to get in the window. Into Rosalinda's room. Rage fueled his steps and he heard Gabrio behind him, running just as hard. If he had his horse, he would run these hombres down and drag them into the desert to rot.

Vengeance is mine.

He shrugged off the voice. These men were breaking into the Santiago hacienda. They were intent on harming Rosalinda. Her niños could be caught in the middle. He had to do something.

Vengeance is mine.

Lucio gritted his teeth. Refused to let his footsteps falter. He didn't slow as Gabrio called out again. This time the man with Carlos turned. His eyes widened. He stepped back. Tapped Carlos on the shoulder.

Vengeance is mine.

Lucio groaned deep within. "Yes, Lord. I know vengeance is Yours. Protect Rosalinda. Her children. And protect these men from me.

He slowed. Tamped down his anger. Allowed Gabrio to catch up. They were both huffing as they trotted the last few steps and stopped. Carlos swung around to face them. His face twisted in a snarl. Lucio opened his mouth to speak, his nerves strung taut. Gabrio's touch on his arm stopped him.

"Why are you breaking into my hacienda?" Gabrio presented an imposing figure. Taller than the vaqueros, he also had the commanding presence of an aristocrat. The man with Carlos stepped behind his compadre. Carlos lost some of his bravado.

"We are visiting *mi novia*, my girlfriend." He lifted his chin as if defying Gabrio to challenge his statement.

"And who is your girlfriend?" Gabrio folded his arms over his broad chest.

"Rosalinda. She is anxious to see me." The cocky grin made another appearance.

"If she is so anxious to see you, why are you prying the window open instead of meeting her at the door?" Gabrio tilted his head to the side.

"She...uh, she was having trouble and wanted some air. We were just helping her."

A clear lie. Told with ease.

Gabrio nodded and rubbed his chin as if thinking. He put his hands on his waist. "So, if we ask Rosalinda, she would agree? She would say she asked you, her novio, to help her with this window. And instead of asking the hacienda owner if you could pry out the window, you decided to harm our house."

"Sí. Because Rosalinda wanted us to." Carlos nodded. Grinned.

Lucio's hands fisted at his sides.

"I would like you to go back to the barn and do the work you were assigned." Gabrio's tone took on a note of threat. "We will assess whether Rosalinda needs help and assist her if she does. I do not want you coming to this house again. Is that clear?"

Carlos and his friend, who must have been one of Gabrio's men from the way he looked at him, scuttled away toward the outbuildings.

"You should have sent him packing." Lucio watched the retreating men. He didn't care about the other man, but he wanted Carlos gone. Now.

"First of all, he is your vaquero. Second, if I tell him to leave, it's much harder to keep an eye on him. I would have no idea if he actually left the area or planned to bide his time and come for Rosalinda." Gabrio shook his head. "How did you hire such a disreputable hombre?"

"He's worked for my father for a few years. Don Armenta didn't care so much who worked for him as long as they did their job without complaint. I haven't been around Carlos much until recently. I can tell you he won't be staying on with us if I have any say about the matter."

Lucio turned back to the house to see what damage the men might have done. Rosalinda stared at him through the window. Her eyes were huge and sparkled with unshed tears. When she noticed him looking, she lifted her chin and tried to put on the haughty look she sometimes hid behind. Tried. And failed.

She backed away from the wall and had disappeared through the door of her bedroom by the time they were examining the windowsill. The pane was still intact. A little adobe mud would fix the damage.

"Shall we go inside and talk with her?" Gabrio quirked his mouth up at Lucio. "This should be entertaining at least."

He followed his amigo around the outside of the hacienda. He still pictured the satisfaction that would have come with slamming Carlos up against the building and setting him straight about trying to force his way into a woman's room. He breathed deeply. Did his best to let go of his anger. Of his desire to exact vengeance instead of letting the Lord work.

They found the women and children all together in Yoana's sitting room. Yoana held Isabel on her lap, with Maria beside her. Leya held Luis as the young boy leaned against her sucking his thumb. Rosalinda huddled in a chair opposite them, looking about as miserable as a woman could look.

"Gabrio. Lucio." Maria jumped up to run and hug them. Lucio couldn't stop his smile as the young niña looked up at him with trusting eyes. "We are getting ready to hear a story. Do you want to stay and listen?"

"Not this time." Gabrio's gaze tracked to Yoana, and he smiled at her. Rosalinda watched the two. Lucio wished he could see inside her head, hear her thoughts. He wanted to know if she desired a closer relationship as much as he did.

"But we're going to hear about Babab and how she tied a red rope around the men and threw them out the window." Maria clapped her hands and trotted back to climb up beside Yoana. Yoana's mouth twitched. She bit her lip. Lucio could see she struggled not to laugh.

"That does sound exciting." Gabrio cleared his throat. "We would like to speak with your mother for a few minutes. Rosalinda?" Gabrio gestured to the doorway.

"But she'll miss the story." Maria's lower lip jutted out.

"We can wait for your mama to return. Meanwhile, I will give you a riddle to solve." Yoana nodded at them.

Gabrio and Lucio followed Rosalinda from the room.

"Let's go in here." Gabrio motioned for Rosalinda to enter a sitting room. She took a seat, perching on the edge of the chair cushion. Lucio could see she wanted to leap up and run away. He wouldn't be surprised if she did.

Gabrio told Rosalinda what Carlos said to them. Several expressions chased across her beautiful face. Lucio thought he detected fear and anger among others.

"Did you ask him to help you open your window?" Gabrio asked.

Rosalinda sat board-stiff, hands folded in her lap. She resembled a figure in a painting, beautiful but not living. She looked as if the slightest touch would break her.

"I…I." She swallowed hard. "Some fresh air is always nice." She licked her lips. Lucio followed the movement, thoroughly entranced.

"But did you ask him to pry open the window?" Gabrio's insistent tone stayed even, not accusatory. She glanced toward the doorway. Lucio fought the urge to lean against the doorpost so her way would be blocked if she chose to run.

"I…I may have given him that impression." Rosalinda folded her skirt with her fingers, her gaze downward, not looking at them. How he wanted to lift her chin and gaze in the depths of her eyes. Learning what drove her to lie to Gabrio would be one more mystery to crack. Because he knew she lied.

"Carlos has been ordered not to come to the hacienda again." Gabrio rose.

Lucio stood too.

Rosalinda stared up at them her eyes luminous in her pale face.

"He won't come here?" She licked her lips again. Fussed with her skirt.

"No. He will be with the men but is not allowed to come to the house." Gabrio nodded at Lucio, who held out his hand to help Rosalinda from her chair.

He squeezed her hand. She yanked free.

"If you have any further trouble with him, come to me or to Lucio. Is that clear?" Gabrio spoke with a firmness that brooked no argument. She nodded, then went out the door, turning to go back to Yoana's sitting room.

Lucio looked at Gabrio. "Do you think she will listen?"

His only answer was a snort.

CHAPTER NINETEEN

Francisco relaxed in the leather chair on one side of the fireplace. Augustín sat opposite him. The small fire took the night chill from the room without overheating them. After the long ride today, and his constant concern about his family, he relished the chance to unwind. He sipped from the glass of white wine Augustín poured for him. The flavor wasn't as good as the red they'd shared last night, but he still enjoyed the taste.

"I detected a softening in your daughter today." Augustín swirled the liquid in his glass. "Given time, I believe she will come around."

"I hope so." Francisco's eyes tightened as he thought back over the day. He and Yoana had been in the kitchen at the same time when the women were finishing up with Teo and his cut. She hadn't run from the room or even to the other side of the room. She may even have sent some covert glances his way, but he couldn't be sure. If so, they were very fast.

He welcomed her curiosity. If she studied him, he wanted her to see the differences in him. He wanted to be around her more, not just to make up for what he'd done to her, but to get over the past too. Every time he saw her face, heard her voice, or watched her movements, the memory of her mother became fresh. Each time, that pang lessened. He wanted to get to the point where he saw his daughter with joy over the woman she had become, not grief over the woman she resembled.

"You are very deep in thought, mi amigo." Augustín's voice cut into his thoughts. "I hope you are not overwrought because of Lucio and Gabrio. They are young men and very protective of their women."

Francisco had been surprised at Lucio's restraint when he and Gabrio caught the vaqueros trying to pry a window open. But then, Gabrio had always been a good influence.

"Is Lucio interested in Rosalinda? She is a fiery one." Augustín shook his head. "She will take a strong hand to keep her in control. She reminds me of someone. Maybe two someones."

Francisco nearly choked on the sip of wine he'd just taken. He coughed, fighting to keep the liquid from going down the wrong way.

"I see you feel the same way." Augustín chuckled.

He didn't want to talk about Lucio and Rosalinda. He wanted to sit here in the quiet with his friend and watch the flames lick at the logs in the fireplace. He wanted to sip the product of Augustín's harvest and enjoy life in the moment. Talking about Lucio and Rosalinda would ruin the ambiance.

"You can't deny she is beautiful. You already love her niños as if they were your own." Augustín refused to let the matter drop.

"Lucio is not interested in Rosalinda. He protects her because she works at our hacienda. He cares for her as he would any other of our employees."

Augustín laughed. Tipped his head back and let loose a sound that filled the room. Francisco sighed at the closed door. He hoped none of the other familia would come to check on them. He didn't want Augustín saying anything to anyone else.

The door to the room flew open. Bare feet pattered on the floor. Francisco leaned around the edge of the chair to see all three of Rosalinda's children in the room. Maria closed the door after peering out into the darkened hall beyond. She didn't slam the door but closed it softly. Then she trotted across the room after her sister and brother.

His heart swelled as Luis and Isabel ran to him and held up their arms. He swept them into his lap, faced the fireplace, and settled them. Augustín reached for Maria and plopped her beside him in the chair. Her little legs stuck out straight, her toes not even reaching Augustín's knees.

The sight made Francisco smile, while also causing a pang of loss. He remembered a cold winter evening when Yoana was not yet four-years-old. He and Josefa had been sitting much like he and Augustín. Josefa worked on some sewing while he read from the scriptures. Yoana had been put to bed, but she sneaked into the room, coming up on the opposite side of the chair from her mother. Trapped by the begging in her eyes, he lifted her beside him, and she snuggled back. They both thought they'd gotten away with something until Josefa put down her sewing and held out her hand to Yoana.

He'd forgotten that treasured memory. The closeness he had once known with his impetuous daughter. The way her little body felt nestled next to him. All that he'd thrown away when Josefa died. His throat tightened, and he fought to breathe. How could one live with such pain of regret? Sometimes he didn't think he could go on.

Isabel twirled one of her curls around her finger. She snuggled tighter against his chest, turning so her cheek rested against him. She reached up her free hand to touch his face, her fingers like the brush of a butterfly's wings. He closed his eyes, thankful for the small gift.

"I wish Teo were here too." Maria's voice startled him, rescuing him from becoming more emotional than any man should be.

"Do you think he is all right?" She peered over at Francisco, asking him instead of Augustín.

"I have heard about Teo's escapades and his bravery. A little scratch on the head will not hurt him." Francisco managed a smile he hoped would comfort the niña.

"I have not heard of Teo's bravery." Augustín spoke up. "He works for me, and I didn't know. Please tell me, little one."

Maria's mouth fell open as if she couldn't imagine anyone not hearing about her friend and all he had done. She spoke about their time in the bandolero camp, painting quite the picture of Teo standing bravely against a grizzly bear bigger than this hacienda. Francisco almost laughed when he met Augustín's gaze and saw the same humor reflected there.

When she finished, Augustín patted his chest as if overcome with the telling and then hugged Maria. "I can see that I will have to speak to Teo and help him have more responsibilities than cleaning stalls in the barn. Maybe he could help with the vineyards. There is always much to do there."

"Could he come and sit with us at meals?" Maria gazed up at Augustín. Francisco couldn't see her face, but she looked so much like her mother he had no trouble imagining the plea in her eyes.

"I will speak to Gabrio and mi esposa, Señora Santiago, and let you know." Augustín leaned down to kiss Maria's wild curls.

A soft knock echoed in the room. Francisco knew their time with the children had come to an end even before Yoana opened the door at Augustín's call. She relaxed when she saw the children in the room with them but tensed again when she met his gaze.

"Maria, Isabel, Luis, your mother will be back soon. Vámanos." Yoana's tone brooked no argument. "Hurry if you want to hear the story before bed." The three culprits slipped down from the laps of the dons and trudged to the door. Francisco bit his lip and avoided looking at his amigo so he wouldn't laugh out loud. Children never changed.

"I am so sorry, señores." Yoana kept her eyes averted as she backed out of the room to follow the niños. Francisco opened his mouth to say the niños were welcome any time, but she had already closed the door.

"I'm sorry Yoana is so wary of you. I would like to have observed the niños' mother if she had come for them. I have seen some of her feistiness, but she seems to change from one minute to the next." Augustín tapped his fingers on the arm of the chair. "Has she always been this way?"

"No." Francisco explained his observation and thoughts, shaking off the hurt of Yoana's rejection. Rosalinda provided an easier topic. Augustín frowned, staring at the fire. They were both silent as the flames crackled and burned down. A chill crept into the room, not uncomfortable but not as warm as before.

"I think we may need to find out what has happened to her." Augustín picked up his wine and sipped again. "The men Lucio and Gabrio fought were trying to get into Rosalinda's room. Why would they do that?"

"I have an idea, but it isn't a pretty one." Francisco explained about Rosalinda's past, as much as he knew. "Some men think a woman like her has no worth as a person, but only as an object for them to use. I wonder if these men had that in mind when they were breaking in."

"If so, I will see that they leave this ranch." Augustín's gaze had a challenge to it. "Even if they are your vaqueros. I will not put up with such behavior here."

"You have my blessing and my help with this." Francisco held up his glass, noting the glow of the flames through the wine. Rosalinda hadn't wanted to live the life forced on her. Did any woman want that lifestyle? He couldn't imagine how. He knew she'd been abused by men many times. He'd seen scars she hadn't been able to hide. Rounded scars left by something hot, like the tip of a cigar. He shuddered at the thought of a man doing such an act on her tender skin. Horrendous.

"Do you object to Lucio pursuing her because of her past?"

Augustín's question brought up myriad thoughts. How should he respond?

"What I think should not be a factor in Lucio's decision. He is a grown man and capable of choosing for himself." He added a gruffness to his response in the hope Augustín would drop this line of questioning.

"I see." They sat silent for a while. Francisco knew he should go to bed. The possible problems with Rosalinda disturbed him more than he wanted to let on. He feared for her children and the way they would be impacted if she chose to return to her former lifestyle. He needed to spend time in prayer, seeking to learn if he should do more than pray. Deciding if he should speak with Lucio. He needed to know God's will in this matter. He closed his eyes, weariness seeping through his limbs.

"Before we retire for the night, I have a matter I would like to discuss, mi amigo." Augustín's comment made Francisco's eyes pop open. What could they possibly have to discuss that prompted such a serious tone? He and his friend had already talked business--the purchasing of horses and of wine. What more did they have to debate?

"My Juana and I have talked many times of how much we miss your Josefa. We remember her well and your love for one another."

Francisco's fingers tightened on the wine glass. He placed it carefully on the table beside him so he wouldn't break the fragile goblet. He did not want to reminisce about his wife. Although the pain had dimmed, he still thought of her every day and longed for her every night.

"As I see the changes in you, I wonder if you are ready to consider your life again."

Francisco's head jerked up. He stared at Augustín. Consider his life? Why? To what extent? "What do you mean?"

"I know you want to make amends with your children, and that is good. However, you are not that old. Perhaps you should think about marrying again. There are many women Juana and I know who would be happy to be considered by you." Augustín paused, the wine in his glass swirling in a mesmerizing circle.

Francisco gaped. Him? Marry? Absurd. "I would never do that." He waved a hand. "I have been a widower too long. I am too set in my ways. There isn't a woman out there who would want to marry me."

"I think you sell yourself short, my friend." Augustín chuckled. "I remember a young man sought after by many young women. The talk of the town." He grinned. "And then you met Josefa, and none of the others mattered. Not even your father's advice mattered."

Here was the crux of the conversation. The real reason Augustín wanted to talk. The thing Francisco had feared all evening.

"I am a curmudgeon. A mean old man." Francisco stood. "You can ask my daughter. My sons. My grandchildren. I am not fit to live with anymore." He straightened his coat, feeling the chill in the air even more.

"But you are a man who has been changed by God. Or, perhaps, one whom God is still changing. Either way, you need to ask Him what He wants for you instead of assuming you know His will." Augustín set his now-empty glass down and stood. He grasped Francisco's shoulder and squeezed. Francisco thought of pulling away, but the weight of his amigo's touch sent a thread of comfort through him.

"I will consider your words." He nodded and clasped arms with Augustín. "Good night, my friend."

He walked to his room without even noting the passageways. He couldn't recall opening the door to the den and exiting. Lost in thought, his mind was consumed with memories of Josefa. Their meeting. Their whirlwind courtship. Their too few years of bliss.

Augustín had it wrong. He wasn't a young man, at least not young enough for a new wife. How would he be able to bear the thought of touching another when Josefa still resided in his heart? He appreciated his friend's concern for him, but he had his familia. Lucio lived with him still, and his other sons lived close enough to visit once they no longer feared he would be a negative influence on their familias.

He had to focus his time on the family he had. The family he'd made with Josefa. If he looked at another woman, she would be a widow with a family of her own. How could he convince her children to accept him when his own couldn't?

The covers snugged up to his chin, he rolled over to look out the window. A bright moon hung in the sky, and light glided through the pane, falling across the end of his bed. Outside a coyote chorus began, their howls filling the night with an eerie beauty.

Yoana...

She would never accept him marrying and having other children. That action would wound her beyond her current hurt. And then there was Leya. Her scars. Her mantilla that covered a face nearly as perfect as Josefa's.

The consequences of his sins dragged him into a fitful sleep.

CHAPTER TWENTY

Rosalinda fled toward Yoana's room, thankful to be away from Gabrio and Lucio. She wanted to confide in them. When she'd been in the bandolero camp and met Gabrio, she assumed he would be like any other man she'd ever met. Yet, as time passed, she realized he was different. He had higher standards than any of the other men. At least among those she'd known. Most of them would have sold their own sisters for a drink of tequila. Like her mother had sold her, except that might have been to save her sister. Slightly more understandable.

As much as Gabrio's presence unnerved her, Lucio unnerved her more. In the past few months, she'd noted his character too. Yoana, and Leya sang his praises. Not in a bragging way but in a way that showed how much they loved him and cared about him. He displayed kindness to the people who worked for him and for his father. Kindness he didn't have to show. He could be like so many of the aristocracy who lorded their position over others. But he wasn't.

Instead, he stole things. Like her heart. Her heart, which she had firmly protected up to now.

"Mama!" Maria's welcome cry, taken up by her siblings, eased the chill running through Rosalinda's veins. Sadness weighed on her. She might have no choice but to leave her children. The only chance her children might have for a safe life could mean giving them up to someone else.

Did that make her as bad as her mother? She hoped not. At least she would leave her niños with someone who would love them and care for them. Not with someone who would use them and discard them. She would not profit from leaving them. She would not favor one or the other. She. Would. Not.

Maria climbed back up beside Yoana. "I'm ready to hear about Babab now. As soon as Mama sits down." Maria shot Rosalinda a look full of impatience.

To appease her eager daughter, she settled into the chair she'd vacated earlier.

"I hear Isabel already told you the story from yesterday." Yoana hugged the child on her lap. Isabel released the curl twisted around her finger and patted Yoana's cheek. Then she twisted the curl again and leaned against Yoana.

Yoana kissed Isabel's head. Rosalinda's heart ached at the sight. She was right. Yoana and Gabrio would take good care of her niños. She didn't have to worry about the children if she decided to leave. But she would. She would worry. And ache at the loss.

"So Babab threw the men out the window? With a red rope around their necks? They must have been bad men." Maria shook her head. "Like Cisto." She slapped her hand across her mouth, her gaze darting to Rosalinda. The fear in her eyes made Rosalinda's chest ache. She didn't want her niña to be afraid of saying something wrong. They'd lived that way too long.

Yoana ignored Maria's slip. She smoothed Isabel's hair down and smiled down at Maria. "I think I should start at the beginning of the story. Isabel may have mixed up a few facts. Ready?" Maria nodded, drew her feet up and rested her head against Yoana's arm.

"Leya said she told you the stories of Joseph and Moses, right?" Maria sat upright. "She even told us about Moses and

Pharaoh and all the bad things that happened. Frogs and flies. Water turning to blood." She stuck her tongue out and made a face.

Yoana's eyes twinkled. "I love that story. This one takes place after Moses died. God appointed a new leader, Joshua, to take His people, the Israelites, into the land where God wanted them to live. Before they could do that, Joshua sent some men to look over the land and the enemies they would be facing in a city called Jericho. Jericho was a big city with very strong walls. The two spies went to Jericho and when they entered the city they met a woman by the name of Rahab."

"Wait." Maria sat up again and frowned at Isabel. "She said Babab."

"Well, her name was Rahab. Isabel may have heard it wrong. We were riding on horseback at the time. Maybe some other sound interfered."

"Oh." Maria sank back. Rosalinda thought about leaving. She didn't want to listen to a story right now. So this woman helped the men. What did that mean?

She sighed. Her children would be upset if she left. Especially Maria. She could stay. Maybe she could pretend to pay attention while thinking about something more pleasant. A picture of Lucio flitted across her mind. Her face warmed, and she was glad Yoana and Leya couldn't read her thoughts.

Before her thoughts strayed farther, Yoana's words caught her attention.

"The real reason Rahab's story is important is that she was a harlot, but she helped the Israelites even though she could have been killed for doing that." Yoana didn't glance her way, but Rosalinda had the impression Yoana watched her. Leya sat silent, a sleeping Luis on her lap.

"What is a harlot?" Maria asked.

Rosalinda remained frozen in place. Her daughter might not know, but she knew exactly what the woman did for a living.

Bumps rose on her arms. She wanted to sink through the chair and disappear.

"A harlot is a woman who entertains men who aren't her husband." Yoana bit her lip as if struggling to find an explanation that would not reveal too much to innocent ears.

"You mean she gives them tortillas and beans and they play games?"

Leya coughed, her hand over her mouth. Rosalinda wondered that the older woman hadn't slipped her mantilla back over her face to hide her expression.

"Um. Sort of." Yoana nodded. "Except they entertain men without anyone else there to chaperone."

"Oh." Maria nodded, her expression serious. She already understood the need for a chaperone for young women. "I see. People thought Rahab was not a nice person."

"That's right. They were judging her when they shouldn't." Yoana pressed her cheek to Isabel's head and met Rosalinda's gaze. Yoana smiled at her, and she relaxed a little.

"The thing is, the leaders of the city were worried about the Israelites. They were afraid of them because they heard that two men from the Israelite camp may have come into their city. They searched for them. If they caught them, the men would be killed."

"But God won't let that happen." Maria straightened and turned to stare up at Yoana.

"God provided Rahab to help them. The lowliest woman in the city was the one God used to assist his people. Do you know why He used her?"

"Why?"

"Because she wanted to know God. She had heard about Him, and she wanted to believe in Him instead of the idols her people worshipped. So she hid the spies on her roof. Then, when it was safe, she helped them escape and told them how to get away."

"Was that the red rope? Did she tie it around their necks?" Maria asked.

"No. Before they left, the spies told Rahab that because she helped them, God would save her and any of her family that were in her house with her when His people returned and attacked the city. They told her to hang a scarlet, or red, cord from her window."

"Did they keep her safe?" Maria's fingers were twisted into Yoana's skirt.

"Yes. Sometime I will tell you all about the battle of Jericho. It's a great story. But I will tell you Rahab and her family were saved when all the rest of the people in Jericho died." Yoana cupped Maria's cheek when tears welled in her eyes.

"But why did they all have to die? Why didn't God want to save them too?" Maria sniffled.

"Oh, He did. God wanted to save them. But only Rahab cared enough to want to know God. The rest of the people chose to believe in false gods and idols. They rejected God. That is why they died."

"So if I rejected God, I would die?" Maria's lip trembled.

"Every person has the choice to live the way they choose. They can live in a bad way or follow God and believe in His Son, Jesus. God gives every person that opportunity."

Maria sniffed. "Even a harlot?"

"Even a harlot." Yoana nodded. "You want to know another exciting part of Rahab's story?" Maria nodded, and Yoana continued. "Rahab married one of the Israelites, a man named Salmon. She was the great-grandmother to King David. Do you remember him?"

"He fought the big giant." Maria clapped her hands.

"That's right. Which also means a woman many thought a worthless harlot ended up being listed in the line of Jesus Christ, our Savior." Yoana smiled.

Rosalinda couldn't breathe. Could this story be true? Would God be willing to love her and to redeem her in spite of her past? Like He had Rahab?

How could this ever be true?

Lucio sat astride his dun the next day and gazed out across the rolling hills toward the west. Far in the distance, he thought he could catch a glimpse of the blue line of the ocean. From here, he had trouble telling where the sky ended and the ocean began. He'd been to the ocean one time as a boy and could still recall the pounding of the waves against the rocks along the shoreline. On the beach, the waves came across the sand in ripples to wash over his feet. He still remembered the tickle as the sand washed from under his toes when the waves receded.

If only he'd had time to take a side trip to the beach. What would Rosalinda's reaction be to seeing it? Or her niños' reaction? Had they seen the rolling waves before or felt the power of the pounding surf? A smile tugged at his lips at the thought of the niños splashing in the water, and their delight in finding seashells on the beach.

Off to the side, his father and Don Santiago sat on their horses, viewing the Santiago holdings. Far below were the hills with the vineyards. Lucio loved the order of the rows of vines. Gabrio sat beside the dons, pointing something out to them. He reined his horse around and rode over to Lucio.

"Your father is very interested in growing grapes and making your own wine. Do you think your rancho would have the right soil and climate to sustain them?" Gabrio leaned forward to rest his arm on his saddle.

"Some of our land might. We get colder in the winter than you do here. Will the vines survive the cold?" Lucio tried to picture the right place where they could start a crop, but all he could think was they would lose valuable pasture. They were known for horses, not grapes or wine.

Gabrio explained the intricacies of growing the crop. Lucio tried to look interested, but he had no heart to learn. Gabrio laughed and clapped him on the back. "I don't think you have heard a word I've said."

"You are speaking in some foreign tongue." Lucio grinned at his friend. "My ears refuse to translate."

"Good thing, then, that your vaquero, Ramón, has been working with our head man. Ramón has some skill with learning this type of farming. He thinks you have some hillsides that are perfect for growing grapes and not as good for pasture." Gabrio turned his horse and headed for the path down the hill. Their fathers were already leaving the hilltop.

Lucio sent one last look toward the horizon and the enticing line of the ocean before following the others back toward the Santiago hacienda.

When he and Gabrio reached the bottom of the hill, their fathers were waiting for them. They rode on at a slow walk. Lucio figured the older men wanted to talk about the proposed vineyard at the Armenta Rancho and how that would work. He had no desire to talk about making changes or to listen to the possibilities. For some reason, he couldn't find any enthusiasm for the project. Instead, he longed for home and the tall mountains that graced the horizon.

"Lucio, I noticed you brought a beautiful señora with you. Is there something we should know?" Don Santiago's eyes twinkled as if he knew how much trouble he stirred up with that one comment.

"Her niños were good friends with Teo, your stable boy. She is friends with Teo's mother, Dolores." Lucio felt the weight of his father's gaze but kept his focus on Don Santiago. "Maria wanted to see Teo. Rosalinda was disappointed that Dolores is not here and hopes she will return before we leave for home."

"I thought perhaps there was more to the story. Traveling with such a beautiful woman and all those vaqueros must have been a challenge. I am surprised you allowed her to come."

Gabrio snorted. "Knowing Rosalinda, there wasn't a way to stop her. She is very determined."

"I see." Don Santiago guided his horse around a washed out ditch at the side of the road. Dirt and rocks dribbled into the cleft at their passing.

"She watches you and seems to want to stay close to you." The don's regard made Lucio want to roll his eyes. He didn't want to face this interrogation. What good could come of airing his uncertainty in front of his father and his friends?

"Isn't it time you married? My Gabrio is your age and very happy to be married to your sister. You need that same happiness. Right, Francisco?" The look Don Santiago sent his longtime friend carried an emotion Lucio couldn't decipher. Had the pair discussed his singleness and the possibility of him marrying Rosalinda? He couldn't picture his father ever giving his permission for such a union.

"Padre." Gabrio sent Lucio a sympathetic eye roll. "Are you taking over from the women and becoming a matchmaker? Lucio is capable of deciding when and whom to marry."

"He is getting older. He needs a wife. Rosalinda is a beautiful mujer. Here in Alta California, where women are scarce, a man must grab one when he has the opportunity. Right, Francisco?" He grinned at his compadre.

Lucio watched his father. The don's expression remained implacable. His eyes cut to the side toward Don Santiago, but he showed no other sign he'd heard.

"I have heard of her past, Lucio." Don Santiago dropped back to ride alongside him. From the corner of his eye, Lucio caught the widening of Gabrio's eyes. He waited to see what more his father's viejo wanted to say.

All joviality left the don. "I also understand the choice was not hers. She did not want to leave her home and do the things she had to do. You cannot count that against her."

"I don't." Lucio tamped down his irritation and spoke with

respect. "No matter, though, because others of the aristocracy will. If I were to marry her, she would be rejected by all the women in the familias with whom we associate."

"Not all." Don Santiago's gazed locked on him and made him want to squirm like a child caught stealing empanadas. "She would always be welcome here. In fact, all the familias I know who matter would welcome her."

"What he says is true." Gabrio spoke up. "You know how Yoana was compromised when she was kidnapped by the bandoleros last spring. In the old country—in España—she might have been rejected from society, but here, as my wife, she is welcome wherever we go."

The dun danced toward the side of the road. Lucio guided him away from another washed-out place. He knew the animal could sense his unease. He wanted to listen to the advice of Gabrio and his father, but he also knew his own father's mindset. Don Armenta would never accept Rosalinda as a daughter-in-law. He would say she'd bring shame to their family. No matter what Lucio's heart said, he had to listen to his head. He had a responsibility.

Maybe it would be best if they prepared for their return trip. Yoana would be sad at their leaving so soon after their arrival. Maria and Teo would be upset too. But back home, he could stay away from Rosalinda more easily than he seemed able to do here. At the Santiago hacienda, every time he turned around, he saw her. And every glimpse of her made it that much harder for him to get her out of his heart and his mind.

Plus, her niños were such a delight. He hated the thought of not having them around. He wanted to be an influence in their lives. They had a chance their mother never had, and he wanted to see them take advantage of that opportunity.

His father and Don Santiago urged their horses to a slow canter. The sun dipped midway toward the western horizon. From the west a giant bird soared into sight followed by another.

The majesty and grace of the bird thrilled him. He'd heard of these condors with wingspans of up to nine feet. He would make sure the niños could see this rare display.

Minutes later when they rode into the yard near the barn, Maria and Teo ran toward them, shouting and pointing at the sky. The women stood outside near the house with Isabel and Luis beside them.

"Did you see?" Maria called as she ran up to Lucio and Gabrio. "Tía Leya says we don't get to see them very often. They look small from down here, but are very big."

Lucio dismounted and swept her into his arms. "I think Tía Leya is right."

Maria wiggled down. The horses were led away. Lucio's father and Gabrio walked together, waving to a vaquero leading his mount from around the side of the hacienda toward the stable. Don Santiago came alongside Lucio. He put his hand on Lucio's arm and stopped him. Lucio turned to his father's long-time amigo.

Don Santiago's expression was serious, but not angry. "Lucio. I know you think Francisco would never understand. But you need to ask him about his courtship with your madre. With Josefa. There may be things you don't know."

CHAPTER TWENTY-ONE

BEFORE HE HAD the chance to ask Don Santiago what he meant, the man strode toward the hacienda. Almost as if he didn't want to talk more. What did he mean? Why should Lucio ask about his parents' courtship? They had come from Spain along with the Santiagos and a few other aristocratic familias. They were married before they came across the ocean. That's what he'd heard anyway.

"Señor Armenta."

Someone tugged at Lucio's arm. He glanced down to see Teo gazing up at him, his forehead still bandaged. The boy had more color today than he had yesterday. He still looked a little pale and not as excitable as usual.

"What is it, Teo?" He put his hand on the boy's shoulder to assure him he was listening.

"Señor, I need to talk with you." Teo glanced over his shoulder at the barn door. This time Lucio thought he detected a hint of fear in the boy's face. Some of the older boys, or the men, must have been picking on him. Common enough with workers, but not a dispute for him to intercede in when this wasn't his rancho.

"Perhaps you need to speak to Gabrio or Don Santiago?" He

knew he should send the boy to the head vaquero here, but he couldn't recall the man's name. His thoughts were consumed with what Don Santiago had said, and the urgency to talk with his father made him itch to get inside.

He patted Teo again. "I'll let Señor Santiago know you are looking for him." He saw Teo open his mouth to speak, but Lucio strode away. He couldn't be delayed. Guilt pinged inside him, and he halted, turning to walk back and call out to the slump-shouldered boy. "I'll let him know."

He intended to keep his word. He expected to see Gabrio inside with their fathers. But when he entered the house, quiet enveloped him. They weren't in the den or in the kitchen. He had no idea where the men had gone. Maybe he could find his father in his room. He strode down the hallway leading to the room he and his father shared.

No one was there.

He backtracked to the kitchen and went outside. A wagon had pulled behind the hacienda. Yoana, Leya, and Rosalinda were beside the wagon talking with a couple. He still didn't see Gabrio or their fathers. Yoana turned to smile at him as he approached.

"Lucio, do you remember Dolores, Teo's mother?" She indicated the woman beside the wagon. "This is her new husband, Roberto."

Lucio nodded at Dolores. He had vague memories of meeting her when she came to the rancho after Yoana and Leya had been rescued. He shook hands with Roberto. Gabrio had told him one of his workers had taken a liking to Dolores, Teo's mother, and married her. He knew Rosalinda would be glad they returned from Los Angeles in time for a visit. They had combined a wedding trip with picking up supplies. That explained the wagon.

"Do you know where…" Lucio and Yoana spoke at the same time. She grinned at him, and he waited for her to speak.

"Do you know where Gabrio and the dons are?"

"I wanted to ask the same thing. They went in the house ahead of me, but I didn't hear them when I went in."

"They weren't in the den?" Yoana looked past him. "Ah, here they are." She smiled as her husband and their fathers rounded the corner of the house and walked toward them. They were deep in conversation, but Gabrio still sent his wife that special smile they often shared. Lucio couldn't help glancing at Rosalinda. The longing, shown in the tilt of her head and the set of her lips, told him she'd noted the look too.

"Ah, the newlyweds have returned." Don Santiago's face split in a wide smile when he saw the wagon. He strode over to Roberto and said something Lucio couldn't catch. Roberto nodded and reached behind to point to a package wrapped up under the seat. Lucio drew closer, curiosity humming.

"Señora Armenta, *mi neura*, my daughter-in-law. I have a gift for you." The don smiled as he drew a long, wrapped parcel from the wagon. He nodded to Roberto, and the man clucked at the team, leading them toward the barn, Dolores walking beside him. Lucio understood the need to walk after the long day's ride in the buckboard.

"Let's go inside, and we'll take a look." Don Santiago led the way into the dining room where the long table stretched out. He asked Gabrio to move the candlesticks and placed his parcel on the table. He unrolled from one side while Gabrio helped from the other. The women all gasped when they saw the contents. Beautiful cuts of cloth in vibrant colors caught the last of the light coming through the window. The fabric gleamed and sparkled.

"I thought you would enjoy a new dress for the winter season and the holidays." Don Santiago stepped back. "You may choose to make these for yourself or share with your familia. Mi esposa, Juana, would be here, but she is not feeling well today. She urged me to do this for you."

"They are beautiful." Yoana stepped forward to hug her father-in-law before running her fingers over the rich cloth. Lucio saw pain and jealousy flit across his father's face. He'd seen the changes in his father, knew he regretted the past, but still he understood Yoana's feelings too. He needed to find an opportunity to talk with her. Or maybe he could talk with Gabrio and ask him to encourage her to give their father another chance. She had accepted him some since they had arrived. At least now she would be in the same room with him. Not much, but a little change.

Leya bent over the new cloth with Yoana, and they were murmuring about styles and colors. Rosalinda hung back, but he could see she wanted to finger the fabric as the others were doing. Had she ever had a new dress made from beautiful material like this? She'd been given clothing when she came to the Armenta rancho, but those had been castoffs and already worn. A desire to give her something just as beautiful as what Yoana treasured burst inside him.

He wanted her to be the one to give him those special glances and smiles.

He glanced over to see his father and Don Santiago in deep conversation. Roberto, Dolores's new husband, had come back while Lucio had been lost in thought. The two older men were listening to him to the exclusion of all other commotion in the room. Gabrio stood to the side of the dons, his face drawn into a frown.

Lucio made his way toward the men. What happened? Had Carlos caused more grief? He hated to think he might be responsible for any problems at the Santiago hacienda. And Lucio still needed to find a way to get his father alone and discuss what happened with his mother. The niggle of doubt Don Santiago planted about the story he knew of his parents had grown into a worm of dread.

He wanted to find out the truth and what that meant for him.

"Let's go to the den and hear the rest of your news." Don Santiago clapped Roberto on the shoulder. "We want to hear all the details. Gabrio and Lucio, please join us."

Lucio glanced back as he followed the men from the room. His mood lightened as he noted Leya and Yoana including Rosalinda in their conversation about the fabric. Rosalinda's face lit as she touched the material in a tentative gesture. When Yoana looked in his direction, Lucio mouthed, "Thank you," to her. She nodded, and he strode after the others to the den.

"Now, what's this about war and unrest?" Don Santiago motioned for Lucio to close the door before turning back to Roberto.

War? Where? Lucio hadn't heard any news in a long time, but he couldn't imagine where there would be fighting in Alta California.

"There were men from Tejas." Roberto's speech faltered. "Texas. They said the families who migrated from the United States of America were talking about seceding from the Union. They want to make Texas theirs instead of Mexico's. Santa Ana won't allow that. Right now, rumors are flying, but there aren't any actions. No fighting." Roberto shifted from one foot to another.

Don Santiago and Don Armenta continued to pump the man for every possible scrap of information he might have overheard. A heavy pall settled in the air. No one wanted war.

No one.

THE FINE CLOTH snagged on her work-roughened fingers. Rosalinda jerked her hand away before she ruined Yoana's gift. She'd never touched or even seen such fine material. From a distance she'd seen women dressed in clothing made from beautiful fabric. She'd always admired the folds of the dresses and the way the garments would flow. She'd never be good enough to wear something like this. Never.

Thoughts of the story of Rahab flitted through her mind as she stepped back. Before she'd been sold to Cisto, she'd been in Los

Angeles and then San Francisco. Had Rahab had a choice about her occupation? Had her mother or father forced her to become a prostitute to help save the family from starvation? No woman would ever *want* to be sold to a man.

As Leya and Yoana continued to chatter about dresses, she thought about what made Rahab appealing to God. Why had He chosen her, a fallen woman, to be so special? Had He made a mistake? Didn't he know what she did for a living? Leya said God didn't make mistakes, but surely, she could be wrong. Having a former prostitute be in the lineage of Jesus Christ, God's Son, couldn't be part of God's plan.

Could it?

She'd been told often enough that a sinner like her didn't belong in church or around good Christian people. Had Rahab received the condemning looks she had? Derogatory, you-are-the-scum-of-the-earth glances from women with their noses in the air?

And had she, as Rosalinda had done, received very different regard from those same women's husbands?

She shuddered.

When she first met Leya and Yoana, she'd been sure they would be like those women. Judgmental and holier-than-thou. But she'd been wrong. Yoana hadn't condemned Rosalinda for her life. In fact, she offered to help her, especially once they were rescued and freed.

For years Rosalinda longed to be delivered. Had Rahab felt those same longings? Had she prayed to the God of the Israelites when she heard about His miracles and His people? Did she pray for a way out of her miserable existence?

Ever since Rosalinda heard Yoana telling the children about her God, she'd felt nudges to learn more about Him. Maybe one day she would learn to read well enough to see for herself what the Bible said about Jesus and His love.

"What do you think, Rosalinda?"

Yoana's question startled her from her reverie. She blinked. Fumbled to recall what the women had been saying. Felt warmth creep up her neck to her face.

"You weren't listening."

Yoana's smile eased her embarrassment. No condemnation. No haughtiness. No meanness. Simply the joy of friendship offered.

"I was." Rosalinda smiled back. She would like it if she and Yoana could become friends. If that were even possible, considering the difference in their stations.

"I think we have figured out what to do with the cloth. The shimmery green will be for Leya. The blue with the gold threads will make a fine dress for me. But this red--"

Yoana lifted the bolt of cloth. The light caught on the fabric, turning the red to orange and back to red. Like the fiery shades in the sky during a beautiful sunset. Rosalinda had noticed this one first. Had felt a fierce pang of longing to have a gown from this material, at the same time knowing that could never be.

"This one will be for you." Yoana and Leya both grinned at Rosalinda.

Her mouth dropped open, and she knew she must look like a fool.

"You're coloring is perfect for this material." Leya pulled a section of cloth from the bolt and held it beneath Rosalinda's chin. She glanced to Yoana and both women nodded.

"Perfect." Yoana rolled the material back onto the bolt.

Rosalinda still couldn't speak. Surely they didn't expect her to believe they would make her a dress from that cloth. Her? Someone of Rahab's ilk before she was chosen by God?

"Now we need to discuss patterns. We can start on the dresses tomorrow." Yoana covered the rolls of cloth in the protective wrap and rolled them tight.

Rosalinda couldn't breathe. She didn't know how to say she

didn't want that dress. She couldn't lie. She couldn't hurt their feelings. But she wasn't worth their friendship.

"I need to check on the children." She grasped at the first thought that flitted through her head. Yoana and Leya both gave her strange looks but nodded. She fled through the kitchen door to the outside.

Across the yard, she saw her children playing. Feliciana played a game with them. They would be fine. She needed to get away to think. She wanted someone to talk to. Someone who would understand. Someone who knew her and her background.

Dolores.

Taking the long way around so her niños wouldn't see her, she hurried along a trail that wound around the hacienda's outbuildings. She thought she knew which little *casa* belonged to Dolores and headed that way.

The door to the *casita*, the little house, stood open. From inside, she could hear humming. She halted. Did she have the right place? She'd never heard Dolores hum or sing before. She'd always been so quiet and obedient. Never happy or lighthearted.

Dolores came to the door, a small rug in her hands. She stepped outside and started to shake the dirt from the rug when she spotted Rosalinda. Her broad face split in a smile. She dropped the mat.

"Rosalinda. Mi amiga." Dolores rushed to her and enfolded her in a warm embrace. In the bandolero camp, they'd never shown such affection for one another. It took a moment before Rosalinda returned her friend's embrace. The connection brought tears to her eyes.

Dolores stepped back, her hands cupping Rosalinda's upper arms. "I didn't get to truly talk with you earlier today. Teo told me you were here, but I didn't believe him until I saw you. That silly niño makes up stories all the time. I've been busy unpacking and getting the house ready and hoped you would come by." She drew in a breath, her chatter ceasing.

Rosalinda laughed. She'd never heard Dolores speak so much. She pulled her into a second hug. "I'm so glad to see you too. You are married now. And so happy. You have to tell me all about your life here." She squeezed Dolores's arms. "I am sorry to hear about the bebé. We heard he died in his sleep." Grief pinched her friend's face. She started to speak. Stopped. "Thank you." Then she smiled, a sad one, but a smile. "Come in. I have water to heat for hot chocolate or cool water. What would you like?"

Dolores ushered her into the cool adobe dwelling. The privacy and quiet folded around Rosalinda, easing her distress.

She helped fix them each a cup of chocolate. Rosalinda sipped and listened in awe as Dolores chattered as much as her son, Teo. She talked about her life here at the hacienda, how she helped to clean the house. How she met Roberto. How he convinced her to love him. How they married and were so very happy.

"What about you?" Dolores clasped her hands around Rosalinda's. "I've talked and talked about me but haven't given you a moment to tell me how you are doing. How is life at the Armenta hacienda? What work are you doing? Have you met any vaqueros who are interesting?"

Rosalinda fumbled with what to say. She hadn't settled into this new life like Dolores had. Men always looked at her in a different way than they did Dolores, whose plain features were pleasant, but not beautiful. How could this woman understand Rosalinda's dilemma?

As the thought flitted past, she regretted her moments of self-pity. She'd had one man who paid attention to her in a way that didn't demean her. She thought. Maybe. Lucio seemed captivated one moment and not the next. His interest was so different from anything she'd experienced, she didn't know if it was true.

"I work at odd jobs where they need me." Rosalinda cupped her cooled mug with fingers that fought not to tremble. "There are many vaqueros at the Armenta rancho. They have those fine horses to take care of and need a lot of men to help. Sometimes I help in the kitchen and sometimes with cleaning. Wherever I'm needed." She shrugged. How could she broach the subject she wanted to talk about?

This new Dolores might not even understand her uncertainty about whether God would find her worthy to love and forgive. About her developing feelings for the don's son. About Carlos's demands, and her fear for her children. She downed the last of her drink.

"I have only been back a few hours, but I have heard some rumors." Dolores leaned across the table, her dark eyes twinkling. "So, is it true? Is Lucio Armenta interested in you?"

CHAPTER TWENTY-TWO

"No." Rosalinda pressed her hands to her heated cheeks. She pushed up from the table, snatching her teacup and carrying it to the dish basin.

"But that is what the women are saying. They have heard from their husbands that Don Armenta's son is pursuing you." Dolores came up beside Rosalinda, leaning around to peer at her face.

Rosalinda turned away. "You know that can't be true. Those are only rumors spoken by women who don't know to mind their own business." A towel hung on a hook. Rosalinda straightened the folds as she tried to calm her galloping heart.

What had these men seen? Or heard? Part of her wanted to scoff at the idea. Another part wanted to bask in the concept that a man of Lucio Armenta's caliber would be interested in her as more than some pretty trinket to be used and tossed away.

"Come, sit down." Dolores urged her back toward the table. "I did not mean to upset you. Would you like some water? I would offer you something to eat, but I haven't been back long enough to fix anything." Dolores clasped her hands in front of her and her brow creased.

Rosalinda dashed the back of her hand across her eyes.

Dolores knew her the best of anyone. And she knew Dolores. Or she had known her. Perhaps her friend hadn't changed too much. Maybe, if asked, she would keep a secret and give advice that Rosalinda could use.

"Dolores." Rosalinda stepped closer and stilled her friend's twisting fingers with her own. "I need to talk to you. At one time I could trust you to keep a confidence. Can I still?"

"Of course." Dolores shook her head as if saying one thing but indicating another. "I listen to the gossip when I have to, but I am not close to the women here. I keep to myself most of the time and don't talk a lot." She stared down at the floor before lifting her gaze to meet Rosalinda's.

"I had a hard time when I first came here. The people heard where I came from. That my…my children's father hanged for his crimes." She brushed her cheek against her shoulder, wiping away a tear. "They were kind when my bebé died, but only when Roberto asked me to marry him did they start to accept me. It will take a long time before I trust any of them."

They hugged again and then sat at the table across from one another. Rosalinda accepted Dolores's offer of water. Silence fell as Rosalinda fumbled for the words to say. How much should she tell her friend?

"Rosalinda, you can say what you want." Dolores's sincerity shone through her eyes. "I will listen. I don't promise to have any answers, but I will listen and keep your confidence."

Rosalinda released a long sigh. Her thoughts had been scattered in so many directions lately. She didn't know what to do or what to even think. The one thing she knew was she needed advice from someone.

"I have done so much wrong." She closed her aching eyes to keep the tears at bay and to avoid the disappointment she knew she would see in her friend's eyes. "After you left the Armenta rancho to come here, I didn't know what they expected of me. I didn't know my place. I was desperate for a friend, so I…I…." She swallowed hard. She could not verbalize anything about those early weeks.

"You reverted to what you knew best. The only way of life you've known since you were a child."

Dolores's firm hold on her hands kept her grounded. She was amazed that Dolores understood. Leya hadn't known of Rosalinda's indiscretions at the Armenta hacienda or at least had never mentioned them.

"Yes. I flirted with the vaqueros shamelessly. They paid me attention when I did, and I needed someone to care about me." She pulled her hands free and swiped at the tears on her cheeks. "I still do. It's like this desperation inside me, crying out for someone to care." She hiccupped a laugh. "I know that sounds stupid."

"No." Dolores's voice was so firm, Rosalinda met her gaze. Moisture glittered in Dolores's dark eyes, but her gaze didn't waver. "No, it doesn't sound stupid. I did almost the same thing. I was so scared. I didn't know what I would do. How I would care for my niños. If not for Gabrio and Yoana, I would have done the same as you."

Dolores spoke the truth. Rosalinda could see that. "How did you find your place here?"

"Yoana helped me so much. I know we used to think she was stupid and haughty in the bandolero camp, but she is very kind and thoughtful. So smart." Dolores sighed and shook her head.

"She taught me about the Bible. That God loves me. Me. Dolores. He loves me so much he sent his Son, Jesus, to pay the price of death for me." A look of wonder lit Dolores's plain features, making her face shine with beauty. Rosalinda marveled at the difference.

"As she taught me, I wanted to know about this Savior she loved. Rosalinda, He loves you just as much as He loves me and everyone else. When I gave Him my life, I had this peace I can't even describe. He changed me. He brought me a gift I never thought to have. He gave me Roberto, who loves me and treats me like I am his greatest treasure." The tears on her friend's cheeks were ones of happiness now. She glowed as if she had a light shining from the inside out. Rosalinda could only stare at her.

"I am going to pray that you can find the peace I have with the Savior and that God will send a man who will love you like you deserve." Dolores squeezed Rosalinda's hands so hard they ached.

"I don't deserve any man's love." Sadness seeped through her. "I have done so much wrong. There is no way God could ever forgive me. I am not a good person like you, Dolores."

"But I am not good. I am quiet, but I am not righteous." Dolores placed her palms flat on the table. "You don't know the horrible thoughts I used to have. Thoughts about what I wanted to do to that monster who made me act like I wanted him. He treated me like a possession. I hated him. Hated them all." She drew in a deep breath and let it out slowly. "Just because I wasn't as vocal as you doesn't make me a sweet person.

"I wanted Lorenzo to die. I watched that hanging and wished I could look him in the face when that rope tightened around his neck. I remembered every hurt he'd ever done to me and to my children and wanted him to die." She shuddered. Covered her face with her hands.

Rosalinda couldn't speak. Dolores always seemed so easygoing. Amenable. Willing to do whatever anyone asked of her. A tiny seedling of hope, deep inside Rosalinda, gained strength. Maybe there *was* some chance for her. Maybe God would be willing to reach out to her also. Maybe He could love her enough to show her how to get away from what Carlos wanted from her and to rescue her daughters.

She got up and crossed to the window. The afternoon waned, but the men would still work for a couple of hours. Time enough for her to get the advice she needed. Or maybe to just unburden herself and see what happened. Maybe talking about her worries would be the impetus to finding a solution.

The children raced across the yard, galloping like wild horses, one of their favorite games in the mountains. Even Luis tried his best to keep up, his short legs churning as fast as he could make them go. Teo and Maria sat near the barn. The other children must belong to the familias of the rancho.

"They are safe."

Rosalinda startled. Dolores stood beside her gazing out the window. She hadn't heard her get up from the table.

"I don't know that they are." She saw the confusion in Delores' eyes. "Safe. I don't know that my children, my daughters, are safe." She proceeded to tell Dolores about the trip here. About Carlos and his threats and demands. About how much she wanted to be away from that life, but how she needed to protect her daughters from falling prey to men like Carlos.

Dolores pressed her palm to her chest. "Rosalinda, you must go to Don Santiago and Don Armenta and tell them. At least tell Lucio or Gabrio. They will help you."

"I can't. And you can't tell either. You *promised.*" Chills raced down Rosalinda's spine as she realized Carlos had come outside the barn to stand close to Maria.

And his gaze was riveted on Dolores's house, where Rosalinda stood at the window.

THE SLIGHT HUNCH in Roberto's shoulders and his nervous folding of the brim of his sombrero told of his discomfort imparting his news to the dons. Lucio understood the importance of tidings of impending conflict, but he chaffed at the delay in getting his father alone. What he wanted would have to wait until this discussion could be tabled.

"Thank you, Roberto. I appreciate your report." Don Santiago walked the vaquero to the door and ushered him out. The man's footsteps quick-timed down the hall to the entryway. Don Santiago shut the door behind him and faced the room.

"What do you think this means for us?" he asked Don Armenta as he gestured at the chairs facing the fireplace.

Gabrio and Lucio pulled two more chairs close, and they sat in a semicircle facing each other.

"I would say talk of war is premature, but we have a history of such conflicts." Lucio's father rubbed his chin, staring at the ashes in the fireplace.

"Not to mention we are a vast country and difficult to manage." Don Santiago tapped his fingertips on the arm of his chair. "If so many familias have moved into our country, the people from *Los Estados Unidos* intend to take over Tejas. I don't know that Santa Ana will be able to stop them. But he will try. Of that, I am sure."

They all brooded for long minutes contemplating the ramifications of the constant expansion west by the United States of America. What did this mean for them? Lucio knew it couldn't be good. Tejas might be many miles away and closer to the United States of America. That made Tejas appealing to them. But, Alta California, also part of Mexico, could be reached by ship and had so much to offer. What if the United States set their sights here? How could Mexico protect this part of their country when they were so isolated?

"I don't see that we can do anything by worrying." Gabrio stood and stretched. "I have chores to oversee. I will leave you two to discuss this." He looked at Lucio and nodded toward the door. "Want to help?"

Lucio studied his father. Don Armenta's unfocused gaze showed him lost in thought. This would not be the time to talk with his father about his marriage. No matter how urgent the issue pressed on Lucio, he would have to wait.

They stepped out into the late afternoon sun. After the dark thoughts of impending conflict, Lucio startled at the light and beauty outside. He stopped beside Gabrio. Had his friend had a similar reaction?

"Our fathers remember the war and fighting much better than we do." Gabrio leaned down to pat one of the dogs that sidled up to him. "I have heard my father worry about the difficulty of holding onto all this territory and how Mexico is too young a country to be expected to defend all its land."

The dog jumped up to put his front paws on Lucio's leg. He rubbed the pup's ears as the dog's tail wagged so fast its body vibrated. "I agree with you. There is nothing that worry or discussion will accomplish. We have to pray and leave this in God's hands."

"In the meantime, we have other matters to see to." Gabrio nodded toward the barn. The children were playing some game, squealing and running around. Lucio didn't recognize most of them, but spotted Isabel and Luis among them. He couldn't see Maria or Teo, but then noticed them seated with their backs against the barn, heads bent close together.

"Do you think Teo and Maria are plotting to take over the world?" Lucio grinned.

"That is possible, knowing Teo." Gabrio chuckled. "But that isn't the matter that concerns me at the moment. Look to their left."

Lucio glanced that direction. Carlos rested his shoulder against the barn, standing not ten feet from the children. He wasn't watching them, but had his gaze focused on one of the casitas that housed the married workers. His intense gaze didn't waver.

"Who lives in that casita?" Dread wormed into Lucio's chest.

"That is the house prepared for Roberto and Dolores. They will be there tonight for the first time as husband and wife." Gabrio stepped back into the shade of the house. "Let's watch and see what is so fascinating to Carlos."

Lucio joined his amigo and waited. Why would the man be watching Dolores's house? Roberto would be working right now. Dolores would be getting their home ready.

The door of the casita flew open. Rosalinda stormed out, her arms rigid at her sides, hands fisted. She stalked toward Carlos. He straightened, and his face split in a grin as if he knew what she would say before she even reached him.

"I think that's our cue to head for the barn." Gabrio's even tone calmed the anger simmering in Lucio's veins. He took a deep breath, praying for wisdom in dealing with this situation. He wanted to storm over and demand to know what hold that miscreant had over Rosalinda. He wanted to drag her away and marry her so no other man would ever look at her that way again. Instead, he matched Gabrio's slow saunter as if nothing untoward was happening in front of their eyes.

They approached from the side. The children had moved their game toward the corrals. Teo and Maria looked up at their approach, but Gabrio motioned them to be quiet. Lucio couldn't take his focus from Rosalinda long enough to do anything. So far, he didn't believe Carlos or Rosalinda had noticed their approach.

Gabrio stopped beside Teo and squatted down. Lucio followed suit. From here they would be able to hear most any exchange between Carlos and Rosalinda. Eavesdropping shouldn't be done, but since Rosalinda wouldn't talk to him, this seemed the only way he could help.

"What are you doing here?" Rosalinda's fists clenched and unclenched as she faced off against the swarthy vaquero. "You stay away from my niños."

"I'm not bothering your niños." Carlos's lips twisted. "Have I touched any of them?"

Rosalinda's eyes narrowed. Her chin jutted forward. She reminded Lucio of a mother bear ready to fight for her young. Had Carlos threatened the little ones to get Rosalinda to do what he wanted?

"Have you given my offer some thought?" Carlos asked.

"I want you to leave my niños alone and leave me alone." Rosalinda said something else, but the words were lost as the laughing horde of children chased each other back in their direction. Lucio strained to hear, to make out the words by watching Rosalinda's lips. But he was at the wrong angle and couldn't see.

He didn't know what she said, but Carlos straightened. His attitude changed. His eyes narrowed. The superior grin faded. Anger darkened his face to the point of giving him a terrifying visage. Rosalinda didn't step back, but she should. The hombre could be dangerous.

Carlos leaned forward, his expression intense. The children raced by, their laughter fading as they ran toward the hacienda.

"...what I want, or you know the consequences."

Lucio caught the last of Carlos's words. He'd heard enough. He and Gabrio stood at the same time.

Carlos must have noticed their movement from the corner of his eye. He flicked a glance toward them. His whole demeanor changed. If Lucio hadn't been watching, he would have thought the man was just flirting with a woman he wanted to impress. Once again, Carlos gave the impression—to those who didn't know him—of an easy-going hombre fascinated with a beautiful woman.

Rosalinda opened her mouth to reply, but Carlos's glance flicked toward Gabrio and Lucio. Rosalinda followed his glance and noted them standing beside Teo and Maria. The children were huddled together, wide-eyed. Maria had paled.

"Do you need help?" Lucio was beside Rosalinda in a few strides. He glared at Carlos.

The man grinned back as if he'd done nothing. "We were just having a friendly conversation."

"The conversation didn't look so friendly to me." Lucio turned to Rosalinda. "Is he bothering you? Or bothering your niños?"

Indecision flitted across Rosalinda's face. For a moment, Lucio thought she might divulge the truth about what was going on. Then her expression shuttered, and he knew.

She wouldn't tell him a thing.

Maybe if he got her away from Carlos. But even then he didn't know if she would talk.

He glanced down as something tugged his pant leg. Teo gazed up at him, his mouth set in a firm line, his eyes begging for attention.

CHAPTER TWENTY-THREE

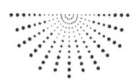

SHE STARED into the warm brown of Lucio's eyes. She could see him begging her to confess what Carlos wanted of her. To admit she wasn't a fit mother. To admit to all her failures. To admit she loved him.

Maybe that wasn't what he expected, but that was what would happen if she opened up to him. He would confront Carlos, and Carlos would tell him all about her early stay at the Armenta rancho. The men she flirted with who still expected the same treatment, even though she hadn't acted that way in weeks. The way she'd shamed herself and her children. Behaving the only way she knew to get what she needed or wanted.

"We were just talking." She took a step back. Something shadowed Lucio's handsome features. Confusion? Hurt? His brows drew together as he studied her. He opened his mouth. Closed it. Seemed to want to say something but looked away instead.

An ache blossomed in her chest. She had to get away. Had to make sure her children would be safe from men like Carlos. How could she do that? Would Yoana take them? Would Dolores? Leya? Who would want to take on three children?

She whirled around before the men could see the tears

clouding her vision. She hurried toward the hacienda, but instead of going inside, she went around back. A flower garden stretched out toward the hill behind the hacienda. She trod down one of the paths, rushing to get away from her past.

In a secluded alcove surrounded by rose bushes and vines, she sank down onto a small bench. Hidden from prying eyes, she leaned forward, elbows on knees and covered her face with her hands. What a mess. What choice did she have but to go back to the only life she'd known? She hated the thought, but what else could she do?

The last thing she wanted was to put her niños in danger of living the life she'd lived. The thought of her precious daughters, so innocent in their youth, learning what she'd learned at a young age, pained her beyond what she could endure. She groaned as she leaned over, clasping her arms across her aching middle.

"God, if You are really there. If You listen to women like Rahab, would You hear me? I don't know what to do. I don't even know if You want me. Why You would want me." Tears burned a trail down her cheeks. "Please, God, please take me. No one else wants me for myself. You are my only hope."

She bowed until her forehead touched her knees. Pressing the heels of her palms against her eyes, she tried to stop the burning tears, to no avail. She wept. For the life she could have had. For the pain of being sold by her mother. For the choices forced on her. For the impending decision facing her. For her inability to change the future.

When her weeping slowed, she realized peace had settled over her. Nothing had changed, but for some reason, her fear was gone. Her worries had faded. She had a sense of rightness. That all would turn out for the best, even though she didn't see how that could happen.

The bushes rustled. She wiped her cheeks on her skirt and straightened.

"I thought I saw you go in here." Carlos faced her, arms folded across his chest, legs apart. His sombrero shadowed his face, but she could see the gleam of his teeth and sense his exultation. "Tomorrow night. The cabin at the far end of the field. The one that looks abandoned. Be there after everyone is in bed. We'll be waiting."

He swiveled and stalked away, not even waiting for her response. She sat frozen. Her fear rose again. Had God even heard her? Had she been mistaken that He might care about her? He'd cared about Rahab. Why not her?

Dusk set the sky ablaze in color as she made her way toward the back door of the hacienda. Her steps dragged. Her body seemed so heavy, as if she slogged through deep water.

The aromas from the kitchen that should have had her empty stomach begging for food made her nauseous. Checking on her niños, she made an excuse about a headache and headed for her room to lie down. Leya's brows knit as she swept her mantilla back from her face to study Rosalinda, but she didn't stop her from leaving.

The quiet of her room should have been soothing but wasn't. Outside, she heard doves cooing, the distant howl of a coyote, and the bark of one of the dogs. Every sound grated like rough cloth against the washboard of her nerves.

"Mama." The door crashed open. Maria and Isabel rushed into the room. Rosalinda sat up on the bed where she'd been staring at the ceiling.

"Mama, Yoana is going to tell us another story. Hurry." Maria grabbed her hand and tugged. Isabel jumped up and down, clapping her hands. She wanted to tell her daughters she didn't want another story about a God who didn't care about her, but she knew her time with her niños was too short to waste. She dragged after them down the hall to Yoana's sitting room.

Yoana and Leya were already seated. Leya held Luis on her lap, his head lolling against her chest. His eyes drooped, showing how worn out he was from the constant running this afternoon.

"She's here." Maria led Rosalinda to a chair, and then she and Isabel sank to the floor in front of Yoana. "What are you telling us tonight?"

"Let's see." Yoana's fingers brushed against the leather cover of the book on her lap. "Is there a story you would like to hear?"

"I want to hear about Rahab's wedding." Maria clapped her hands. Isabel followed suit. Rosalinda didn't want to hear about the harlot's marriage. Why did God love this woman so much but not her?

"That would be a good story." Yoana nodded. "But first you have to hear what happened before Rahab could get married. Would you like to hear about the Battle of Jericho? That is the town where Rahab lived."

"A battle?" Maria frowned. "I don't want to hear about a bunch of guns shooting."

Yoana shook her head. "The Israelites didn't have guns, remember? And, they didn't even have to fight to win this battle."

"No fighting?"

Yoana went on to tell the story of the Israelites and how Joshua listened to God before they started their assault on the walled city of Jericho. Rosalinda couldn't help but be fascinated that the Israelite army would march around the city every day without saying anything. Had the inhabitants of Jericho taunted them as they marched?

"Then on the last day they did something different." Yoana leaned over and brushed a lock of hair back from Isabel's forehead.

"What did they do?" Maria folded her hands under chin, eyes alight.

"They marched around the city again, the priests blew their trumpets, and the Israelites shouted. One loud cry." Yoana waited, smiling down at the girls.

"That's all?" Maria tilted her head to the side. "How did they win the battle then?"

"Well, when they shouted, those thick walls surrounding the city fell down!"

Maria gasped. Isabel glanced at her sister and gave an exaggerated gasp too. Rosalinda almost smiled at their antics as she listened to Yoana continue telling how God knocked down the walls and defeated the city for the Israelites. Her daughters *ooh*ed and *aah*ed as they listened.

"*Now* did Rabab get married?" Maria bounced as she sat on her knees in front of Yoana.

"Ra*hab*." Yoana enunciated the name. "Here's something for you to think about. Rahab gave her life to God and helped the Israelites. God promised to protect her and her family. Then the Israelites came and marched around her city preparing for battle. Rahab's house was part of the wall, as were many of the homes. Rahab might have thought God abandoned her as her home shook from the footsteps of the Israelites. All the people she knew feared the Israelites and their God, yet they refused to change.

"She had to listen to all of them die when the walls fell down. Her house probably shook, but she had to trust that God would still save her when everyone else she knew didn't live. That kind of faith is hard to have." Yoana slid off her chair to face Maria and Isabel.

"There are times when God says He will be there for you, but you can't see that He is. You might think He's abandoned you, but He hasn't. Can you remember that?" She hugged the girls, and they hugged her back.

Rosalinda sat immobile as she watched. Had God wanted her to hear this story? Was He saying that like Rahab she needed to have faith that He would work even when she couldn't understand His ways? Was He at work on her behalf in some mysterious way she couldn't see?

HIS BOOT HEELS clicked out his impatience on the hard wood

floors as Lucio strode through the hacienda. He paid little attention to the ornate furnishings in the drawing room or the china set adorned with the Santiago S symbol and the flourishes of gold. He had to find Rosalinda and make sure she was all right before he left the rancho with his father, Don Santiago, and Gabrio.

He had no time to talk with Teo to find out what the boy wanted. Instead, he and Gabrio had been hailed by their fathers as Rosalinda fled from them. Their fathers insisted on getting ready to go to a nearby rancho to impart the news from Tejas. Lucio wanted to reiterate that Texas was far enough away. They could wait until tomorrow to share the word they received from Roberto. They shouldn't be riding at night. No one listened to him, not even Gabrio.

He heard Yoana talking in her sitting room. As he approached the doorway, he could see her kneeling in front of Maria and Isabel, talking to them. A step farther and he could see Rosalinda. She sat in a chair, hands folded in her lap. With her hair clasped at her neck, her high cheekbones were emphasized. Her hazel eyes, darker tonight, were wide as she listened to Yoana. Some strands of her hair had come loose and curved around her jaw, ending in a long wave almost to her waist.

His mouth went dry.

Maybe it *was* best for him to leave. She would be safe here. Ramón would watch over the familia. Would Manuel and Alberto? The men knew to watch out for Carlos and to try to find out what he'd been up to. If anyone could find out, Ramón could. He had a way of hearing things that Lucio would never be privy to.

Although everything in him longed to call Rosalinda away to tell her good-bye, he slipped back down the hallway without any of the women seeing him. Before he left the house, he closed his eyes and said a quick prayer that God would watch over all those dear to him. Rosalinda was in the forefront of his thoughts.

God would understand.

He hoped he would get the chance to talk with his father. The ride wasn't long but would take a couple of hours. Perhaps longer, since they would be traveling after sunset.

"Ramón." Lucio called his friend over before he mounted and gave him instructions. Ramón's mouth set in a grim line as he learned about the latest interaction between Rosalinda and Carlos.

"I'll keep an eye on him. Don't worry about anything." Ramón waved as they rode from the yard. Lucio wanted to have peace about this trip, but a niggling worry at the back of his mind kept him from relaxing and enjoying the ride.

They were over halfway to the Dominguez rancho when his father's stallion shied at something, stumbled to his knees, and threw Don Armenta. In the moonlight, Lucio saw his father's leg connect with a boulder and could almost hear the snap of bone. By the time he swung off his horse and reached his father, pain was etched on the older man's face, although he made no sounds of distress.

Gabrio knelt beside him and ran his hands down Don Armenta's leg. "I think it's broken, but the bone isn't protruding. We are closer to the Dominguez rancho. My father and I will ride ahead and bring a wagon back. Your father can't ride this way."

"My horse." Don Armenta started to lift up, looking to the side for his stallion.

"My father checked him over. He has a slight limp, but I believe he is sound." Gabrio nodded to Lucio and went to check on the black.

Don Santiago and Gabrio led the horse away, promising to bring help as fast as possible. Lucio sat with his father under the pale moonlight. Was it possible...?

Had God orchestrated this opportunity to give him the time needed to talk about his parents?

Now that the moment was here, he had no idea what to say or how to start.

He took off his poncho and folded it to put under his father's head. Gabrio left his as a blanket to keep Don Armenta warm in the chill of the desert night.

"I can see you have feelings for her."

His father's words startled him. "For whom?" He regretted the words the moment he spoke. For too many years he'd pretended ignorance with his father.

The don's lips quirked. "For Rosalinda."

Lucio sighed. Knew he had to admit the truth. Hated what was to come. His father would surely object and have very valid reasons why Lucio should send her away.

"I am coming to love her. She is a strong woman and learning to be a good mother. She's endured a life of hardship many women would never survive." He clamped his lips together to stop the tide gushing from his mouth.

"She is a fine woman. I didn't think so at first, but I've watched her. She needs a chance to show who she can be." His father's tone was thoughtful, but Lucio detected an underlying current of doubt.

"She is at a crossroads in her life, Lucio. She needs direction to choose the right course. If she chooses wrong, her whole life will be ruined. As well as that of her niños. You need to help her."

Too stunned to speak, Lucio stared at the man who had for years been so strict and difficult but now seemed so different. What brought on the change? Maybe something that happened with Yoana. Maybe God had worked a miracle.

"Padre." Lucio cleared his throat, unused to addressing the don in such an intimate manner.

"Augustín told me he mentioned my courtship of your mother." Don Armenta shifted and groaned. "You think I don't approve of Rosalinda, and there was a time I wouldn't have. But Augustín talked to me. Reminded me of my past, of my story with Josefa, your mother."

"What story?" Lucio settled against the boulder his father had hit when he broke his leg. His heart pounded as he waited to find out this secret past.

"Your mother came from a very poor family. I came from a very wealthy one." Don Armenta shifted. He winced and sucked in a breath as his leg moved.

Lucio waited for him to continue.

"Augustín and I were best friends. He was betrothed to Juana, and I was betrothed to her sister. Two weeks before Augustín and Juana were to wed, we both received paperwork to come to the Americas and claim our land. We planned a double wedding, but Juana's sister fell ill. She'd always been sickly. Weak."

In the distance a coyote yipped. Another coyote joined the plaintive chorus.

"I have to say I didn't much care for Juana's sister. I knew her, but she was selfish and cared for no one else. I planned to be obedient to my father and marry her anyway, but I was secretly glad when she became ill. Part of me hoped I would not have to marry her. I'm sorry for that, because she died of the illness the day after Augustín's wedding."

Yes, but what about his mother? But Lucio knew he couldn't hurry the story.

"The night before his wedding, some of our friends and I treated Augustín to a night out partying. The place we went to provided women for us." His father cleared his throat, a pained look on his face. "Your mother was one of those women."

Lucio stared. His *mother?* A woman like Rosalinda?

"Her family had fallen on hard times. She had to provide for her younger siblings, and finding legitimate employment was nearly impossible for young women. Please do not think ill of her." His father's eyes pleaded for understanding.

"I know you may find this impossible to understand, but I fell in love with your mother that night. I stole her away. Paid for her to be mine. Convinced her to marry me even though my friends advised against it. I hid our marriage from my parents until the day our ship left port for the Americas. My father was furious when he found out, but the distance kept his anger at bay."

"My mother..." He'd had no idea. None at all.

"Your mother lived a very similar life to Rosalinda's. She was forced to live that way to protect her familia."

Lucio leaped to his feet. "No."

CHAPTER TWENTY-FOUR

Lucio strode down the road away from his father. He shouldn't. He should be there in case Don Armenta needed him. But he had to have a few minutes to process what his father revealed to him.

His brothers didn't know about their mother's past. They couldn't. Their father didn't say—or even hint—about any indiscretions on her part to anyone. If Gabrio knew, would he have said something?

Lucio shook his head. His mother. His sweet, fun, ready-to-laugh mother. An impulsive beauty, much like his sister. When Mama died, they all lost something so precious they floundered for years trying to find a way to live without her. How could she have lived such a life before she married his father?

Guilt burned through him. He knew his mother's character. She'd loved her familia as much as humanly possible. She'd given her life to save Yoana. How could he doubt her? If she lived such a life, she'd had a good reason.

What did he know about a poor family and the trials they faced? What would he do if his nieces and nephews didn't have enough food to eat? Would he become a bandolero to steal sustenance for his loved ones? From what his Father had said, his mother had no other choice.

And Lucio...what right did he have to sit in judgment on those who had less than he did?

No right.

Still, the thought hurt. The thought of his mother being degraded. The thought of Rosalinda being forced into such a life. The horror brought tears to his eyes. Did God weep over all the injustice in the world too? Did His heart ache even more than Lucio's did at that moment?

Yes. He imagined God wept over His people all the time.

"God, I'm sorry for being so self-righteous. Please help me understand what you want me to do. You know the feelings I have for Rosalinda. Show me what to do, Lord. Show me." He bowed his head and wept. Tears of sorrow and anger for the hurt done to his mother. For the hurt done to Rosalinda. For the sins that remained so prevalent in this world.

His emotions spent, he strode back up the road toward his father. When he knelt beside him, Don Armenta's breathing was even. He slept, a low moan escaping with every few breaths. Lucio placed his hand on his father's arm and prayed. Prayed he would recover and have the opportunity to reconcile with his children.

That they all would learn what a giving, loving man he'd been to their mother.

The moon had risen to bathe the hills in shadowed light when Lucio heard the creak of a wagon and the clop of horse hooves. He lifted to his feet, his muscles protesting from sitting so long on the hard ground.

"Whoa." A man Lucio didn't know pulled the team to a halt. Gabrio jumped from the seat and strode toward Lucio and his father.

"How is he?" Gabrio knelt down much as Lucio had earlier.

"He's been sleeping, but he's in pain. Thank you for bringing the wagon." Lucio dropped down beside Gabrio. "Do you think we could take him back to your hacienda? I know the trip is farther, but I believe he will be more comfortable there."

"My father thought so too. He is talking with Don Dominguez, and then they will catch up to us. They will keep your father's stallion long enough to make sure his leg isn't injured and then bring him back to our hacienda." Gabrio stood, as did Lucio.

"We have padding and blankets in the back of the wagon to make your father comfortable. I'll have Tito bring the wagon closer, and we can lift him in as gently as possible." Gabrio motioned to the man on the wagon seat.

They took their time, but even though they were careful, Don Armenta still cried out as they lifted him. He passed out before they got him in the wagon, which was for the best. Once they had him settled, Lucio sat down beside him.

"I'll ride back here. We can tie my horse to the back of the wagon, or you can ride him, Gabrio." Lucio pushed more of the padding under his father's head to keep him from hitting against the boards.

"I'll take your mount and ride back to the hacienda. I can let the women know what happened so they are ready when your father arrives." Gabrio swung astride the dun and rode ahead.

Although Tito drove with care, the wagon jounced in some of the ruts of the road. Don Armenta didn't cry out again, but he groaned from time to time as he roused.

Several hours passed before they pulled the wagon into the yard beside the Santiago hacienda. Lamps blazed. Exhaustion pulled at Lucio, but he forced himself to stay alert and climbed down. When they'd put his father in the wagon, they situated blankets underneath him so they could use them to carry him into the house. He and Gabrio hoped that would keep the jarring to a minimum.

The door flew open. Yoana raced outside, followed by Leya. Lucio hid his surprise. Yoana had yet to speak to their father, despite being presented with plenty of opportunities. Perhaps this accident would bring the two of them together in a way nothing else could have done.

She skidded to a halt at the back of the wagon, her hand clasping the sideboard, her face the color of sand in the moonlight. "Is he...?" She faced Lucio, her eyes luminous, mouth curved down.

"He's been in and out of consciousness. We hit a rock a few minutes ago, and that hurt him. I think we should move him before he comes around. Do you have his room ready?" Lucio gave his sister a quick hug.

"We're ready. One of the women and her husband, who both work here, are good at setting bones, and she is a *curandera*. I had them come over to be ready when he arrived." Yoana stepped back. Gabrio came up behind her and enfolded her in his arms. She pressed against him for a moment, then stepped away so he could help with Don Armenta.

Lucio and Gabrio discussed strategy, then beckoned two more men forward to help with the task. Having the blankets in place worked. They kept them as tight as possible to keep the jostling to a minimum. When they had the don ensconced in his room, the couple Yoana spoke of were ready to check him.

His father's skin had turned sallow, his cheeks sunken. Lucio couldn't ever remember him looking so frail. He'd never thought of his father as old because he'd always been so strong and rarely ill or injured. Now he realized how much he'd taken for granted.

The woman approached, her eyes lowered, her manner deferential. Lucio thought she must be used to dealing only with the injuries or sicknesses of the workers, not of the familia of the hacienda or their friends. He noted her nervousness, but before he could think of how to put her at ease, Yoana took the woman's hands in hers and held them tightly. She leaned close, her smile tenuous yet genuine.

"¿Cómo está?"

The woman's shoulders lifted as she stood upright, more

confidant. "His leg is broken, but the break is clean. We believe if we set the bone and keep him from walking, he will heal. There is no break of the skin where infection could set in." She paused and glanced back at her husband, who was making Don Armenta comfortable and preparing the leg for splints.

"We will need to give him a few days in bed and then get him up. Sometimes when people stay in bed too long, they get an infection of the lungs that is more dangerous than the broken bone. I will burn herbs to help."

"We'll see that he gets up then." Lucio made a mental note to be there and help his father as much as possible, even if this meant delaying their return home. He could always send Ramón back to take word to Emiliano.

"Thank you." Yoana released the woman's hands, and she returned to help her husband.

Gabrio ushered them out so they could talk without disturbing Don Armenta if he awoke. Lucio walked in a daze. Should he share what his father told him about their mother with Yoana? Would she want to know? Would any of his siblings believe him if their father died? It would be only his word.

And what did it mean that his father divulged this information now? Did he approve of Lucio pursuing Rosalinda, or did he only speak from the stress of the moment?

So many questions…

And so few answers.

"Is there something I can do to help?" Rosalinda stopped beside Leya in the hallway outside the room where Don Armenta rested. Leya held a steaming cup of chocolate. Rosalinda breathed in the mix of cinnamon and chocolate and almost snatched the cup from Leya's hands.

Her quaking hands.

The surface of the liquid rippled like a lake when there were earth tremors. Not sloshing from the cup, but with plenty of circular waves.

"¿Está bien?" She put her hand on the older woman's shoulder and could feel quivering and tension in Leya's frame. "What is wrong? Has he taken a turn for the worse?" Rosalinda hadn't heard anything since getting up this morning. Most of the household had been awake in the night after the news about Don Armenta's injury. Only her children—her very energetic children—slept the night through.

The stress of the past weeks and her restlessness at night weighed on her. She wanted to escape this conflict and sleep for a week. Oh, to have someone trustworthy to talk to, other than Dolores. Someone who would understand both sides of the issue.

Rahab, would you have understood?

"Está bien." Leya exhaled a shaky breath. "I know Don Armenta loves his chocolate, so I brought him some. But now I'm not sure I should go in alone. I don't know if anyone is sitting with him." She bit her lower lip and stopped talking. Leya didn't usually chatter on like this, another indication of her nervousness.

Rosalinda didn't fully understand why Leya would be nervous, but she had heard about Don Armenta's demeanor before she came to the Armenta hacienda. He'd been very difficult with both Yoana and Leya, and he was one of the reasons Leya wore a mantilla to hide her scar. He hadn't wanted others to see her and know about her shame. Rosalinda ached for what Leya had to endure, both during her abduction as a young woman and after her rescue. To have known a loving family and then to be shunned by them would have been devastating.

"Do you want me to go in with you? Dolores has my niños, so I have the time."

Leya's smile told her all she needed to know. "Thank you."

"Let me knock and see if Don Armenta is able to receive visitors." She stepped forward and rapped lightly on the door. Soft footfalls approached. The knob turned and the curandera peered out at them. The shadows under her eyes spoke of a long night.

Rosalinda glanced at Leya, but she didn't make a sound.

"Is Don Armenta awake? We brought him some hot chocolate and would like to sit with him." From the corner of her eye, Rosalinda saw Leya nod.

"He's been awake off and on." The woman swung the door wide for them to enter. "I will take a break and let you sit with him. I'll check back in. Be sure to let him sleep if he starts to drift off."

She left as soon as they were inside, closing the door softly behind her. The heavy aroma of fresh herbs filled the room. There were two chairs near the bed where Don Armenta rested. A small table was at the head of the bed beside him. The cup rattled in the saucer as Leya set it down.

Don Armenta's eyes were closed. His breathing was even and deep, so they sat quietly. Leya's head bent forward. She must be praying for her brother-in-law. Rosalinda studied his features. His complexion had a bit of sallowness, but for the pain he had to have experienced, and his age, he looked pretty good.

How handsome he must have been when he was younger. Rosalinda could see Lucio in the set of his father's chin and mouth. Did Lucio get his eyes and the color of his hair from his mother? Don Armenta's hair was streaked with gray, but the darker bits were not at all like Lucio's.

The don's eyes opened.

Rosalinda blinked. Stared down at him, then smiled. Had Leya noticed him waking up? "Good morning, Don Armenta. ¿Comó está?" Rosalinda hadn't meant to ask that. How would he be feeling? He'd be hurting, of course. But, being a man, he would never say that.

Leya's head snapped up when Rosalinda spoke. She reached for the still steaming cup of chocolate. "We brought you something warm." Her hands trembled the tiniest bit as she lifted the drink.

"I could smell the cinnamon and chocolate before I opened my eyes." He started to raise up, winced and relaxed back into the bedding.

"Let me get the extra pillows and put them behind your back so you can sit up to drink." Rosalinda stood and circled the bed where the extra items waited on a low table. She tried to be gentle as she eased him up and wedged the pillows behind him. He only groaned once, so she counted that a success, seeing as her healing skills were nonexistent.

As Rosalinda returned to her seat, Leya held out the chocolate to Don Armenta.

He started to take it, then dropped his hands to the covers and shook his head. "I'm afraid I'll spill all over Señora Santiago's bedding. Maybe later I'll be stronger." His face had paled.

"If you allow me, I will help you." Leya waited, statue still. At his nod, she moved to perch on the bed beside him. She lifted the cup to his lips, with the saucer beneath to catch any drips. His gaze stayed steady on her.

Could he see her eyes through the dark mantilla?

Rosalinda felt like an intruder in a tender moment, but she knew neither Don Armenta nor Leya intended their encounter to be intimate. Or was she wrong…?

Was there something between them? Something more than being in-laws? They *had* spent a good amount of time in close company on the trip here. Don Armenta had been very accommodating and entertaining, though Rosalinda hadn't seen him interact much with Leya.

He reached one hand up to steady Leya's, his fingers cupping around her hand. She stilled.

If only Rosalinda could see Leya's face. Her eyes. Then she would know how her friend felt about this familiarity.

Don Armenta finished his drink, then leaned back against the pillows. His hand dropped to his lap, and he smiled at Leya as she placed the cup on the table and moved back to her chair.

"Thank you. That was delicious. A perfect blend of chocolate and cinnamon. My Josefa used to make it just that way."

Leya waved her hand to the side. "It is a family recipe our mother learned from a woman brought over from the New World."

The silence in the room stretched out, so Rosalinda leaned forward. "Is there anything we can bring you? Something to read? Perhaps you would like to visit with one of the men. Don Santiago hasn't returned yet, but Lucio and Gabrio are here."

"I would most like to speak with Yoana." Don Armenta nodded at Rosalinda and then turned to Leya. "Do you think my daughter would be willing to talk? I have so much to say to her."

"I will see." Leya brushed at her jaw and revealed a glimpse of her smile. "You were not awake when they drove the wagon in last night, so you did not see how distraught Yoana was over your injury."

Hope lit his eyes. Don Armenta's features were even more handsome as he smiled. "She was distraught?"

"Yes. She cares for you very much. I will talk with her and see if she will come visit you."

Don Armenta's eyes drifted closed and open. He must still be so exhausted.

Rosalinda stood and rounded the bed a second time. "Let me help you lie back."

With careful movements, she extracted the extra pillows until he lay supine, his eyes closing. Rosalinda motioned with her head toward the door. Leya picked up the empty cup.

"Leya."

His voice, heavy with sleep, halted them both.

"Leya, don't forget to bring Yoana. And you." His arm lifted and dropped back down. "I need you here."

CHAPTER TWENTY-FIVE

WHEN THE DOOR closed behind Leya and Rosalinda, Francisco opened his eyes. His leg ached like he'd caught it in a bear trap and tried to gnaw it free. His jaw ached almost as much from gritting his back teeth to keep from showing his discomfort to the women.

The one positive so far from this injury had been Leya helping him with the chocolate. The clean fragrance of her as she leaned close made him want to cringe away because he knew he didn't smell very pleasant. He still wore his clothes from last night. Dirt. Sweat. Horse. They all combined for an unpleasant scent.

Her delicate hands and fingers as she cradled the cup, and the slight tremor in both, made him glad to wrap her hand in his to lend support. That was why he'd done it. Not because he craved an excuse to touch her. Skin soft as butterfly wings. He rubbed his fingertips together at the memory of the touch.

When she brushed her jaw, nudging aside the mantilla, he'd caught a glimpse of her smile. His heart leapt anew in his chest. He hadn't seen Leya's face in years, but he remembered what she looked like. So much like Josefa. In looks. Not in demeanor. Where Josefa was lightness and laughter, Leya was down to earth, practical. So opposite and so much alike. Kind. Thoughtful. Giving.

After all these years, it had finally happened. He could smile at the memory of Josefa. He missed her still. He always would. But since the trip out here, he'd realized it no longer carried the sharpness of devastating loss. And then there was Leya...

She stirred a different emotion. For so long he'd ignored or avoided her. Now he wanted to know her more. On the trip here, he'd enjoyed being close to her while conversing with Rosalinda.

How God had changed his heart would forever remain a mystery, but he thanked Him every day.

A soft knock sounded on the door. Had Leya found Yoana so quickly and convinced her to meet with him? His pulse picked up. "Please, God, help me to mend the hurts I've caused Yoana."

"Come in." He tried to project his voice enough to be heard through the door, but the person only tapped again.

"Come in." He panted with the effort. His leg throbbed at exertion no matter how trivial. The old anger gnawed at the edges of his nerves. Who would stand out there knocking, knowing he had no way to get to the door? Did they want him to fall and break something else just to be polite and open the door for them?

Another soft tap. He opened his mouth to bellow or, more likely, whisper louder, when the knob turned and a slit of light appeared. He lifted a little to stare. No one there. The door swung wider. His gaze dropped lower. Wide eyes stared at him. Two sets of wide eyes, one brown, one hazel.

Teo and Maria.

His frustration took wing. He smiled. Lifted his hand and gestured them inside. Maria scampered across the room, while Teo eased the door shut, then followed his friend to Francisco's bedside. They stood there side-by-side, staring at him.

"What are you two up to? Do your mothers know you are here?" He smiled, glad for the distraction while he waited for Yoana to come. Or not.

"I want to go riding, but you hurt your leg." Maria's green-brown gaze snared him with her longing and trust. Ah yes. He'd told her yesterday he would take her for another riding lesson soon.

"Lo siento." He opened his hand and almost couldn't speak when she placed her small one in it. Such trust. "I would love to take you riding. I will heal up as fast as I can, and we'll go. ¿Está bien?"

She nodded. Leaned close to place a feather-soft kiss on his cheek. Rubbed her mouth over his stubbled cheeks and giggled.

The ache in his heart rivaled that in his leg as memories surged of Yoana's tiny arms wrapped around his neck and her giggling after kissing his stubbled cheek at the end of a long day.

He cleared his throat. Teo hadn't laughed at all. He didn't know the boy as well as he knew Maria, but he had the sense Teo had something on his mind. He seemed so serious, and Francisco didn't recall him being that way before.

"Have you asked Lucio for a riding lesson?" He squeezed Maria's fingers. "Or maybe Ramón would be able to take you."

"They're too busy." Maria heaved an exaggerated sigh. "Do you think you could take us anyway? As soon as they bring your horse home?"

"You won't have to walk." Teo nodded. "Someone can carry you to the horse, and then you'll be riding."

How to explain the pain involved when riding with a broken leg? "We'll see what happens when my stallion is back. Have you heard when Don Santiago will be here?" He chafed at not having the counsel of his old friend before meeting with Yoana.

The door cracked open. Flew wide.

"What are you doing in here?" The curandera who'd tended him had returned. Her mouth pursed as she swept into the room. She shook her finger at Teo and Maria. "Don Armenta needs rest, not children bothering him. ¡*Fuera!*" She shooed them much as one would chickens in the garden. He almost laughed.

"Wait." Francisco smiled when the trio halted and turned to him. At last, his voice carried. "Teo, come here."

The boy trudged toward him, circling around the stout woman. Something bothered him, and Francisco needed to know what.

"What is wrong? Why did you come here today?"

"I wanted...." Teo glanced around at the woman, who stood hands on hips, glaring at him. "I need to talk to you about something I heard. One of the men talking."

"Teo, this isn't my rancho. You must talk to Gabrio or Don Santiago. They are in charge here."

"But this is one of the Armenta vaqueros, as well as some of the Santiago men." Teo's gaze pleaded with him.

Rustling sounded outside the door. The healer cleared her throat. "Señora Santiago. I am not sure how these niños got in here. I am getting them out." She pushed Maria toward the hall. Francisco caught a glimpse of Yoana waiting beside the door. Joy and hope vied within him. She had come. An answer to his fervent prayers.

"Señor. Don Armenta." Teo tugged at his sleeve. Disappointment saddened his gaze as if he knew they had no chance to talk now.

"Teo, please look for Lucio and Gabrio. Talk with them about what you heard if it's that important." He hated the dejection on the boy's face and the slump in his shoulders, but he couldn't miss this chance to be with Yoana. Mending their relationship had to be more important than listening to gossip from the workers.

"Teo." He waited until the boy turned and met his gaze. "If you can't find them, come back and talk with me. ¿Entiendes?"

Teo nodded and trudged from the room. The woman followed the children out. Yoana came in, closed the door and leaned against it, studying him as he lay in bed.

He hated weakness. Always had. Always would. Especially in front of someone who had good reason to despise him. Still, perhaps she needed to see him vulnerable before she would listen to him apologize.

He hid his surprise that she'd come on her own, not bringing Leya with her. Yet she had always been strong. She faced down a grizzly bear in the mountains to protect Teo and Maria. She wouldn't back down from him.

"Please, sit." He motioned to the chairs Leya and Rosalinda used earlier. Yoana stayed where she was a beat too long, showing her defiance. Head held high, she crossed the room and sank on to the chair.

"Thank you for coming." Francisco's mind went blank. He'd had a pretty speech prepared in case he ever got the chance to talk to her, but all those words fled. She sat straight, her hands folded in her lap. So proper. So beautiful.

So like her mother.

Please, God, give me the right words. Help her to hear what I have to say. He drew in a breath and forced his muscles to relax as the pain washed over him.

"Yoana." He swallowed hard. This might be his only chance to get this right. A long explanation or a simple one? He settled for simple.

"I'm sorry. Please forgive me." He bit the inside of his lip to keep from saying more. He wanted to pour out his heart to her, yet he didn't want to overwhelm her. There was nothing he could say that would make up for all he'd put her through. Nothing.

She stared at him. He couldn't see any softening in her expression. She clasped her fingers so hard her fingers were almost white. Her braid hung over her shoulder. Her features were like stone. He couldn't remember a time she'd been so expressionless.

Please, God. Please help.

He started to speak. Curled his hands into fists. Kept quiet.

After an eternity, he saw moisture welling up in her eyes. He longed to touch her. To somehow let her know how much he loved her. That he hadn't been so despicable because he didn't care, but because he cared too much.

"Why do you hate me so?" Her choked, hoarse voice pushed the words out with great effort. He almost blurted out that he didn't hate her, but he knew she would never believe him.

"May I tell you a story? A story about your mother and me? I told your brother part of our history, but you need to hear it. Maybe then you will understand." He raised his hand as fire flashed in her eyes and she opened her mouth to speak.

"I'm not trying to excuse the way I treated you. There is no excuse. I'm only saying you might find a way to understand my deplorable behavior." He paused. Saw her get hold of her emotions.

"Please, Yoana."

She nodded. A brief tilt of her head, as if agreeing with him about anything hurt her. He told her the same story he'd told Lucio the night before. The more he told, the more emotion filled her features. He understood. She struggled to understand how her mother could have lived the life of a harlot.

"I fell in love with your mother the first moment I saw her. I don't know why. There was just something. I can still see her in that room, her head thrown back, laughing with one of the other girls. I knew. I just knew she was special." Now it was his voice that was hoarse. He reached for the water cup on the table by his bed and took a sip. Yoana waited, still not speaking.

"I married your mother in secret. My parents did not approve. In fact, when my father found out, he threatened to kill her. He never wanted to see either of us again. The one thing your mother asked before we left for the Americas was to bring her younger sister. She knew Leya would be forced into the same life she'd been leading, and she couldn't bear that happening. We secreted her away and left with the Santiagos, who were also newly married."

Yoana's eyes widened in surprise, probably because he and

Josefa had never talked about why they brought Leya with them. They hadn't talked to their children about España at all.

"Josefa, your mother, was the light of my life. She taught me about laughter and love, two things that were absent in my family. We were very strict, my father authoritarian and harsh. I had never known familia could be loving until your mother."

"So you reverted back to being like your father after Mama's death?" Yoana didn't ask but made a statement of fact.

"Yes. When your mother died, I lost my reason for living, the light that kept me afloat." She started to speak, but he held up one hand to stop her. "I realize now how wrong I was. I had you and your brothers to live for, but at the time I couldn't see that. I saw only my grief, a living, voracious beast that took over my life. I was wrong to react that way, but it is what happened. And I know asking you to forgive me may be beyond what you can or will do, but I don't know what else to do." His throat tightened. He took another sip of water to ease the ache.

"Why are you asking now? And why should I believe you?" She swiped at her eyes. "Before I married Gabrio, you spoke to me. For the first time in years. I hoped you had changed. I wanted you to. But you didn't." She blinked rapidly and looked away.

"You're right." He rubbed his hand over his face. If only he could wipe away the past as easily as he brushed the moisture from his eyes. "As for why I'm asking now…" He cleared his throat. Faith was a private thing, but she needed to know. "A couple of months ago I was out riding. Alone. My horse fell, much as he did last night, and I was thrown."

Yoana whirled to face him, eyes wide. "Lucio didn't tell me about this."

"No one knew." He gave a wry smile. "Stubborn old men don't like to tell about their weak moments. I was knocked unconscious. Nothing broken, but I had a boulder of a lump on my head. I thought I might die. I…." He swallowed hard. The fear he'd felt that day had been overwhelming.

"I met Jesus that day. I'd always known about Him, but this time, I saw He was real." He slanted a glance at her. "Do you understand what I mean?"

She nodded.

"Since then, He's shown me the many attitudes I need to change and atonements I need to make." His gaze held hers. "You, most of all. Yoana, I don't want to lose you. Please forgive me." A wave of pain washed over him. Exhaustion crept up his limbs, making them too heavy to move. He sank back against the bed, fighting to stay awake, but knowing this was a losing battle.

Yoana stood. Said something. Walked to the door. She opened the door, and Teo waited there. She left.

Teo came to his bedside and whispered in his ear.

Francisco tried to focus but drifted to sleep with the sound of Teo's voice in his ear.

CHAPTER TWENTY-SIX

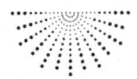

THE AFTERNOON WANED by the time Lucio woke. He hadn't gotten to sleep until late morning, but the few hours he did get were much needed. He sat up and rubbed his hands over his face. How was his father doing? "God, please use this to Your glory. Help my father to heal. Heal the rift between Yoana and our father."

He ran his fingers through his hair. He'd have to ask Leya or Yoana to give him a trim so he didn't look too shaggy. The son of a don had standards to keep. That had been drummed into him at an early age.

Standards...

His thoughts drifted to Rosalinda. To the story of his mother and her past. A little thrill raced through him that maybe his father would approve Lucio's attraction to Rosalinda.

Lucio looked out the window. Could he overcome societal expectations to make Rosalinda his wife? But even as he thought that, he realized he didn't care. Societal expectations! What did they matter? He wanted to marry her, no matter what.

His exhaustion fled.

He washed, shaved, dressed, and left his room, his movements urgent. The desire to see Rosalinda drove him. His pulse thrummed through him. His senses were on alert as he stepped out into the hallway. He heard chatter in the direction of the kitchen and headed that way.

Gabrio stood as Lucio entered the warmth of the kitchen. Gabrio had been seated in a corner near the doorway, a cloth draped over his shoulders, as Yoana trimmed his hair. Lucio halted. Had they heard his earlier thoughts?

"Your turn." Yoana motioned to the seat with her head as she shook the trimmings from the cloth. "We need to talk. Rosalinda can cut your hair."

He lost his train of thought. He'd meant to ask something. Something important. But the sight of Rosalinda, her hand on her hip, her lips tilted in a saucy smile, made his mind go blank. The thought of her hands touching him, even if only to trim his hair, sent him toward the chair without hesitation.

He dropped to the seat. Yoana pinned the cloth around his shoulders. She shooed everyone but Rosalinda and Gabrio from the kitchen with a promise to keep an eye on the food. Lucio and Gabrio snorted a laugh at the same time. Yoana glared at them.

Rosalinda fisted her hands on her hips and glared at Lucio from behind Yoana. His laughter died.

"Lo siento, mi hermana." He caught Yoana's hand and tugged her back to him. Gave her his best forgive-me eyes and waited.

She yanked her hand from his and cuffed him lightly on the side of his head. "I'll have Rosalinda here to help with the food. You won't starve to death, though you deserve to. Both of you." She turned her glare on Gabrio. He held up his hands, palms out. She stalked toward him, and he grabbed her and swung her around.

Yoana grinned and smacked Gabrio's shoulder. "Let me go, or I'll blame the burned meal on you." He kissed her first, a quick peck on the lips, and let her go.

Rosalinda moved behind Lucio. He tensed, anticipating her touch. Yoana pulled a chair up and sat facing Lucio, her expression as serious as he'd ever seen.

"I spoke with our father this morning." She glanced at Gabrio, who pulled a chair beside hers and sat down, taking her hand in his. Lucio didn't know what to say. Or to feel. Relief that they'd finally talked, yes. Trepidation over Yoana's expression? Absolutely. What did Don Armenta say to her?

"How is Father? I meant to ask." He should have asked first but hadn't been able to think straight. The source of his lack of focus ran her fingers through his hair. Good thing he'd already asked about their father, because once again his attention narrowed only to Rosalinda. And the incredible sensation of her touch.

"He is in pain, but too stubborn to say anything." Yoana frowned, silent, her gaze unfocused. She shivered. Honed in on Lucio again.

"That isn't why I wanted to talk to you. He told me about Mother."

Lucio had been leaning back, almost groaning as Rosalinda combed his hair. Yoana's statement wrenched him back to the present. He jolted forward. Rosalinda yanked his hair.

"Ouch." He rubbed his head as Rosalinda muttered behind him. Yoana's gaze didn't waver. What should he say? Her expression gave him no clues.

"He told me more than he told you, or that's what he said." She shared what their father said. Lucio's eyes widened. So that was why Leya came with his parents to the Americas. He hadn't ever considered why his tía had come over. Why had they never asked these questions? Probably because their mother died so young and their father turned into an irascible, unapproachable bear.

"He asked me to forgive him." For the first time, Yoana's lips trembled, and she pressed them into a line. Tears glittered in her eyes.

He couldn't imagine how hard that must have been for her.

Rosalinda gripped his shoulders and pulled him back against the chair. He tried to relax as he fumbled for words to comfort his sister. He had none.

The light tug on his scalp preceded the snip of scissors. The sweet scent of cinnamon wafted in the air. Had Rosalinda been helping with some baking or making hot chocolate? He loved the smell. Memories of helping his mother, of drinking cinnamon-laden cocoa with her and his siblings, took him away from the room. He had trouble picturing his mother at all, only a vague memory of the sound of her laughter, the brush of her lips on his cheek when she tucked him in at night. And light. She always brought light and joy.

He shook off the memories. Yoana needed him here and now, not in the past. And not entranced with Rosalinda, no matter how hard it was to concentrate with her touch on his hair.

He studied his sister. "What are you going to do?"

Yoana sighed. Glanced at Gabrio. Squeezed his hand. Met Lucio's gaze. "Forgive him. As a Christian, I have no other choice. I thought I had already done so until he showed up here. All the hurt and anger returned. I've been trying to figure out how to truly forgive once and for all. It isn't easy."

Gabrio tugged on her until she leaned against his chest. He kissed the top of her head, and Yoana closed her eyes. Longing, swift and sharp, sliced through Lucio. Rosalinda's hands stilled. Her fingers were twined in his hair. He couldn't breathe at the sensation. To draw her close and snuggle her against his chest... that would be heaven. But how would she react to affection that didn't come with the price of servitude? Or slavery.

Rosalinda untied the cloth from around his neck and swept it away from him without spilling any of the hair down his neck. He didn't want her to step away, but he had no reason to ask her to stay close. Other than wanting her there.

He scooted toward Yoana. He needed to finish with her. Then he could find Rosalinda and see if she would be willing to pursue a relationship with him. To marry him.

Pots rattled. Yoana sat up, turning to look toward the stove. "Thank you, Rosalinda. If I'd let the meal burn, I would be banished into the desert."

"I don't think so." Gabrio gave her a hug, stood, and put his chair back. "I'm going to see if my father has arrived. I thought I heard horses out by the barn." He raised his eyebrows at Lucio.

"I'll join you in a moment." Lucio stood and moved out of the way as Yoana began to sweep the floor.

Gabrio left, and Lucio took the broom from Yoana. She stared up at him, eyes wide.

"Maybe you should go with Gabrio." He waited a beat for her to understand. She glanced toward Rosalinda, who was stirring the contents of a pot, grinned, and nodded.

He set the broom against the wall. Wiped his palms on his pants. Walked up behind the woman he intended to marry and slipped his arms around her.

Rosalinda jumped. The spoon flew in the air and clattered to the ground. She whirled around. Face to face with him. Her hazel eyes went wide. The green, gold, and brown mix mesmerized him.

He gave her time. Time to understand his intent. Time to realize he wouldn't force anything. Time to know this would be something they both wanted.

She cupped his face with her hand.

He needed no more invitation.

THE TOUCH of his lips against hers spiraled warmth and sweetness through her. Rosalinda slipped her hand around the back of Lucio's neck, savoring the closeness as he drew her to him. After a moment he pulled back, his warm eyes studying her, something in those depths she'd never seen before.

Could it be...? Did he truly care for her? The woman who must betray him or risk her daughters?

Her limbs weakened as the truth struck her soul. She loved this man.

Love. She'd never thought she would ever meet a man worthy of her love, one she could care about. But Lucio had never pushed her. Never forced himself on her. Never taken her for granted. And through his kindness and patience...

He had won her heart.

"Rosalinda." He breathed her name, but no more. His lips came down on hers once more and stole her breath. If he continued kissing her, she would lose her courage to do what she had to do. She would be like her mother, sacrificing her daughters for her own wants and needs.

She pushed against him, her heart pounding, wanting to break. "Lucio. This isn't right." Her palm against his chest, she watched confusion, and then understanding, wash over him.

"What isn't right? Us? Together?" He brushed a lock of her hair behind her ear. She closed her eyes and savored his tenderness. Never had a man done this. How could she push him away?

"Rosalinda." He waited until she opened her eyes and met his gaze. "I love you."

His words sliced through her defenses. Words she'd heard many times but never believed. But from him, they were truth.

Painful truth.

"Lucio. You can't." She choked on the words. Swallowed hard. Ran her hand along his strong jaw one last time. "This won't work."

"Why?" He waited only a moment for an answer she couldn't give. "If you think your past is a stumbling block, it isn't. Rosalinda, I want to marry you."

He sank to one knee in front of her. She covered her mouth with her hands, unable to move or speak. He tugged one arm until he had her fingers wrapped in his. Kissed the back of her hand.

"Rosalinda, will you marry me? I love you and want to live the rest of my life with you at my side." The earnestness in his eyes nearly undid her. Oh, how she wanted the same. How she longed to throw caution aside and say "Yes." But she couldn't. For his sake. For her daughters' safety.

"I...." She pressed her lips together fighting back a myriad of emotions. A flood of longing and regret. "I can't marry you."

Hurt. Disbelief. His sorrow tore at her heart.

"I want to." She couldn't deny this one small concession. "I love you too, but I can't marry you." She yanked her hand from his. Before he could stand, she stepped to the side and fled the room. She heard him call after her, but she didn't stop. She passed Carmen at the back door, glad the woman would be checking the meal and feeding the family, because she couldn't face any of them again. Not with what she had to do.

They'd been so kind to her. Taught her so much. Showed her what love could be. Helped her meet Jesus, her Savior. Surrendering to Carlos felt like a betrayal of all the Armentas had done for her, but what else could she do? Her children were precious and worth more than her life.

Lucio might love her now, but what if they met someone from her past. How would he feel if a man commented on indiscretions when he saw her? Would Lucio be able to set aside her past for a new start? Would their friends and family be able to see her and not the degradation? Would they love her niños?

So many questions raced through her head. Nausea rolled in her stomach. She pressed her fist to her abdomen and bent over, focusing on drawing in one breath at a time. "God, what do I do? I've never loved a man before. Never even wanted a man." She shuddered. "But Lucio is different. He sees me. Wants to know me, who I am. What do I do?"

Tears burned her eyes and spilled down her cheeks. She couldn't think only of herself. She had her niños to consider. Lucio and his father spent time taking her children for rides, playing with them, or telling them stories. But did that mean they wanted to accept them as their own familia? She didn't know. How could an aristocratic familia put aside her past, despite what Yoana said their mother had done in her youth?

A confusion of thoughts chased through her mind.

Beyond the garden, in the direction of the stables, she heard a commotion. Men called out. Horses whinnied. What had happened? Were her niños involved? Dolores had promised to watch them, but she knew her little ones.

She wiped her damp cheeks, rose, and straightened her dress. Lifting onto her toes, she tried to peer past the vegetation without being seen, but the vines and plants were too thick. She stiffened her spine and walked along the winding path. She would have to face everyone sooner or later. Had anyone overheard Lucio's proposal? Had he told anyone? Most of her friends would think her stupid to turn down the son of a don, but she had no choice.

The stable yard was a hive of activity. Don Santiago had returned from the nearby rancho, and he must have brought half the household with him. Horses stamped and neighed. Men called out. Teo ran from the barn to take the reins of Don Santiago's mount.

Teo.

Without Maria.

She frowned. Teo and Maria were inseparable. She helped with his chores, and when he had free time, they played together or sat and talked. She stared at the open barn door, willing her daughter to make an appearance. Teo led the horse around the side of the barn to the corral.

Maria still hadn't come outside.

Rosalinda's heart thudded a heavy rhythm. Her chest tightened. She couldn't breathe. Isabel and Luis were not in sight either. She turned from the action in the stable yard and raced toward Dolores and Roberto's house.

Where were her children?

"Dolores!" She banged on the doorframe. The door stood open. She could hear Dolores's off-key singing in the back of the house. Maybe the niños were there with her.

"Dolores." She called out again and stepped inside. Her friend's singing stopped. She came from the bedroom, a rag in her hand.

"Dolores, where is Maria. Where are my niños?"

"Maria is with Teo. So is Isabel. Luis is down for a nap in the house with Leya watching him." Dolores wiped a drip of sweat from her brow. "The others are probably in the barn."

Her daughters!

She tried to tamp down her mounting panic. Of course, her daughters were waiting in the barn for Teo to get done with his chores. They hadn't come outside because there were so many men and so much confusion. She nodded at Dolores and rushed back outside, hurrying toward the stable.

She almost ran into Teo as he trotted around the far side of the barn. She grabbed his shoulders to steady them both. "Teo, where are my niñas? Are they here?"

His eyes flashed with something she couldn't read. He glanced at someone behind her. "They aren't with you?" He looked over his shoulder toward the house.

Could they have gone inside with Leya and Luis? No. As soon as the men rode into the yard, the pair would have been in the midst of the commotion.

She held tight to Teo. "When did you last see them?" Her stomach twisted. Fear burned up her throat.

"I saw them a little while ago when I had work to do. I haven't seen them since then." Teo pulled away. "You should look in the house."

The chaos had slowed somewhat. Rosalinda lifted her head, fighting the despair drifting though her. Lucio stood near Don Santiago and Gabrio, his gaze riveted on her. She expected hurt. Or anger. Rejection. Instead...

Love and longing reached out to her.
A movement behind Lucio caught her attention.
Carlos. Leaning against a fence post.
His gaze was also riveted on her.

CHAPTER TWENTY-SEVEN

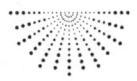

LUCIO DIDN'T HEAR what Don Santiago said next. Over near the corner of the stable he caught sight of Rosalinda, her hands cupping Teo's shoulders, her face a study in intensity. Even from this distance, he could see the tension in her stance, the fear on her face.

She glanced up. Saw him watching her. He'd been so hurt when she turned down his proposal and ran. But peace flooded his soul, as if God touched him and said, *"Wait."*

She must fear her past would come between them. Or that he didn't love her like she needed to be loved. That she would never be accepted for herself.

Her gaze tracked beyond him. Gabrio said something. Lucio ignored him. Rosalinda's beautiful features twisted—and Lucio started at her sudden rage. She stalked toward him, her hands fisted in her skirts.

No...not toward him. She looked past him as if he wasn't there anymore.

He swiveled. Carlos stood behind him, the picture of the relaxed vaquero. Lucio wanted to wipe the smirk from the hombre's face. What had he done this time to anger Rosalinda? Would the man never stop tormenting her?

Carlos's eyes roved over Rosalinda as she stalked toward him, and his grin widened to a leer. Lucio stepped around Gabrio, though his friend fell in beside him, and headed for the coming clash.

Rosalinda didn't even glance Lucio's way. The color in her cheeks had darkened her skin. Her chin jutted forward as she approached Carlos. No fear radiated from her, only determination and anger.

She was magnificent.

She stopped two feet from the vaquero. Hands fisted on her hips, she glared at him. "What have you done with my niñas? I want them back now."

Carlos laughed at her. She slapped him. In the blink of an eye, all humor left the man. He grabbed the front of Rosalinda's dress with one hand and yanked her to him. With his other hand he restrained her swinging fist. He leaned close and said something to her, and she kicked him. Hard.

Carlos grunted. Tossed Rosalinda away. Bent forward in obvious pain. Lucio caught Rosalinda and kept her from falling. She scrabbled to get her feet under her and pushed away from him. Mouth set in a thin line, she leaped back at Carlos.

Lucio snatched her around the waist. Gabrio grabbed her arm before she could swing her fist around to hit Carlos. Lucio and Gabrio grinned at each other. Rosalinda's fire reminded them of Yoana.

"Stop." Lucio turned Rosalinda to face him. Her hair had come undone. Strands fell across her face in wild disarray. Her eyes snapped. He wanted to drag her close and kiss her. If they had some privacy, he would do just that.

"Rosalinda." He kept his voice calm. "Stop. Talk to me."

He saw the moment her senses returned. Her tense muscles

relaxed. She blew a strand of hair away from her nose. Glared up at him, but without the venom she'd shown for Carlos.

"Release me." She put her palm against his chest. "Please."

"Tell me what is wrong. Why are you so upset?" He eased his hold but didn't release her.

"My niñas are missing." Tears filled her eyes, the green orbs shimmering, drawing him in. "I don't know where they are."

"Why do you think Carlos has them?"

"I...." She swallowed. Looked down. "I thought he might have seen them."

"Mi corazón." He paused to let the endearment sink in. She was his heart and would always be his heart. "Mi corazón, you did not ask him like you would a man who *might* know something. You attacked like a mama bear fighting for her cubs."

Her cheeks flushed. A single tear tipped over the rim of her lower eyelid and trickled down to her chin.

He brushed the drop away and cupped her cheek. "Tell me why you think Maria and Isabel are missing. Have you checked with Leya? I know she had Luis earlier."

"The girls were with Dolores and Teo. Teo hasn't seen them." She glanced back around at Carlos. "I just know. They are missing. And--" She bit her lip. "I will go inside and ask Leya."

"I'll walk with you." He pulled her arm through his and nodded at Gabrio as he led her away. Behind him, Gabrio barked some orders, and the men dispersed.

Rosalinda shivered.

Before they entered the house, Lucio turned her to face him. "What did Carlos say to you?" He didn't believe her girls were just missing. He figured Carlos had done something to threaten or frighten Rosalinda, but he would never have the temerity to actually take her children...

Would he? For what purpose?

"He..." She shook her head. "I don't know. Nothing."

He waited a long minute, studying her. Why wouldn't she tell him? She was probably trying to protect him from getting into another fight with Carlos. If only he could convince her to trust him so completely she would share everything with him.

"Let's go find Leya." He reached around her to open the door. The cool hallway echoed with their footsteps. Don Santiago was still outside with his men and the men who came from the Dominguez rancho. They would be inside soon to check on his father and see how he'd fared through the night.

A pang of need to check Don Armenta rang through him. As soon as he had Rosalinda and her niños settled, he would do so.

Leya sat in a rocking chair sewing some of the new material brought from Los Angeles. Luis slept on the bed nearby, his arms flung out, soft snores lilting in the stillness. Leya smiled when she saw them, her mantilla on the stand beside her. Her expression turned serious when she noted Rosalinda's distress. She set aside the cloth.

"What is it?" She rose and reached for Rosalinda's hands, folding them in her own. She cast a questioning glance at Lucio, but he nodded toward his corazón. Rosalinda needed to be the one to ask.

"Mi niñas. Maria and Isabel. Are they with you?" Rosalinda's voice cracked.

"No. They went with Dolores to help Teo in the barn. I haven't seen them since then. Why?" Leya's brow creased.

"They are missing." Rosalinda broke off, her body shaking. Lucio stepped closer. He put his arm around her. Had he been mistaken? Were Maria and Isabel truly missing? But why? What could have happened to them that Teo wouldn't have known?

The little ones loved his father. Perhaps they were there. He took Rosalinda's hands in his own. "Stay here with Leya. I will check on my father and see if your niñas have gone to speak with him. I heard Maria and Teo were in there earlier today. Maybe the niñas went to see him again." Lucio shared a glance with his tía, and she nodded. She would take care of the distraught mother while he searched for Maria and Isabel. He would set this rancho afire to find them.

His father slept. Brow creased, low moans punctuating his breathing, he didn't rouse when Lucio stepped into the room. The curandera wasn't here. She must have stepped out for a few minutes when the don fell asleep.

He backed out of the room and closed the door with care.

The front door opened before he could turn the knob. Don Santiago almost ran into him as he crossed the threshold. He jerked to a stop. Stared at Lucio, his face turning grim. Behind him, Gabrio and the other men quieted.

"What has happened?" Don Santiago asked.

As fast as possible, Lucio filled them in on the missing girls. Gabrio took charge of the men from his rancho while his father led their guests into another room to visit. They would not be able to help with the search and would only impede the progress since they didn't know their way around.

For the next hour they searched every possible hiding place, house, and outbuilding. They questioned Dolores and Teo to no avail. Lucio had a suspicion Teo might know more than he claimed, but he couldn't figure out what. The boy's responses to their questions seemed genuine, his concern real.

"I don't know where else to look." Gabrio lifted his sombrero and wiped his forehead. "None of the horses are missing. I thought maybe the little ones figured out how to saddle one and went for a ride, but that can't be."

Lucio had wondered the same thing. He knew how much Maria loved to ride and how adventurous she'd become.

"I have to tell Rosalinda." He led the way as they went back to the hacienda and down the hallway to where Leya and Rosalinda had been. They walked in to find Leya in tears. Luis played with some blocks on the floor, but...

Where was Rosalinda?

"She's gone." Leya put her hand to her chest, tears trickling down her cheeks. "She made an excuse to leave and didn't come back. I don't know where she is."

WHAT WAS SHE TO DO? Well, she knew what she had to do, but she didn't know if she could. Go back to the life she'd led before. Could she do that? Even to save her daughters?

Rosalinda sank once again onto the secluded bench in the garden. Birds twittered around her. Bees buzzed. The wind caressed her face with cool fingers.

"God, please help me. I want to be loved by You. Chosen by You. But I'm not strong like Rahab. I don't know how to be strong." She pressed her fingertips against her eyelids, trying to shut out memories. Memories she'd suppressed to keep her sanity. Those early days and weeks of her slavery. The horror. The fear. The hopelessness. She couldn't face the thought of Maria and Isabel being subjected to such horrors. She had to do something.

"God, what do You want me to do?" Silence fell on the garden. Even the wind died as she waited for an answer from a God Who chose to be silent.

The image of Rahab, waiting in her home while the Israelites marched around the city filled her mind. Rosalinda heard the taunts. The sound of thousands of feet marching, marching, marching. Felt the vibration echoing through the floor.

Had Rahab been afraid? That God had forgotten her? That she'd misunderstood? Afraid she needed to do something other than have faith and wait?

What about when the walls came crashing down? The sound must have terrified those who weren't killed by the falling stones. Did Rahab's house shake? Did she huddle in her home with her family gathered around, awash in fear and doubt? Or did she watch out the window, waiting for God to follow through on His promise to protect her and her family?

Rahab would have stood strong, watching the scarlet cord

where it disappeared out her window. Maybe she praised the God of the Israelites instead of giving in to fear. Maybe in her heart she sang a song of rejoicing to Him, even as her friends and neighbors rejected Him and taunted her.

Rosalinda lifted her face to the sky. Tried to think of a song to sing, but the only songs she knew were not ones praising the Lord God, Creator of all. "Thank You. Thank You for loving me even when I can't feel that love. If I believe in You, I have to believe in Your promises. Leya read me the verse that says You love me. Right here. Right now. As I am."

Tears traced a path down her cheeks. She swiped them away with the back of her hand. "I don't know what to do, but I thank You because You have the answer. You know where my niñas are. You can keep them safe. Lord, guide my way. Strengthen the little faith I have."

Head bowed, she sat in the quiet, waiting and listening. A bird chirped, joined by another. She opened her eyes. A butterfly, its pale yellow-green wings opening and closing in slow motion, rested on the back of her hand. She hadn't even felt the butterfly light there. She stared at the perfection and beauty, closer than she'd ever seen before.

And she knew.

God cared for this fragile creature, but He cared for Rosalinda and her children even more. The butterfly lifted into the air, circled above her hand, and floated away.

The light dimmed. Dusk settled across the garden, muting the colors. Stars winked on above her. A sudden urge to speak to Teo and Dolores settled over her, so Rosalinda made her way to the edge of the garden closest to their house.

The grounds were quiet. Compared to the earlier chaos of riders and horses, this scene held peace. Comfort filled her. And again...

She knew. All would be right. Somehow God would protect her and her babies.

She crossed the yard, her focus on the lights gleaming in Dolores and Roberto's windows. She could smell roasting meat and chilies. She drew a deep breath. She loved chilies.

At the door, she paused before knocking. *Is this what You want me to do?* For the first time in her life, she didn't want to plunge ahead on her own, but wanted instead to see what He desired. The imperative pressed on her heart and mind. She needed God more than she'd ever needed anything or anyone in her life. Her welfare and that of her niños depended on Him. And only on Him.

She knocked.

Teo swung the door wide, his sweet face already creased in a smile. When he saw her, his excitement faded. He dipped his head and stepped back, allowing her entrance to the home. When he'd closed the door behind her, she turned and sank to her knees in front of him. "Teo, I need to know they are safe. Please." She kept her voice pitched low so no one else would hear her murmured inquiry.

His jerky nod spoke volumes to her heart. He knew. He knew where Maria and Isabel were and that they were protected. This special boy, Maria's best friend, would never call her daughter safe if she were in the hands of someone like Carlos.

"Teo, who is it?" Dolores called from the kitchen, the clink of pots telling of her work.

Rosalinda stood. Squeezed Teo's shoulder to thank him. "It's me, Dolores." She followed Teo to the kitchen where Roberto sat at the table, his hair still damp from washing up, probably at the horse tank outside. Most of the men washed there before going in for the night.

"Rosalinda, come in. Have a seat." Dolores wiped her hands and grabbed another plate to put on the stack by the stove. She gestured to an empty chair. "We're just eating. Join us. Do you remember my husband, Roberto? Roberto, this is my friend, Rosalinda."

Roberto pushed his chair from the table and stood. He nodded his head toward her. "Welcome. It is nice to meet you formally. I have heard much about you, and saw you when we arrived from Los Angeles, but I didn't get to speak with you."

Dolores dished up food and carried the plates to the table. She waved off Rosalinda's offer to help. "Sit. We aren't at the camp anymore." She went back for a plate for Teo and one for herself, and they all sat down.

Rosalinda couldn't eat. Her stomach ached with the decision she'd made and the need to talk with Dolores and Roberto. She pushed the food around, put a small bite in her mouth, and listened to Dolores chatter about her day and her new home.

When Teo left the table to go do one last check on the horses at the stable, she noted he slipped a wrapped bundle of food inside his shirt. Relief washed over her, but she kept her focus on his mother, trying to listen to what she had to say.

As soon as the door closed behind the boy, she held her hand up to stop Dolores. "I need to talk with you and Roberto. I don't have much time, and this is very important. Will you listen?"

Dolores glanced at her new husband. He sat up straighter and wiped his mouth. They both nodded. Rosalinda drew a deep breath and started the speech she'd rehearsed in her mind for the past two days. She prayed they would do as she asked and not reveal her plan before she could put everything in place. They had to.

Her children's lives were at stake.

PURPOSE STRENGTHENED her spine as Rosalinda stepped out into the night. Crickets chirped. Something skittered across the dirt. A coyote sang in the distance, his plaintive cry echoing the sadness of her heart.

She tried to make her feet move. They were refusing. She'd come to the decision that she would do whatever it took to keep her niños safe. Hearing Maria and Isabel were missing. Seeing

Carlos's expression. Feeling the fear throughout her being. All those had come together to convince her this had to be done. She knew God understood her heart. This might not be His plan, but He seemed to be leading her in this direction. "Please, God." She couldn't find any other words to pray. She groaned from the depths of her soul.

She stopped in front of an isolated cabin. Dim light shone behind closed curtains. She didn't remember walking here. Men's voices, their lewd talk, filtered through the broken pane in the window. Lewd talk...

About her.

CHAPTER TWENTY-EIGHT

"What do you mean she's *gone?*" Lucio tore his gaze from Leya and sent a frantic glance around the room, half expecting to see Rosalinda hiding in the shadows or behind a curtain. She wasn't.

"I sent Yoana to look for her before she went to sit with your father, but she couldn't find her anywhere. She even checked with Dolores."

Luis scrambled up from the floor and ran to Leya. His lower lip trembled as he lifted his arms to be picked up. "Mama." He sniffled.

Lucio didn't want to upset the boy anymore, so he nodded at Leya and turned to leave. "I'll check with Yoana and see what I can find out. I'll be back."

"I'll be praying." Leya's strained smile eased into a more peaceful one. He knew his tía would follow through on her promise. He'd never known anyone to have more faith than she did.

"Thank you." Before he could shut the door, his tía called out to him. He turned back.

"I know you have feelings for Rosalinda. She has them for you too. Be patient. She has a good heart, but she has been hurt so much. She will be worth the wait." Her words and her smile warmed and encouraged him.

He nodded, his throat too tight to voice his thanks.

He hurried to his father's room. Scents of the evening meal wafted on the air. His stomach rumbled, but he had no time to indulge in food.

He tapped on the door before easing it open.

Yoana looked up from a book of figures she had open. She glanced at their father and motioned Lucio in, then put her finger to her lips. "He's still sleeping." She spoke low as she leaned toward him when he sat down next to her. "This is best for him."

"Yoana, I have to find Rosalinda. Leya said you searched for her and didn't find her." He clasped his hands together to keep from grabbing her.

"I thought I looked everywhere, but realized I didn't check the garden. There is a bench there, secluded, where she likes to sit. I've seen her there a couple of times and forgot to check there. You can find it by following the path that leads to the right." She put her hand on his arm as he started to rise.

"Our father wanted to speak to you. He was very distressed when you weren't in the house. Can you wait until he wakes?"

He glanced at his father. Don Armenta's eyes were open, but hooded. Was his father awake or not? Lucio stepped over to the bed and leaned down. His father grasped his sleeve and tugged. Lucio knelt and leaned close.

"Teo needs to see you. He can help you find her." Don Armenta raised up to speak but sank back when he finished. His eyes closed again, his face pale.

Lucio squeezed his father's hand before rising. "I'm going to find Teo. Something is wrong, and I'm afraid for Rosalinda and her niños."

"I am too. Go." Yoana waved her hand toward the door. "Gabrio will be here in a few minutes. I'll tell him where you've gone."

Night folded across the land. Stars gleamed above. A beautiful night, but he had no time to enjoy the heavens. His long strides ate the distance between the hacienda and the small cottage where Teo lived with his mother and Roberto. Dolores answered as soon as he knocked, as if she'd been waiting for him. She directed him to the barn to find Teo.

The barn door stood cracked open. A lantern hung inside near the opening. The rest of the stable was hidden in shadows. Lucio listened, but didn't hear anything. Before he could call out, Gabrio startled him by stepping inside.

"Yoana said there might be trouble. Is there a problem in the stable?"

Lucio shook his head. "My father said I needed to talk to Teo. The boy has been trying to tell me something, but I've been so busy I haven't taken the time to listen. His mother said he would be here."

"Then let's look." Gabrio lifted the lantern and strode down the center aisle of the barn. The shadows danced on either side as they passed.

"Teo." Gabrio paused toward the end of the long row of stalls. "Teo, we need to talk with you. Now."

They heard scuffling from the room that held feed and tack for the horses. Teo leaped out the door, his face a mask of guilt. Lucio didn't care what the boy had been up to. He needed answers about Rosalinda and her daughters.

"Teo, you need to tell us what you heard." Lucio motioned the boy to come to him and knelt in front of him. Gabrio set the lantern down and knelt beside him.

"I tried to talk to you." Teo's lips trembled.

"You aren't in trouble. Rosalinda is missing. So are Maria and Isabel. We have to find them. Can you help?" Lucio clasped the boy's hand trying to convey the urgency and need.

Teo nodded. "I heard men talking. They didn't know I was there

in the hay." He sniffed and rubbed his toe in the dirt. "The men said they are making Maria's mother meet them in a cabin where a lot of men will enjoy what...she can offer." He frowned. "Maybe she is making tortillas for them." He scratched his head with his free hand.
Lucio's pulse stuttered. Why would Rosalinda do this?
"They said if she doesn't come, they will take Maria and Isabel to Los Angeles and sell them." He cocked his head to one side. "Why would someone buy little girls?"
Lucio couldn't speak. This was the hold Carlos had over Rosalinda. This would be why she hadn't talked to him. This was the reason she turned down his proposal.
"Do you know where Maria and Isabel are?" Gabrio's tone was firm but calm. "We have to make sure they are safe. Then we will find Rosalinda."
"I helped them to hide." Teo glanced over his shoulder at the tack room. "I brought them some food."
Relief swept Lucio, followed by rage. "Where are the men meeting Rosalinda?"
"I don't know." Teo frowned. "They said the cabin, but they didn't say which cabin."
"Está bien. Listen to me." Gabrio caught Teo's arm. "I want you to take Maria and Isabel to the hacienda. Give them to Leya or to Yoana. Not anyone else. ¿Entiendes? They will be safe."
Teo nodded and ran for the room where the girls were hidden. Gabrio and Lucio stood. Lucio wanted to rush out in the night and begin checking every cabin, but that would waste far too much time.
"I think I know where they might be." Gabrio dragged his hand down his face. "Let me get a couple of the men I trust, and we'll go there."
They headed for the bunkhouse where the workers stayed. The room seemed empty compared to the usual hubbub of the evening. Lucio pressed his lips together. These men would pay...

Gabrio called out to Manuel, Alberto, and two other men. They all followed him outside.

He explained the situation to his men and asked if any of them had heard anything. Manuel and Alberto shook their heads. The other two shifted from side to side. When pressed, they gave the details they'd heard. Including the cabin where the travesty would take place.

Gabrio stared long at the men. "Because you were honest and didn't participate, I will let you stay on as workers here. But know that you are being watched. You should have come to someone about this plan. You knew it was wrong."

They shuffled their feet and didn't meet his gaze.

Gabrio turned to Lucio. "Let's go. I'll show you the cabin, and we'll get her out. When she's safe"—his gaze hardened—"we'll deal with the men." He pointed at one of the two men he'd chastised. "Find Ramón, the Armenta's head vaquero. Bring him to the cabin. Hurry."

The walk wasn't far but seemed to take an eternity.

Please, God, keep Rosalinda safe from harm. Any kind of harm. Lucio understood she wanted to protect her niñas, but if only she had trusted him enough to talk to him, then—

When has any man in her life been trustworthy?

The thought tightened his chest. Rosalinda wasn't the only one who needed to learn about trust and love. He drew a deep breath. *God, show me how to help her feel safe.*

As they approached a small cottage set away from the others and isolated by trees, they could hear raucous laughter and shouting ring out in the night. Gabrio's hand on his arm kept Lucio from running forward and yanking the door open.

HER STEPS FALTERED as she approached the lone cabin. The darkness folded around her offering no comfort. The stars overhead were cold and distant.

Alone. Once again, she was alone.

The door swung open. Sallow light spilled on to the path, grasping her toes with greedy fingers. Carlos leered at her from the entry.

Fear. Hatred. Disgust. All those feelings swirled in a miasma that turned her stomach upside down. "You will leave my daughters alone!" She forced her voice to be strong so he wouldn't hear her fear. "You give your word."

He sauntered toward her. Stopped. Rubbed his jaw as he studied her. She could hear the rasp of the stubble and smell his rancid body.

Before she could react, he snatched her to him. His fetid breath washed over her, and she tried not to grimace. She could do this. For her ninas. But...

She didn't want to. Oh, how she *hated* doing it.

"Let's go in and discuss the terms. Perhaps I will only take one of your daughters. You can choose which one."

Carlos's chuckle shivered down her spine. She shoved at him hard enough to make him stumble back.

Choose which one? Had this been her mother's option too? Such a ghastly choice, with no way to make it right? In that moment, she understood. She would never agree with what her mother did. But she understood.

Rosalinda straightened. "No. You agreed to leave them alone if I came with you." What would she do if he went back on his word. A few hours could do atrocious things to childhood innocence. She *would* protect her babies. But Carlos couldn't know how her heart raced with fear. He would exploit that.

"Come in and see." He grabbed her arm and dragged her toward the meager light. The open door didn't beckon so much as threaten. She cringed inwardly, but she kept her spine straight, her expression closed.

Men packed the small room. Every eye turned to her when

Carlos pulled her inside. Some greedy, anticipating. Some reluctant, even uncertain.

But all there of their own choice.

"We are ready to begin." Carlos waved a hand as he dragged her over by the fireplace and made her step up on the stone ledge. Her arm ached from his tight grip.

"As you can see, she is here and eager to meet with you." Carlos chuckled and pinched her cheek.

She glared down at him, then gritted her teeth into a semblance of a smile. A predatory one. "What about my niñas?"

Carlos's buoyant facade wavered. "We will talk later. After we are done here and are on our way to Los Angeles." He winked at her. "We will make good money there." He lowered his voice as he stepped up beside her and leaned close to her ear. "Here too."

You are loved. God's truth whispered across her heart. She looked out over the sea of faces, and God's love gave her courage and insight.

Carlos didn't care about his word. He would not keep it. But he was not brave either. He bullied her with false pretenses. If she allowed him to intimidate her, she would never be free. Even worse…

By listening to this man…by fearing for her daughters…by questioning her faith, she was keeping God from guiding her footsteps.

Men surged forward, vying for her attention. For her. The past rushed back to collide with the present. She clamped her lips tight to keep from losing what little she had eaten today.

She didn't belong here. She couldn't do this anymore. She closed her eyes, shutting out the sight of men eager to use her. Men she despised.

The memory of Lucio came. His dark eyes glowing with love. His gentle touch that had nothing to do with forcing her to his will. She wanted to cry with the loss of him. He would never want her after this.

The clamor faded to the background as she shut down. She'd learned to do this as a child, to endure what she couldn't escape, but…

Something was different. Something interfered. Some*one* interfered.

I love you with an everlasting love.

She felt the nudge to her soul almost as clearly as she felt Carlos's fingers digging into her arm.

God? Did God truly care about her? She thought of Rahab standing in her house while destruction rattled the walls and the cries of the doomed echoed in the air. She wanted deliverance from this life as much as she imagined Rahab wanted a new life for herself and her family. She wanted to follow God with everything in her. To become a new person He would call His own. She wanted a chance to know the love of a man who cared about her.

She wanted Lucio.

God, what do I do? Are You there? She held out the scarlet cord of her heart and soul to Him. Peace rained down on her, rivulets refreshing her parched heart and soul. She waited as the men around her vied for a chance to be the first to be with her. She waited to see what God would do.

She waited. And then…

"No." Her voice quavered in the din.

Silence folded around her. The men quieted. She opened her eyes. They were all staring at her. Carlos's grip loosened.

And she knew exactly what God wanted her to do.

She yanked her arm free. Stepped down to the floor. Her heart bounded in jackrabbit hops as she crossed to the door. The men tumbled aside like falling stones, their faces stricken. They did nothing to stop her. She could feel the peace of God around her, like a wall of protection. She couldn't restrain a smile. Her soul leaped.

She reached for the latch and swung the door open.

Lucio stood there, gun out, hand extended to the door.

His eyes widened. His arm opened. She stepped forward into his embrace, barely noticing Gabrio, Ramón, and the other men behind him. All prepared for a battle God had already fought and won for them.

For her.

"Take her back to the house." Gabrio spoke from beside Rosalinda. Her face buried against Lucio's chest, she didn't look up. She breathed in the scent of him.

At last.

She was home.

"Let's go, mi corazón."

She kept her gaze downcast as Lucio led her along the moonlit path toward the hacienda. Before they had gone far, she halted. The wonder of God's deliverance eased, and she could think again.

"Mis niñas. Are they safe?" She fisted her hand in Lucio's shirt, gazing up at him.

"They are." He cupped her face with his hand, his thumb tracing a path along her lower lip. "Teo hid them away. He overheard the plans those men had and prepared better than we did. I'm so sorry I failed you. Did they--." He looked away, as if he couldn't bear to ask more.

She told him all that happened. How much the story of Rahab meant to her. How God intervened on her behalf in a way she might never understand.

"The men in that cabin are all being told to leave." Lucio tugged her tight against him as if he never wanted to let her go.

She hoped he didn't.

"Gabrio will see to his men, and Ramón will see to mine. You won't have to be around them ever again." His breath teased across her ear sending shivers down her spine.

How was it possible that she of all women should be so connected with a man? A good man. A godly man. She could stand here in his embrace forever.

He lifted her face until she met his gaze. The intensity of his emotions burned in his eyes. He slowly lowered his head until his lips touched hers. She gasped. Reached behind his neck when he started to pull away. Tugged him down. Kissed him until they were both breathless.

Incredible.

He lifted his head. Smiled at her. She must look like a besotted girl being kissed for the first time. But that's what it felt like.

No, that's what it *was*. The first time she'd ever been kissed as God meant a man to kiss a woman.

She traced her fingers over his full mouth. Such wondrous, new emotions flooding her.

He kissed her again. She didn't want it to end.

When it did, she pressed her hand to her chest, trying to calm the rapid beat. Trying to catch her breath. He smiled at her.

Went to his knee.

"Rosalinda, I love you beyond what words can express. Will you marry me?"

Her throat tightened to the point that she didn't think she could speak. But she did. "Yes." She half sobbed. "Yes, I will marry you!" She dropped to her knees in front of him. "I love you, Lucio Armenta. I love you beyond anything I ever believed possible."

He stood and helped her to her feet. Kissed her one more time. She looked forward to more. A lifetime of more.

"Let's go check on our children." He tucked her hand in his arm and led her toward the hacienda…

And the beginning of her life.

EPILOGUE

"Are you ready, mi amigo?"

Lucio steadied his father as Augustín stuck his head in the door of Don Armenta's room and smiled. He came in and crossed to the bed where papá wiped the sweat from his brow.

Sweating. The don was sweating. From pulling on a pair of pants and fastening them. Lucio hoped he wouldn't try to do too much today.

"God has given us such a beautiful day, so we will have the wedding outside. Benches and chairs are set up. The bride is getting dressed." Augustín plucked an embroidered jacket from the bedpost and brought it to Father, chattering nonstop about the wedding preparations. The food. The guests. The excitement.

"Look at your son. He is as nervous as I've ever seen him." Laugh lines deepened beside Augustín's eyes. "I think he wants to post guards in case his bride decides to slip away before the wedding." He chuckled. "Of course, my esposa, Yoana, and Leya will not allow that to happen. Right, Lucio?"

"Rosalinda will be there." Lucio didn't want them to see his doubts as he helped his father slip on his jacket and adjust the sleeves. His father insisted on walking, although he would be hobbling on crudely fashioned crutches. They planned for him to arrive early enough to avoid most of the guests seeing him totter like an ancient viejo to his assigned seat, holding their breaths lest he tumble and injure himself even more. The don's fears, not his. He was glad to see his father recovered enough to get out of bed.

"We have benches and chairs set up. Yours will be a little more comfortable than most. Ready?" Augustín handed Father the crutches, then stood opposite from Lucio to assist his friend in getting up. By the time they'd helped the don gain an upright position, with the wood supports firm under his arms, they were all breathing hard. Still, his papá hadn't fallen back on the bed as he'd done when learning to use the dratted sticks.

"Give me a minute." Francisco closed his eyes. His breathing steadied. "Está bien." He nodded at his friend. "Lead the way."

The distance that should have taken no more than two minutes to walk took an eternity. Or felt like one. Each hop forward had to jar his father's injured leg. Sweat beaded the don's upper lip. They passed no one. Lucio and Don Santiago kept up a running patter about the day's festivities, while his father focused on walking. The crutches wobbled. Lucio's breath caught. He prepared to grab his father if one of the crutches broke. He couldn't fall again.

When Augustín opened the front door, they all blinked in the bright sunshine. Gabrio hurried toward them, his face creased in a smile. "Don Armenta. How good to see you up and about."

His father inhaled a deep breath. "It is good to go outside. You've all kept me cooped up."

Gabrio didn't seem to take offense at the slight surliness in the don's tone. "Let me help with this step."

Augustín stepped back to let Gabrio take his place. Lucio and Gabrio lifted Don Armenta down without losing his balance--or his dignity.

"Gracias." Father nodded at Gabrio. "You are a blessing to my familia."

His father took in the distance from the hacienda to the lawn where the wedding would take place. Lucio touched his arm. "This may seem monumental, Papá, but we will take it one step at a time."

"You have plenty of time, mi amigo." Augustín took his son's place. "We can go a few steps and stop to admire the view."

Don Armenta nodded at his friend. How his father hated showing any weakness, but since his injury, he'd mellowed, almost as if he were allowing God to work in him and through him.

As the don reached his chair and sank into it, he smiled. Relief showed in the relaxing of his shoulders and the bit of color that returned to his cheeks.

Concern knit Augustín's brow. "¿Está bien?"

Father held up his hand, palm out. His lips pinched together. "Está bien. Go ahead. See to your duties. You too, Lucio. I will bask in the sunshine." His tight smile resembled more of a grimace.

Lucio took his leave making sure to keep his father in sight. The next half hour brought a parade of people by to see him. He could almost hear the conversation as people would ask how his leg was healing or to congratulate him on the upcoming wedding of his son.

People drifted in. The workers and vaqueros filled up the benches in the back. One of the men brought his guitar and opened with a lively melody. Another joined him, singing a familiar ballad in a high tenor. His father tapped his fingers on his leg, a sure sign he enjoyed the music.

"Don Armenta." Teo raced toward the don before Lucio could catch him. The boy's face glowed. Maria and Isabel were close behind. Lucio froze, expecting the children to leap on their friend and jar his body, but Teo skidded to a halt a few feet away. He held out his arm stopping the girls. "We have to be careful, remember." Teo's loud admonishment could be heard as a song ended.

Gratitude made Lucio's knees weaker than the thought of

standing in front of a crowd and saying his vows to Rosalinda. He shouldn't be shaky. He had no misgivings, but the responsibility of taking on a complete family kept him awake long into the night.

He strode toward his father and the children, who should already be with Yoana.

"My mama is marrying Señor Lucio." Maria clapped her hands and twirled around.

Lucio halted, not wanting to give the children the opportunity to beg him again to let them stand up with him.

"He is like a fish," Isabel said.

Lucio snorted. These kids came up with the wildest ideas.

"A fish?" His father didn't laugh, but his mouth twitched. "Why is he like a fish?"

Isabel put her hand over her mouth, suddenly too shy to speak.

"Because Rahab married a fish." Maria patted Isabel on her head. "In the Bible. And Mama says God loves her just like He did Rahab."

"Rahab married a fish?" The don mimicked what they were saying, confusion plain in his furrowed brow.

"Do you know about Rahab?" Maria asked.

Don Armenta shook his head, and she launched into the story, complete with details about a harlot who made tortillas for men who were not her husband. Lucio had to hold his breath to keep from laughing aloud.

"Girls. Teo." Yoana came down the aisle with Leya, who carried Luis. They took seats near him, and Yoana motioned the niños to the chairs on the far side of Leya. She turned to their father and gave his arm a light squeeze. "It's good to see you up and outside, Papá."

"I have to ask." The don leaned toward Yoana,.

"¿Sí?" She bent closer. From where he stood, Lucio could still hear.

"Who is Rahab, and why did she marry a fish?" He tried to be quiet, but in a moment of silence, his voice must have carried more than he intended. Leya's hand clapped over her mouth, pressing her mantilla to her face. Yoana choked. She bit her lip and glanced toward the niños.

"I will tell you later." She patted their father's arm.

She winked at Lucio, and he slipped away in the crowd before his daughters-to-be spotted him. He had to find Gabrio and get in place. His skin prickled. His pulse thrummed.

"There you are." Gabrio motioned Lucio to join him beside the tree near the front. "What happened? Is Rosalinda ready?" Gabrio glanced toward the hacienda.

Did everyone think his bride would run away?

"I'm just…" How could he put his fear into words?

"I get it. I do." Gabrio pulled him around the tree where they were blocked from view. "When I married your sister, I loved her more than I could say. But, on the wedding day, I realized how hard this job would be. I would be responsible for more than myself."

"That's it." Relief wobbled Lucio's knees. "I will have a wife and three niños. What if I'm not up to the task?"

"You aren't." Gabrio grinned. Lucio stared up at him, his mouth open. "What I mean is you are not good enough on your own. I found that out early on. Without God's guidance and being able to lean on Him, I would never be enough for Yoana. Will you let me pray for you?"

Lucio bowed his head. Gabrio's powerful prayer washed away his worries, his uncertainties, his insecurity. He could trust God to help his new family and to guide him as a husband and father.

Rosalinda watched Dolores disappear through the open door, her pale blue skirt swirling in the light breeze. Delores flashed a quick smile in her direction before facing forward and walking down the aisle to where she would stand next to Rosalinda as she took her vows.

The flowers fisted in her hands trembled. A couple of the petals drifted to the floor. Tears burned her eyes. The doubts she'd had about marrying Lucio threatened to drown her. She should turn and run. Run fast.

"You are a precious jewel." The words Leya read to her this morning refreshed her mind, heart, and soul, chasing away her doubts. God loved her. Lucio loved her. She loved both. Getting married would be easy compared to her past. She had God, and soon a loving husband, on her side.

She stepped out. Yoana turned to smile at her almost sister-in-law as she took hesitant steps toward the seated people, all of them staring at her. Yoana stood and everyone followed her lead.

Rosalinda froze. So many faces. Staring at her. Were they judging her? Thinking her unworthy? Seeing her past? Her frantic gaze darted from one blurred visage to another. She couldn't see Yoana or Leya.

She took another hesitant step. Froze again.

Her frantic gaze swept the crowd.

At the front, a hand waved above the crowd. Rosalinda's gaze zeroed in. Don Armenta. He beamed at her, and she relaxed a fraction. He pointed. Her gaze followed the direction he motioned…

Lucio.

The love in his gaze stole her breath, her thoughts, her trepidation.

She didn't remember walking down the aisle. Saw no one but her husband-to-be. Her love.

The vows were probably beautiful. She must have said all the right words. Lucio's touch as their hands clasped kept her from focusing on anything but him. He leaned in to kiss her. The sweetness. The promise. She didn't want the kiss to end.

Laughter startled her. Warmth heated her face. Lucio grinned and pulled her back for a second shorter kiss. The crowd applauded. Rosalinda laughed too.

They faced the people gathered for their wedding. Dolores handed Rosalinda her bouquet. When had she given the flowers to her friend? Leya brought the niños to them. Lucio carried Luis, and they walked together down the aisle, a new family.

Time flew by as guests ate, listened to music, and chatted. Rosalinda talked to everyone but knew she'd never remember a single conversation. When Lucio stopped to speak to Ramón, she took the opportunity to seek out her new father-in-law.

As she approached, Don Armenta straightened. He'd been nodding off and looked like he needed a nap. She leaned down to kiss his cheek.

"Papá." She held her breath as she lowered to the seat next to him. Her face heated. What would he think of her forward manner? "¿Está bien? ¿To call you, Papá?"

"Of course." He blinked. Swiped at his eyes. "Welcome to my familia, mija."

Her breath shuddered. Her eyes stung. His daughter. "Thank you, Papá." She leaned over to kiss his cheek again, grateful God had blessed her with a father at last.

"I have something to tell you. I have forgiven my mother. I still don't believe she loved me like she loved my sister, but that could be twisted by my memories. I do understand how her choice meant life or death for my sister. She would never have survived what I went through." Sadness stole her words. She pushed away the melancholy and smiled to ease the distress evident in his gaze. "But what those men meant for depravity, God has turned to something beautiful for me and my niños."

"God used the bandoleros to work on more than one of us. I can't thank Him enough." He cupped her hands between his and squeezed. "Now you had best find that husband of yours and get ready if you are to be away from here before nightfall."

"That would be me." Lucio's voice came from behind her. Her heart thumped, and she turned to look up at him.

Lucio grinned at her. "Your husband? I will have to get used to hearing that."

She jumped up to hug him, and he swept her over backward in a kiss. Don Armenta applauded.

Lucio lifted her back up. "We need to get ready." They were planning to ride to the ocean and would be back by the end of the week to begin the trek home. She hoped the don would regain his strength and be ready to travel.

"Are you ready to go inside, Papá? You have been up for a long time." Yoana and Gabrio came up arm-in-arm. Yoana reached for her father's crutches, but Gabrio got them first. He helped the don stand, and they began the tortuous trek back to the house while Lucio and Rosalinda went inside to change for their trip. Music played in the side yard. People were dancing. A woman's low voice wove a melody in the air. Such a perfect day.

"You are so perfect." Lucio halted Rosalinda in the empty kitchen and pulled her into his arms. His kiss trickled delight through her. She shivered, stretched up for another kiss.

"Do you mind if we say good-bye to my father again before we leave?" Lucio smoothed a strand of hair from her brow.

"Not at all." She took his hand and led the way to the don's room.

Yoana and Gabrio had just gotten Don Armenta into bed. Lucio and Rosalinda stopped in the doorway. The don leaned back against the pillows. Glanced up at Yoana. Her gaze was riveted on Gabrio, her cheeks flushed with color. Don Armenta grinned.

Yoana put her hands on her hips. "What is so funny?"

"I believe you have news to tell me but are afraid to say the words. When is the *bebé* going to be here?"

Rosalinda gasped and glanced at Lucio. He met her gaze, eyes wide.

"Papá. How did you know?" Yoana feigned outrage, but Rosalinda could tell it was an act.

"I always knew when another Armenta was coming. You have the same glimmer as your mother did. In fact, you are much like your mother in so many ways." He paused. "Thank you. Thank you for forgiving me, for letting me be your papá. I will come back to fight with Augustín to see who is the most honored abuelito."

Lucio ushered Rosalinda into the room. They were starting their good-bye's when the patter of small feet heralded the arrival of Teo, Maria, and Isabel. The children raced past the adults to reach the bed. They were sweaty, and their clothes were not as neat as before, but they were so happy.

"Señor Armenta." Maria lifted his hand, hugging his arm to her cheek. "I forgot to finish telling you about the fish."

Yoana snorted. Clapped her hand to her mouth. Gabrio's eyes twinkled. His lips twitched. Rosalinda caught the glimmer of mirth in Lucio's eyes, but had no idea what fish they were talking about.

"I have been waiting all day to hear about this fish." Laughter tinged the don's reply. He sat forward as if he'd really waited to hear from Maria all day.

"Rahab married Salmon." Maria held up one finger as if giving a lecture. "Carmen said Manuel traveled way north one time, and there is a fish called a salmon. So Rahab married a fish. That is why my mama married a fish too." She giggled as she glanced over her shoulder at Lucio.

Rosalinda's mouth fell open. What would Lucio think?

His father's mouth twitched. He pressed his lips together. Maria's finger still pointed upward. To the side, Yoana had her face buried in Gabrio's shoulder. They both shook with silent laughter.

"I am sure Rahab's Salmon was a man, not a fish." Lucio's fingers squeezed hers as he spoke.

"His parents named him after a fish?" Maria's nose wrinkled.

Don Armenta guffawed. "If you keep calling me Don Armento instead of abuelito, I will start calling you little trout. Then *you* will be a fish." The three children burst into giggles.

"We have to go, abuelito." Maria kissed her new abuelo on the cheek, and the trio raced from the room.

Rosalinda and Lucio said their good-byes, along with more congratulations for Yoana and Gabrio. They slipped outside into the cooling afternoon air. Ramón waited with their horses, already packed for the trip.

Lucio helped her into the saddle. He smiled up at her before swinging astride his dun. She followed him from the hacienda looking forward to their future.

A future filled with promise.

GLOSSARY

Abuelo(a) – Grandfather/mother,
Abuelito(a) – Grandpa/Grandma
Ándele – Come on, Hurry up
Bambino – Baby
Bandolero – Bandit
Baño – Bathroom
Bebé – Baby
Bienvenidos – Welcome
Buenas tardes – Good afternoon
Caballo – Horse
Casa, Casita – House, small house
Compadre – Good friend
Corazón – Heart
Curandero – Healer
Dios – God, con Dios – with God
¿Dónde está? – Where is it/he/she?
Dulce – Sweet
Entiende – entender, to understand
Esposo(a) – Husband/Wife

GLOSSARY

España – Spain
Está bien – All right
Familia – Family
¡Fuera! – Get out!
Gatito pequeñito – tiny kitten
Gracias – Thank you
Gustan – Like, Pleasure
Hacienda – House
Hermano(a) – Brother/Sister
Hombre – man
Horchata – Sweet drink made from rice
Loco – Crazy
Lo siento – I'm sorry
Los Estados Unidos – The United States
Madre – Mother
Mantilla – Shawl or scarf
Mejor amigo(a) – best friend
Mijo(a) – My son/daughter
¡Mira! – Look!
Mujer – Woman
Nietos – Grandchildren
Niño(a) – child
Novio(a) – boyfriend, girlfriend
Pan del cielo – bread of heaven
Por favor – please
Puta – Prostitute
Qué bonita – How pretty
¿Qué es? – What is it?
Senor(a) – Mr./Mrs.
Sí – Yes
Sorpresa – surprise
También – Also, Too
Tía – Aunt

Vámanos – Let's go
Vaquero – Cowboy
Ven Acá – Come here
Viejo – Old man

AUTHOR'S NOTE

Thank you for joining me in this journey to with Rosalinda and Lucio. Their story drew me in and made me want to see what would happen with them—and with Rosalinda's delightful children.

That may sound odd to you. You may think I have everything planned out before I write the book. The opposite is true. For *The Ranchero's Love*, I knew the hero and heroine would be Lucio and Rosalinda. I also knew they would be traveling to visit Lucio's sister, Yoana. The rest of the story played out as I wrote – almost like writing down the scenes of a movie you are watching.

For instance, when I started, I had no idea Carlos would show up on the pages, or that Francisco would join the group and have such a major role to play. I didn't know the history behind Lucio and Yoana's mother and how that would impact Lucio's outlook toward Rosalinda.

As I wrote, the idea of being judged for your past, or what others perceive you to be, became a critical part of the story. I wondered

AUTHOR'S NOTE

– what if you had no control over what happened to you? What if you want to change but don't know how to be different? What if you feel trapped by how others see you? How do you break those bonds?

I hope *The Ranchero's Love* gave you as much opportunity to consider these issues as it did for me. Writing Rosalinda's story made me consider how I treat people, and how I want to be treated by others.

In both Romans 2:11 and Acts 10:34, we read that God doesn't show partiality. *The Ranchero's Love* helped me explore that idea. No matter your past, no matter what you've done—or haven't done—God loves you, and He wants to have a relationship with you. He loves You with an everlasting love.

Thank you again for joining me in this journey. I would love to hear from you. You can find me on my website, as well as on other social media platforms: www.nancyjfarrier.com.

Nancy J. Farrier

ACKNOWLEDGMENTS

There are always so many to thank at the end of writing a book. Writing is usually a solitary effort, but publishing is a community work. Without help from so many valuable people, I wouldn't have managed.

∼

First, to my editors, Karen Ball and Louise M. Gouge. Thank you so much for taking what I wrote and making the story so much stronger. You are amazing, and I love working with you.

∼

For those who proofread early copies – and all found mistakes I missed – my heartfelt thanks. Marie, Junie, Anne, and Alyssa. You are the best. It is still my dream to give you a book to proofread, and you'll say, "What mistakes?"

∼

Of course, to my favorite cover artist, Ardra Farrier, a huge thank you. This book cover was a labor of love with the emphasis on labor. Working full time, planning your wedding, plus designing a book cover, may have been a tad overwhelming. Thank you for your gorgeous design.

I would not be able to write without the encouragement of so many other authors. Thank you to the FHL chapter of RWA and OCCRWA. You are always there with what I need. Writers make up an incredible community. Such a blessing.

As always, all I do is for the glory of God. I am able to be who I am because Jesus Christ gave His life for me and loved me with an incredible love. By His example, I try to share that love through my stories.

ABOUT THE AUTHOR

Nancy J. Farrier is a multi-published, award winning author of historical and contemporary Christian fiction. She writes Southwest fiction with real life issues. She lives in Southern California with her husband and cats. Nancy loves reading, bicycling, and needlework.

Please connect with Nancy J. Farrier here:

ALSO BY NANCY J. FARRIER

Land of Promise Series
The Ranchero's Love
Bandolero

Brides of Arizona
The Cowboy's Bride
A Bride's Agreement
The Timeless Love Romance Collection
8 Weddings and a Miracle
The Immigrant Brides
Painted Desert

Made in the USA
Monee, IL
28 May 2020